INDIAN SPORTS

CONVERSATIONS AND REFLECTIONS

Vijayan Bala

ZORBA BOOKS

ZORBA BOOKS

Published in India by Zorba Books, 2018

Website: www.zorbabooks.com
Email: info@zorbabooks.com

ISBN Print Book - 978-93-87456-74-7
ISBN Print eBook - 978-93-87456-75-4

Zorba Books Pvt. Ltd.(opc)
Gurgaon, INDIA

Printed at Repro Knowledgecast Limited, Thane

ABOUT THE AUTHOR

Mr. Vijayan Bala who is 66 years young (born on 10 October 1951) is basically an educationist who has taught English in reputed schools such as Don Bosco (Park Circus), Modern School, Barakhamba Road, New Delhi and St. Xavier's, Old Delhi; been Vice Principal at the Army Public School, Dhaula Kuan, New Delhi and finished off as Prinicipal, Raunaq Public School, Ganaur near Sonepat. In the schools he has worked in he was greatly involved co-curricular and sports activities. He has been a mentor for English teachers of Bal Bharati Schools, Delhi NCR and has also conducted workshops for English teachers in different schools. He has also written English help books for ICSE and ISC students .

In the field of Sports, he has written freelance from the age of 18 for annual publications such as INDIAN CRICKET, magazines such as Sportsweek, Sportsworld, Weekend Review, Sun and Alive and Woman's Era (the last two are Delhi Press publications) and newspapers like Hindustan Times. He has been on the statistical committees of the Board of Control for Cricket in India and the Cricket Association of Bengal. He has also written two books on Cricket Statistics published by Vikas, Delhi and Konark, Delhi with forewords by Mr. Vijay Merchant and Mansur Ali Khan Pataudi respectively and a sports quiz book (with a foreword by Col. Rathore – Olympic medalist and Union Minister) published by Roli Books, Delhi. He has been a commentator for All India Radio and Doordarshan covering Cricket, Hockey and Football. He has also passed the state level umpiring exam held by the Delhi and Districts Cricket Association.

Rekha Yadav, (IRPS)
Executive Director/E(Sports)
&
Secretary, Railway Sports Promotion Board

भारत सरकार
रेल मंत्रालय, (रेलवे बोर्ड)
नई दिल्ली-११०००१
GOVERNMENT OF INDIA
MINISTRY OF RAILWAYS
(RAILWAY BOARD)
NEW DELHI-110001

FOREWORD

I have known Mr Vijayan Bala for close to 5 years now. Our first interaction was when he was doing some research on Railway athletes to be included in the Sports Quiz Book he was working on. I found his enthusiasm endearingly infectious and one got the general sense that Sports for him was a labour of love.

An educationist by profession, Mr Bala has taught in the most reputed schools of India viz. Don Bosco (Park Circus Kolkata), Modern School, Barakhamba Road, St Xavier's, Old Delhi and took on the administrative responsibilities as Vice Principal of Army Public School, Dhaula Kuan and Principal RPS, Gannaur near Sonepat. Passionate about sports from a very young age, he actively freelanced with publications and newspapers like Indian Cricket, Hindustan Times and any sports aficionados' staple.....Sportsweek and Sportsworld. A qualified state level cricket Umpire, Mr Bala has been a commentator for All India Radio and Doordarshan covering the games of Cricket, Hockey and Football.

So when I learnt that he is compiling a book of interviews which he did with India's sporting heroes over a period of years; ranging from likes of Leslie Claudius and P K Banerjee; Olympic medallists like Col. Rajyavardhan Rathore, Sushil Kumar, Sakshi Malik to rising stars like Manika Batra, I could not but be thrilled at the prospect of new insights into different facets of these legends.

I wish him the very best for his forthcoming book which I am sure will be of interest to all people connected with sports.

Rekha Yadav

PREFACE

I have always been passionately involved in sports and players since the age of seven so much so that I started maintaining scrap books on cricket and hockey from that age. The desire to know more about players and to understand them better made me try and specialize in the art of doing interviews .

My first interview was of S Venkataraghvan, then vice-captain of the Indian cricket team that defeated West Indies for the first time in a Test series in 1971. That piece was published in the Hindustan Standard, Kolkata in July 1971. My last interview appeared in the Woman's Era (August First) issue this year. I should mention here that I kept on writing, broadcasting and doing interviews of sports personalities for various newspapers and magazines in different periods of my life without disturbing my studies or my main calling which was educating students. The pieces I wrote and the interviews I did were many. However, in this compilation I have selected 77 interviews of players, administrators and umpires whom I met at different stages of their careers. I am confident that this compilation of interviews will help and inspire all those involved in the field of sports as quite a few of India's greatest sporting moments have been covered in it.

I am grateful to Mrs. Rekha Yadav, Executive Director (Sports) and Secretary, Railway Sports Promotion Board, for kindly consenting to write the foreword.

Finally, I wish to thank all those who gave me opportunities to write – in particular Divesh Nath – my one-time student and now Editor friend - as he has constantly supported and encouraged me in bringing out this book.

Bala

(VIJAYAN BALA)

CONTENTS

1971-1976

1982-1987

1996-1999

2002-2006

2012-AUGUST 2018

1971-1976

S. Venkataraghavan, L. Claudius, Naresh Kumar, S. Mewalal, S. Manna and Gurbux Singh

S. VENKATARAGHAVAN –INDIAN OFF-SPINNER AND VICE-CAPTAIN

HINDUSTAN STANDARD, KOLKATA – 18 JULY 1971

26-year old Srinivasaraghavan Venkataraghavan, the off-spinner from Tamil Nadu, was the vice-captain of the Indian team that went to the West Indies. Venkat returned home as India's leading wicket-taker with 22 wickets in the Tests. The West Indies captain Gary Sobers, referred to Venkat as "a brainy bowler." **India defeated West Indies for the first time in a Test series and that too away from home.**

I met Venkat at his residence in Madras and had a chat with him about cricket and his career.

Did you model yourself on any bowler?

I never modelled myself on any bowler. I feel it is best for one to have his own style of bowling. Of course, suggestions and tips are helpful.

What type of wickets (barring dust bowls) do you like bowling on?

I prefer the hard and fast wickets because they give both batsmen and bowlers an equal chance. I do not like the slow type of wickets.

Does the presence of a top-class off-spinner like Prasanna in the same team cause any undue bother?

We are different types of off-spinners. In fact, the presence of Prasanna results in a healthy rivalry and brings out the best in both of us.

What do you think are the factors that go up to make a good and successful cricketer?

To be a good cricketer, one must have natural talent but to be a successful one, a player must have to practise very hard especially in the fielding department.

Who is the best batsman you have bowled to in Test cricket?

I have bowled to many of the world's leading batsmen like Sutcliffe, Reid, Sobers, Kanhai, Butcher, Hunte, Lloyd. Boycott, Edrich, Graveney and Cowdrey. It is really difficult for me to say who is the best.

What were the kind of wickets you met with in the Tests during the West Indies tour?

The wicket at Jamaica was the fastest, the others were slow and offered a little turn.

What is your comment on the Indian performances?

Gavaskar's batting was brilliant but it was Sardesai's double century in the first Test which boosted our morale. Our bowling and catching too were excellent and the team played as one whole.

What is your opinion of the West Indies team at present?

The West Indies batting is as good as ever with the presence of stars like Sobers, Kanhai and Lloyd and promising players like C. Davis, D. Lewis and M.Foster. But it is their bowling which left a lot to be desired. They had no bowlers of the pace and experience of Hall and Griffith. Dowe was fast but very erratic. The spin rested too much upon Noreiga and Sobers.

Could you mention the names of any outstanding young West Indies players?

Alvin Kallicharan, the left-handed batsman from Guyana was most impressive. We will definitely hear a lot about him in the future. Norbert Phillips, the fast bowler from the Windward Islands, was very promising. He was really quick but at times his action was suspect. I did not see much of Julien, Rowe and Desousa so I would not like to comment on them.

Everybody talks about the difficulties faced under English conditions, but nobody explains what exactly English conditions are? As you have toured England before could you elaborate?

The wickets in England vary enormously as the soil can be of chalk (South England), clay (North England) etc. English wickets are seldom dry (too much rain) and hard. The ball moves more of the seam than in the air. The shine on the ball lasts longer. In most grounds there are no sight-screens. Conditions like humidity and whether or not a ground is enclosed by seating accommodation or trees affect the movement (swing) of the ball in the air.

How would you rate our chances against England in the forthcoming Tests?

England is a well-knit side. A tough tour is definitely ahead but should we acclimatize ourselves quickly and the weather is favourable we should do very well.

LESLIE CLAUDIUS – FIRST INDIAN HOCKEY PLAYER TO PLAY FOUR OLYMPICS

SPORTSWEEK - 19 DECEMBER 1971

Padma Shri Leslie Walter Claudius, whom I met for the first time at his spacious flat in central Calcutta, impressed me at once by his simplicity, friendly behaviour and his love for hockey– a game in whose annals his name is indelibly carved.

Claudius, who played at right-half for India, is perhaps the highest capped Indian player and also shares a unique honour with another player of having represented India in four successive Olympic Games (1948 till 1960). Talking to Claudius on hockey, I soon realized, was an education.

Claudius was born on 25 March, 1927 at Bilaspur. His father worked in the Railways. After studying upto Junior Cambridge at the Railway School, Bilaspur, Claudius joined the Railway Auxiliary Force in 1944. The next year, he played football for the B.N. Railway team in the I.F.A. shield Tournament.

His hockey career began at the age of 19 in 1946 in unusual circumstances. The regular centre-half of the B.N.R. team was injured and Claudius got a chance. That year, B.N.R. lost to Port Commissioners in the final of the Beighton Cup Tournament 1-2. It was the first time Claudius played in a Beighton Cup final.

In 1947, when the Railway Auxiliary force was disbanded Claudius joined the Calcutta Port Commissioners. He made his Bengal debut in 1948.The same year, saw Claudius come into national reckoning. He was a stand-by in the Bengal team that year. Moreover, he was unable to participate in the Beighton Cup Tournament, the same year, as he had a fractured finger. His excellent performances in the Aga Khan Tournament at Bombay earned him a place in the Indian hockey team for the 1948 London Olympic Games.

In 1950, Claudius left the Port Commissioners and joined the Calcutta Customs. In December that year, Claudius was selected to represent the Indian team on a tour of East Africa. In 1952, he was a member of the Indian team at the Helsinki Olympics. In 1954, Claudius went to Malaya with the Indian team. Then in 1955. he toured New Zealand and Australia with an Indian team.

Claudius then represented India in the 1956 Melbourne Olympics – his third successive Olympics. In the Asian Games at Tokyo in 1958, Indian suffered its first setback in international hockey when Pakistan won the title on goal average. I asked Claudius the reasons for India's defeat and he remarked, "The team that represented India had only half a dozen hockey players, while the others, who made the team, had no credentials of hockey." About the manager he said, "He did not bother to find out whether the goal average rule would be applied. The draw, too, was arranged in such a way that Pakistan always met a team after India had played against it."

In 1959, Claudius captained the Indian hockey team on their tour of Europe. The team also took part in the Munich Hockey Festival. At Munich, Claudius was adjudged the 'Best Player' of the tournament. Claudius captained India in the 1960 Rome Olympics. It was his fourth successive Olympics. That year India lost the title for the first time to Pakistan.

About the Rome Olympics, Claudius said, "It was both the happiest and saddest moments of my life. I was captaining India for the first time in the Olympic Games and it was for the first team India failed to win the Olympic title. I took the defeat as a slur in my hockey career."

Claudius never recovered from that defeat and did not represent India after 1960. He played for Bengal till 1962 and for Customs Club till 1965 - the year in which he received the Beighton Cup winners medal for the first time in his hockey career.

When I asked Claudius which was the most thrilling and exciting match of his career, he said, "The match between the Punjab and Bengal in 1956 National in Punjab. In 1952, Bengal had defeated the Punjab in the Nationals at Calcutta. It was for this reason, they wanted to avenge the defeat However, it was not to be. We scored an early goal and then managed to hang on to our lead till the final whistle."

Talking about India's chances in the Munich Olympics next year, Claudius said, "Frankly speaking our chances are not as bad as people make it out to be. In the recent World Cup Tournament at Barcelona,it was bad tactics and poor selection that cost us the first position. For Munich, preparations should begin right now."

Claudius, today, is a Preventive Inspector in the Calcutta Customs. He is happily married and has four sons. Apart from his family and his work, he is interested in Western music and dancing. In fact, he is incharge of the entertainment section of a club in Calcutta.

NARESH KUMAR – GOOD TENNIS PLAYER, CAPTAIN, MANAGER & COMMENTATOR

SPORTSWEEK – 23 JANUARY 1972

At 43, Naresh Kumar, a former Indian Davis Cup player, is still nearly as fit as he used to be in his prime. This is mainly because Naresh still plays competitive tennis whenever he gets a chance. I met this very pleasant veteran at his office and the interview was a wonderful experience.

Naresh Kumar was born at Lahore on 22 December, 1928 in a well-to-do family with practically no sporting background. His father was a businessman. Naresh and his parents have lived in Calcutta most of the time.

Naresh did not play any tennis at school – St. Xavier's, Calcutta. However, he represented his school in athletics, hockey, football and cricket. Naresh went to Lahore for his college education in 1942 as there were rumours of Calcutta being bombed. While doing his Intermediate at Lahore Government College, (1943-45), Naresh took to tennis seriously. He was a reserve in his college tennis team.

In 1945, Naresh returned to Calcutta and joined City College to take a B.Com. degree at the age of 19. It was during this period, Naresh played a lot of competitive tennis. In 1946, he was selected to represent the Calcutta University. However, the tournament was not held that year. He was also the National Junior champion in 1945 and 1946.In 1948, Naresh won the Delhi, Bihar and Bengal Championships. In the Bengal Championships, he defeated Sumant Misra, the then National Champion; while in the Delhi Championships, he defeated Narendra Nath, another top player of that time.

While playing in England, the following year, Naresh won the men's doubles title at Beckenham in partnership with Sawhney.

Naresh considers this a great win, as at Beckenham, tennis of the highest quality was played. Moreover, the pair whom Naresh and Sawhney defeated were the previous year's winners.

Naresh Kumar made his Davis Cup debut in 1952. He continued to be a member of the Davis Cup till 1961. In 1961, against the United States, he could not play as he was not well on the day of the match. He has also been the non-playing captain of the Indian Davis Cup team for a few years. He remarked, "Perhaps, the only non-playing captain to pay his own expenses."

When I asked him which was the best match he had played, Naresh replied, "The game in which Krishnan and I beat Budge Patty and Gardner Mulloy on the Centre Court at Wimbledon in 1958. Patty and Mulloy were the winners of the doubles title the previous year."

Naresh considers Lew Hoad and Rod Laver as the best players he has played against. In fact, he thinks them to be the best players he has known.

About the Indian players, he has played with, Naresh said, "I would love to have Krishnan as my partner."

As regards Indian tennis today, Naresh said, "Premjit Lal and Jaidip Mukherjea are still good and are in fact excellent Davis Cup players. The point is they cannot improve anymore. How long they will be able to continue at the present rate only time can tell. The younger players can only make the team, when Lal and Mukherjea call it a day. This is because Lal and Mukherjea have the experience which the youngsters do not possess. At present the best thing would be to keep two youngsters – Vijay Amritraj and Gaurav Misra – in the Davis Cup squad with Lal and Mukherjea, to enable them to play the preliminary matches and get Davis Cup experience."

About the shortage of quality tennis balls in our country today, Naresh remarked, "The Government should take drastic steps to ensure that proper supplies of quality tennis balls are made. The companies manufacturing tennis balls have the necessary technical know-how, but intentionally manipulate the market to create an artificial scarcity."

Today, Naresh Kumar is the Managing Director of a Company dealing in coals. He is married and has three children – two daughters and a son. Apart from his work and tennis, Naresh is a writer. He is an expert on tropical fish and has a book to this credit on that subject.

S.MEWALAL– SCORER OF FOOTBALL GOLD MEDAL WINNING GOAL IN 1951 ASIAD

SPORTSWEEK – 28 MAY 1972

Many may not be aware of the contribution made by British Military teams to the development of football in India. In Calcutta and Bangalore, one still hears from the veterans of the past generation of the achievements of these teams.

Mewalal started with his early life story. In 1936 Sergeant Barnett of the 9th Border Regiment, after seeing the 10-year-old Mewalal play football on the road, asked him to join his club- Morning Star. Thus, began the career of Calcutta-born Shew Mewalal, who later became one of the greatest centre-forwards India has produced.

After playing three years for Morning Star club, Mewalal had the distinction of being the only Indian to play for Police Club - a purely British team, in the 1939 season. The following year he joined Napier Sporting Club (now known as Kidderpore Club) and played in the second division till 1944. He then represented Aryans for a couple of years before joining Bengal and Assam Railway (now known as Eastern Railway) in 1948. He played for that team till 1956. In 1956, Mewalal played for Mohun Bagan after which he joined South-Eastern Railway. He played a year for the South-Eastern Railway, when a serious leg injury forced him to retire from competitive football.

Mewalal made his debut for Bengal in the Santosh Trophy Tournament at Mysore in 1946. He represented his State till 1956, excepting 1948, 1952 to 1955. In the Santosh Trophy Tournament, he scored in all 37 goals, including five hat-tricks.

He represented India for the first time in the 1948 London Olympics. After the Olympics, the Indian team played some exhibition matches in the continent. In those matches, Mewalal scored 20 goals including three hat-tricks.

The following year, Mewalal went with the Indian team to Afghanistan. In 1950, he toured the Far East. He also represented India in the Quadrangular Tournament held at Colombo, the following year.

His moment of glory came in the final of the first ever Asian Games Tournament at Delhi in 1951, when he scored the goal that brought India victory and the title. Mewalal's last appearance for India was in the 1952 Olympic Games at Helsinki. About India's crushing 1-10 defeat at the hands of Yugoslavia in that tournament, Mewalal remarked, "We were badly beaten as the climate was very cold. Moreover, playing bare – footed in those conditions was nearly impossible."

When I asked Mewalal, which was the best match of his career, he said. "The match against Orissa in the 1950 Nationals when I scored two goals."

Mewalal today, is an Assistant Welfare Inspector in South-Eastern Railway. He is a qualified N.I.S. coach and is at present a National selector. Since his retirement from competitive football, Mewalal has devoted all his spare time to coaching youngsters. His devotion to the game to which he owes what he is today, is indicated by the fact that he has called his home 'Football Bhawan'. He is married and has three children.

S. MANNA – CAPTAIN OF THE 1951 ASIAD FOOTBALL GOLD MEDAL WINNING TEAM

SPORTSWEEK – 2 JULY 1972

Not many Indian footballers have had as long a playing career as Padma Shri Sailen Manna, a former Indian captain. Manna was perhaps one of the best right full-backs our country has produced for nearly two decades. Essentially a team player, Manna was most effective with his uncanny anticipation, forthright tackling and hefty first-time clearances. His height always helped him to get the better of his opponents in the air.

Born on 24 October, 1924 at Howrah in a family devoted to sports, Manna started playing football at school. However, he took to the game seriously only after joining the college in 1941. That year, he was a member of the Calcutta University side which won the All-India Inter-varsity Football Tournament.

After playing two years for Howrah Union Club – then a Calcutta second division side – Manna joined Mohun Bagan and played for them till 1960. Manna was appointed captain of Mohun Bagan in 1950 and under his stewardship, the club won the Durand Cup five times (three times in a row), the I.F.A. shield six times (four times in a row) and other leading tournaments in the country. Manna made his debut for Bengal in 1944. He continued representing his State till 1954 and in the process captained the side for a number of years.

He represented India for the first time in the 1948 Olympics at London. That year, he was the vice-captain. The following year, Manna captained India for the first time on the tour of Ceylon. After the tour, he continued to captain India in all major

International tournaments such as the 1951 Asian Games at Delhi, the 1952 Helsinki Olympics, the 1954 Asian Games at Manila and the three Quadrangular tournaments. He also captained India on quite a few other foreign tours. His greatest success as India's captain came in 1951 when under his leadership, India won the football title at the first-ever Asian Games.

When I asked Manna as to which match he considered as the best he had played he remarked, "I have played a number of matches which could be termed as my best. However, of the lot, perhaps the best was the 1953 Santosh Trophy match against Hyderabad. Hyderabad in those years had an exceptionally good forward line."

Manna considers the East Bengal forward line of the early 50s as the most difficult set of forwards he has played against. The five forwards were from the South of India and the first letters of their names when put together formed a South Indian dish- VADAS (Venkatesh, Apparao, Dhanraj, Ahmed and Saleh). **He was also full of praise for the great left winger S Raman – the 1948 Olympian.**

About Indian football today, Manna said, "The standard of football has fallen a great deal. At present, there is a total absence of skilled players. The main reason for this is the improvement in the technique of the game. This has made the game more mechanical."

Today, Manna is an Assistant Administrative Officer in the Geological Survey of India. He is married and has one daughter.

GURBUX SINGH – INDIAN COACH'S ANALYSIS OF HOCKEY FAILURE IN 1976 OLYMPICS

SWARAJYA (CHENNAI) - 18 SEPTEMBER 1976

Gurbux Singh was a member of the Indian Olympic hockey team to Tokyo in 1964 and Joint Captain of the team in the 1968 Mexico Olympics. He was also the coach of the Indian Hockey team for the 1976 Montreal Olympics. I spoke to him on his return from Montreal and he brought out the shortcomings of the Indian team which led to its dismal performance there.

Hockey lovers in India were stunned by our 1-6 defeat against Australia and 1-3 defeat against Holland in the pool matches of the recently concluded Montreal Olympics. Can you explain why we lost so badly in those two matches?

As regards the game against Australia, there are two reasons for our defeat – one technical and the other psychological. Let me explain the technical one first. Before the game I had instructed the defenders to mark the Australian right flank (inside and wing) and centre-forward Ronald Riley closely. They failed in their duty and the result, of course, is now well-known. Again, when the team was down 1-3 at half-time, the players felt that their team was out of the tournament and so gave up all hope. Another point that should be mentioned about this defeat is that, on that day,contrary to my instructions, our goal-keeper did not wear a mask. Now as regards the defeat against Holland, I must say that it was just unfortunate that we lost 1-3. In that game, we outplayed Holland in the first half but just failed to score. In the second half too, we played very well but Holland scored of two stray long corners – one of them going through the goalkeeper's pads.

What sort of problems did the astro-turf pose?

Good hockey is possible on astroturf but playing regularly on it tells on one physically. Playing on this surface is very tiring and also injurious to the ankles and calf and thigh muscles. As a result, no team was able to play consistently well in the tournament. If astro-turf is to become a permanent feature in international hockey, then the International Hockey Federation should, first, allow a country to take more than 16 players and secondly insist on a larger time-gap between the matches played by a country.

Do you feel that it was a mistake on India's part not to have participated in the pre-Olympic hockey tournament on this surface at Montreal last year?

In retrospect, yes, it was because we lost the experience of playing a tournament on astro-turf.

By the way, a question on the choice of the final 16. How was it that such a talented player, like Prabakharan, could not make the final 16?

Prabhakaran was not fully fit, being troubled by an injured thigh muscle. In fact, we tried him out as a right-winger and a centre-forward too, but he failed to impress. It was for these reasons that we included Syed Ali. Syed Ali, who is normally a left-winger, also played very well both as a left-inside and a right-winger.

Do you feel that it is necessary for India to change its traditional 2-3-5 system of play?

We adopted the 2-3-5 system of play at Montreal and despite our defeat, I still feel it is the most effective way of playing winning hockey. In fact, New Zealand, Australia and Pakistan adopt this system of play.

Now, before I come to the drawbacks of Indian Hockey, could you say what were the qualities that enabled New Zealand to become Olympic Hockey champions?

New Zealand is a team that plays extremely well as the under-dog. Their approach is very defensive and they usually score from stray chances.

What drawbacks in our play did the Montreal Olympics bring to light?

The hockey tournament in the Montreal Olympics brought to light a number of defects both in our play and approach to the game. First of all, our ability to score goals- field and penalty corners – is very poor. Secondly, our defence lacks depth –being particularly slow in recovery. Thirdly, the sticks used by our full-backs are too heavy for comfort and effective use. Fourthly, unlike the European teams, we are very slow in counter-attacks. And finally, Indian umpiring should be standardized with that of their counterparts abroad. Let me illustrate this point. Indian players who are not used to being tackled from the left at home are in great difficulty abroad because umpires there permit this type of tackle.

And finally, do you feel Indian hockey can stage a come-back?

Of course, it can. In fact, if the drawbacks I have mentioned are immediately looked into, there is no reason why we should not be on top of the hockey world again.

1982-1987

Swarup Kishan, Md. Shahid, Dilip Doshi, Nonita Lall, Bula Chowdhury, Gaurav Ghei, P.K. Bannerjee, Diana Eduljee, Sandhya Aggarwal, B.S. Chandrasekhar, Mansur Ali Khan Pataudi, V.K. Ramaswamy and Mohinder Lal

SWARUP KISHAN – A QUALITY INDIAN CRICKET UMPIRE

WEEKEND REVIEW (19-25 SEPTEMBER 1982)

Indian cricket umpires have quite often faced considerable criticism from players of Test sides touring India. However, one umpire whom players (both foreign and Indian), have always had a good word for is Delhi's Swarup Kishan- both Gooch and Miandad rate him very highly.

I met this big built 52-year old umpire on the eve of his birthday (12 July), at his Directorate of Audit Office, where he works as an officer, to ask him to relate his experiences as an umpire and to talk on umpiring in general.

Swarup, when did you first start umpiring cricket matches?

I started umpiring cricket matches in 1948-49 for school matches. I also umpired league matches that year.

Could you relate your rise to the status of a Test panel umpire?

I became a Ranji panel umpire in 1966, after passing the exam conducted by the Board of Control for Cricket in India. After six years, in 1972, I was selected for the All-India panel. It was in the 1978-79 Test against the West Indies at Bangalore that I made my Test debut. To date, I have umpired in 10 Tests.

What are the main qualities required by a person to become a successful Test umpire?

The three main things required for one to be successful Test umpire are, first of all, a thorough knowledge of the game, and its rules; secondly, confidence in oneself; and, lastly, the ability to control the game. This last quality depends a lot on whether the players have a regard for you, that is to say, have confidence in you.

Is it a must for one to have played the game to be a good umpire?

It is not essential but it is certainly useful to have played the game. This is so because you know how players feel and react to different situations during a game. Again, practical experience in any field is far more useful than mere theoretical knowledge.

Have you played any cricket in your younger days?

In my younger days, I played cricket for the College of Commerce side and even captained the Delhi Audit Team. You will be interested to know that I also captained the Faculty of Law side in Badminton.

Which moment in your Test career as an Umpire do you remember most?

I cannot forget my first Test. It was against the West Indies at Bangalore in 1978-79. After the West Indies first innings, India began its first innings. Of the first ball of the Indian innings, Gavaskar was out caught and I was the umpire at the bowler's end. This incident I still remember to this day.

In which Test centre in India, have you found Test umpiring a challenge?

Without a shadow of doubt, Calcutta, because of the huge crowd. Even though Calcutta's Test crowds are probably the biggest in the world, they are very good and sensible. The crowd understands every bit of the game and it is both a pleasure and a challenge umpiring in front of them. Again, the arrangements for umpires at Calcutta are superb.

In our domestic cricket, we have the system of neutral umpires. Is it a practice worth following?

As far as we umpires are concerned, we do not mind umpiring anywhere. However, by stopping this practice, the Board can cut down on a lot of unnecessary expenditure. Again, this system is strenuous and also results in a lot of time being wasted. For example, if a Delhi umpire has to umpire a match at Trivandrum, he spends seven days travelling (by train) and only does three days actual umpiring. Thus, the same umpire could have umpired two matches in his zone in the same period and at much less cost.

Finally, Swarup, how long do you intend continuing umpiring?

I shall continue umpiring till I am fit and able. At Test level, the 1984-85 season will be my last as, after the season, I would have crossed 55 years of age (55 is the retirement age for Test umpires).

MD. SHAHID – A BRILLIANT HOCKEY FORWARD

WEEKEND REVIEW (17-23 OCTOBER 1982)

22-year-old Mohammad Shahid, the left-inside of the Indian side for Asiad 1982, is one of the finest forwards in the world today. Shahid, who works for the Railways, was selected for the World XI after the Champions Cup at Amsterdam. I met Shahid in the practice camp before the Asian Games and spoke to him about his hockey career.

Shahid, how did you take to playing hockey?

For me it was the easiest thing possible as our family is deeply interested in the game. My father was a useful player while my brother. Asmatullah. has played for UP in the National Hockey Championship.

Were you coached by anybody?

I was extremely lucky to come under Jhaman Lal Sharma, a former Indian hockey international. Mr. Sharma helped me a lot in improving my game.

When did you first play for your state?

I made my debut for U.P. in the National Hockey Championships in 1978, at the age of 18. I played for them in the following year too, before joining the Railways. Since 1980, I have been playing for the Railways.

When did you first play international hockey?

I got my first taste of international hockey in 1979,when I was selected to represent India in the Junior World Cup tournament at Versailles. The next year, I made my international debut in the senior level too, when I was selected to represent the Indian senior side in the Quadrangular at Kuala Lumpur.

Which game has been the most memorable one you have played in?

Obviously, the match against Pakistan in the Champions Cup at Amsterdam. After 16 minutes play, we were down 0-3 but thanks to our team's never-say-die spirit and Rajinder's superb hat-trick we managed to win 5-4.

Which match of yours do you consider your best?

I would consider my performance in the match against Pakistan in the Quadrangular at Kuala Lumpur as my best. In fact, I played extremely well in that whole tournament. I was adjudged the best player of that tournament. I consider that a tremendous achievement as I was quite an inexperienced player in international hockey then.

Your combination with Zaffar lqbal makes India's left flank one of the best in the world today. How has this come about?

Zaffar *bhai* is a good elder brother to me. Moreover, having played together since 1980,we have developed a great, understanding. Fortunately, both of us have talents which, when used together, can shatter any defence in the world.

What are the qualities that go to make an outstanding inside-forward?

To be a good inside forward, one has to possess the qualities of stick-work, body dodge and the art of combination with the wings and halves.

Shahid, you have been accused of dribbling too much- I mean hanging on to the ball too much. What do you feel about this criticism?

Yes. I used to dribble too much. But remember one thing. God does not make any one perfect. This habit of over-dribbling is my defect. However, I must say that I have been getting rid of this defect over the last few tournaments.

What do you feel about the present Indian side?

We have a tremendous side which has youth as its forte. Remember, it takes four to five years to build a champion side. So, in a couple of years time, we should have a great side. We are also lucky to have such a great coach like Balbir Singh looking after us. He is working on our main drawback—'lack of finish' among the forwards. I feel that when the Asiad comes, we will be at our best.

DILIP DOSHI – ONE OF INDIA'S FINEST LEFT ARM SPINNERS

SUN - 27 NOVEMBER 1982

34-year old Dilip Rasiklal Doshi of Bengal is India's and perhaps the world's best-left arm spinner in Test Cricket today. I have known Dilip since 1968 and the greatest thing about this bespectacled spinning wizard is his modesty. Success has not affected him in the least and he is the same unassuming and extremely friendly Dilip whom I got to know nearly 14 years ago. I met Dilip recently in Delhi and he spoke on his career and various aspects of cricket.

You had to wait eleven years before making your Test debut. What advice would you give to young cricketers aspiring to play for the country?

All I can say is that one should never lose heart. I always believe that if one has talent and self-confidence, he will ultimately get the break.

Do you feel coaching is a must for one to become a great player?

As I have never been coached, I do not believe that coaching is all that essential for anyone to become a great cricketer.

You seem to be like wine - the older you grow the better you become. How is it so?

Well, experience is the best teacher for slow spin bowlers. So it is not surprising that I am getting better with age. A spinner learns to bowl with better control as he grows in experience. Most important of all, he also realizes at what pace to bowl on different wickets. You also learn to bowl the correct line to different batsmen.

You have been playing cricket in England for a number of years. In what ways has playing in England helped you?

Yes, I have been spent ten educative cricketing years in England. I have learnt a tremendous lot from cricket there. In England, by playing regularly on varying conditions and against players of the highest calibre one learns a lot. Moreover, having regularly bowled on such beautiful batting wickets at Trent Bridge and Birmingham has also helped me to be a better bowler.

Would you say that wickets in England are much easier than what they used to be in the past?

Yes, you are quite correct. For the last three years wickets in England have been totally covered. That has brought a lot of runs back to the game in England. Although seamers do get something out of the wickets, the wickets are in general slow and good for batting.

The cold climate of England must surely be a big handicap for spinners. How did you overcome it?

Yes, it is quite a tough thing for spinners (particularly those from abroad) to bowl in the English cold. However, since I have overcome the mental block, I have not been physically affected by it so much. My philosophy that one should not be unduly bothered about things beyond one's control has helped me a lot in solving this problem.

Do you feel limited overs cricket has killed the growth of spinners?

Limited overs cricket has certainly made life difficult for the slow bowler. Since people play some unusual strokes in limited overs cricket, they do not hesitate to do so in Test cricket too. So this has also made the job of spinners more difficult. Again as a result of limited overs cricket, spinners mainly concentrate on restriction. Therefore, you can say that limited overs cricket has killed the growth of spinners.

Which performance of yours in Tests to date would you rate as your most outstanding one?

I have had quite a few good performances in Tests. In fact, I consider all my performances in difficult conditions as good ones. However, I cannot forget the third and final Test against Australia at Melbourne in 1980-81. In that Test, India scored a dramatic win and I took 5 for 142 in the match off 74 overs despite bowling with a broken foot.

Did you fracture your foot before the Test or during it?

I broke my foot on 1 February 1981 when batting against Victoria at Geelong. Within a couple of hours I knew the suspected result but decided to keep it between the doctor and myself so that I could play in the Melbourne Test that started on 7 February.

How did you manage to bowl in the Test with that injury?

It was a difficult thing for me but I felt my country needed me throughout the Test. I had to put the injured foot in a bucket of ice during every interval to keep the swelling down. Only after we won the Test did I tell Sunil and the Manager about the injury. I am glad I took the right decision and stuck to it.

Could you tell readers about that Melbourne win?

Our win at Melbourne was truly a historical one because it helped us to share a Test series with Australia in Australia for the first time. The Australians had the fairly easy target of scoring 143 for a win with a little more than a day to get them in. Considering their powerful batting line-up, the odds were in favour of an Australian win. However, magnificent bowling by our bowlers (particularly Kapil and Ghavri) and Sunil's shrewd handling and field placing made life extremely difficult for the Australian batsmen. We had to attack if we had to win and the pressure we applied helped us to bundle out Australia for 82 and win the match. Kapil took 5 for 28 while Ghavri and myself got a couple of wickets each.

NONITA LALL – ONE OF INDIA'S BEST WOMEN GOLFERS AND A GOOD COACH

WEEKEND REVIEW (3-9 JULY 1983)

22-year-old Miss Nonita Lall (star woman golfer of Delhi), is back from a tour of Singapore and Kuala Lumpur after having represented India in the Queen Sirikit Cup tournament in Singapore. India, who finished at the bottom last year, did much better this year to finish sixth out of nine countries. I met Nonita (who with a handicap of 4 has the highest rating among women golfers in our country) at her residence recently and chatted with her about her golfing career in particular and women's golf in general.

To what would you attribute the Indian side's improved performance in this year's Queen Sirikit Cup tournament?

The two-week training-cum-practice camp we had prior to our departure was obviously the main reason for our improved performance. This camp was supervised by Brandon D'Sousa, a Calcutta-based golfer who has just turned professional. At the camp we used to play over 27 holes for about three hours everyday. This strenuous practice under humid conditions did a lot to improve our stamina. The other main reason for our improved performance was the fact that we went well in advance for this tournament to get used to the conditions.

What were the playing conditions like in Singapore?

Since the Australian and Japanese players are very big strikers, the courses were made much longer. Again, the humidity was extremely high and on the first two days of the tournament there was very heavy rain. Lastly, one has to play on hilly courses.

In which other tournaments did the team participate in on this tour?

On this tour, we also participated in the Subang Open in Malaysia where we finished second out of ten countries. I finished fourth in the individual event. After that we returned to Singapore and participated in the Jurong Open, Ranjit Grewal emerged winner while I finished third.

When did you start playing golf seriously?

I started playing golf seriously only four years back. Basketball was really my game both at school and college. You would be interested to know that I captained the school, college and Delhi Varsity basketball sides and also represented the State side in the Nationals.

Have you been coached in golf?

Yes. By my dad. I have learned all my golf from him.

Was he a good golfer in his younger days?

He was a good golfer who was and still is very involved in the game. In fact, he has accompanied the Indian side as non-playing captain on quite a few occasions.

How many hours a day do you practise?

I practise golf four to five times a week for about two to two and a half hours everyday. I do not play over the weekends. I am lucky that I work as a teacher in a school and so I have my afternoons free for golf.

Could you mention some of your notable performances in your career to date?

Since 1979, I have won the Western India title in December 1980, Northern India and the West Bengal titles in February 1983. The season 1982-83 has been a good one for me in that I also finished runner-up in the Madras Open in August 1982 and the P.G. Sethi memorial tournament in January 1983.

In your golf career, to date, which has been your most memorable moment?

Obviously the final round of the Northern India Championship in February 1983. With the last round to go I was eight strokes behind the leader. I was therefore determined to play my best in the final round. I had birdies in the eighth and ninth holes and played well in the last nine which is relatively easy in Delhi. I finished the round at one over par which, apart from being a course record, was also the best ever round played by an Indian woman. It was this remarkable performance which to a great extent helped me to win the title.

What are the problems faced by Indian women golfers?

The first main problem is the absence of good coaches. I firmly believe that to become a top-level golfer one needs a good coach to help one out Again, golf is a very demanding game which requires hard work and perseverance. Children, particularly girls, must take to it at a young age but unfortunately, the interests shift in the cases of most children and so the dedication is lacking. Marriage also upsets the careers of some golfers as at times the in-laws do not approve and of course, children have to be properly looked after. Lastly, it is a very expensive game which many people cannot afford.

How do you rate the prospects of women's golf in India?

You will be happy to know that on our recent trip, the Australian and Japanese golfers who had seen us last year felt that we had improved greatly. Thus, there is no dearth of talent in our country. I am of the opinion that we can become really good golfers if first of all we are provided with good coaches and secondly we are given more frequent opportunities to participate in international tournaments.

BULA CHOWDHURY – NEW INDIAN SWIMMING SENSATION

WOMAN'S ERA – AUGUST (FIRST) 1985

Bula Chowdhury, the 15-year old swimming sensation from Bengal is the National record holder in the Butterfly event. I met Bula at the lounge of the Nehru Stadium Complex after she returned from a strenuous practice session at the Talkatora Swimming pool under the guidance of Eric Arnold, the reputed Australian coach.

Bula, you look extremely tired. What is your training schedule like?

Our training is partly in the morning and the rest in the evening. We have weight-training exercises for an hour from 5.30 a.m. to 6.30 a.m. This is followed by two and a half hours practice session at the Talkatora pool from 7.00 a.m. In the evening we have practice for two and a half hours from 5.00 p.m.

Why are you undergoing this training?

This training is part of the preparations for the 1986 Asian Games.

Bula, let us go back to your early days and your career so far. When and how did you take to swimming?

Our family, which is not very well-to-do, comes from Hooghly district in West Bengal. Though there are no established swimmers in our family, I, like any other villager, liked swimming as there were a number of pools near our place. I started swimming at the age of 5. Soon after, I joined the Chattra Swimming Club.

When did you first participate in State-level competitions?

In the age-group State Championship, I have been regularly representing my state since 1978 while at the senior level I first represented my state in the Delhi Nationals in 1982. Presently, I am the National Record holder in the 100 m and 200 m Butterfly events for women.

Have you been coached?

Yes. I have been coached by Pashupati Kundu, who still guides me when I have problems. Of course, I have received training from Jonke, a German coach prior to the New Delhi Asian Games in 1982. Right now I am being coached by Eric Arnold, an Australian.

How do you find the foreign coaches?

The two foreign coaches who trained me have helped me a lot. They use more advanced methods than our own coaches. I wish we could be under foreign coaches for a longer period.

I understand you will be going for training to Australia for six months. When will you be going there?

Eric Arnold, who will be my coach in Australia, has said that I will be going to Australia in July 1985 and will be trained there till March 1986. Arnold has his own swimming centre in Newcastle. A number of international meets will be held in Australia then. So I will get plenty of opportunities to compete with the best and learn.

When did you make your international debut?

At the junior level, I first represented my country in the Asian Age-Group Championship in Hong Kong in 1983. I got the bronze medal in the 100m Butterfly event. At the senior level, I represented my country for the first time at the South Asian Games at Seoul in 1984. I performed fairly well equalling the Asian Games meet record in the 100m Butterfly events.

Could you tell us about your international career to date?

After Seoul, I was selected to represent India in Friendship 1984 in Russia. The standard in that competition was very high. Though I could achieve very little, it was a great learning experience for me. After that I represented my country in the South Asian Games in Kathmandu last year. I won four golds in the Championship.

Do you have any other interests?

I like seeing movies but honestly, swimming for me is everything.

Finally, has swimming affected your studies?

I am a student of class X at R.R. Balika Vidyalaya, Hind Motor. My studies have been affected but my school sees to it that I do not suffer academically.

GAURAV GHEI – AN IMMENSELY TALENTED YOUNG GOLFER

CHILDREN'S WORLD – SEPTEMBER 1985

THE 1984 S.S. Prakash Trophy, awarded by the Delhi Sports Journalists Association to the most promising junior sportsman, went to 16-year-old Gaurav Ghei, a golfer of great promise. I met Gaurav at his residence in Delhi and spoke to him about his golfing career.

Gaurav captained the Modern School golf team, which represented India in the eight-nation Aer Lingus International Schoolboys Golf Championship held in South West Ireland on 12 May. India finished fourth. Gaurav was satisfied with the result, taking into account the extremely difficult course and inclement weather.

Gaurav's success story began from the time he was a toddler. He used to accompany his father, an accomplished player himself, to the golf course, not bothering about the heat, cold, or rain. He thus picked up the basics of the game.

He began competing in 1980, but success and fame came his way only a couple of years later. Participating in the Junior age- group at the national level in 1982, Gaurav was the runner-up in the Northern India Sub-Junior Golf Championship (Calcutta) and sixth in the Junior event.

The year 1983 saw many laurels coming Gaurav's way. He won the Northern India Sub-Junior and Junior Golf titles for the second time and finished fifth in the Asian Junior Golf Championship at Jakarta. Later that year, Gaurav finished runner-up in the All India Amateur Championship (Seniors)played at Delhi, becoming the youngest finalist in the history of the championship to date. Gaurav entered the international arena at the senior level in 1984, when he represented India in the Indo-French tie at Paris and the Sri Lanka Amateur Golf Championship at Colombo. He has won the Junior Championship of Northern India, again, this year.

Gaurav feels that our country has a dearth of good coaches. So while our players rely on talent to win, the players abroad win through a combination of talent and technique.

Young, talented, disciplined, and determined as he is, with a fair amount of international experience, there is no reason why Gaurav cannot become one of India's finest golfers.

P.K. BANERJEE– INDIAN FOOTBALL OLYMPIAN AND CHIEF COACH

HINDUSTAN TIMES - 18 SEPTEMBER 1986

The Indian soccer side was having its last workout at the Nehru Stadium, New Delhi before leaving for Seoul to participate in the Asiad. The Chief coach, Mr. P.K. Banerjee, a veteran of two Olympics (1956 at Melbourne and 1960 at Rome) and three Asiads (1958 at Tokyo, 1962 at Jakarta and 1966 at Bangkok) was supervising the practice. After it was over, I chatted with the 50-year-old Banerjee who was also India's chief coach in the 1982 Asiad at Delhi, on the Indian soccer side's prospects at Seoul and Indian football in general.

Pradip da, when did you take charge of this side?

I was given this side in May this year. Since then we have had a camp at Shillong where the weather is similar to what we are going to experience in Seoul, and other camps at Delhi and Siliguri. It was a pity that our final camp could not be held at Shillong due to very heavy rains. That camp was shifted to Siliguri where we were provided with an excellent ground as well as other facilities. Apart from training, our boys made a short tour to Russia and also participated in the Merdeka Cup. I am extremely grateful to former Olympian Arun Ghosh, the team's assistant coach and Dr. Tandon who was in charge of the physical conditioning of the team.

We read excellent reports about our side's performances in this year's Merdeka tournament. What are your comments?

Our side did put up a fairly good show in the Merdeka tournament, losing in the semi-finals to Czechoslovakia 0-1 very late in the game. However, our finishing needs to be improved further.

What do you feel are our prospects in the forthcoming Asiad?

Our team has improved a lot tactically and also from the point of view of physical fitness. However, we really have no gifted player in our team even of the calibre of fullback, Sudhir Karmakar, and forwards Habib and Inder Singh (Indian Soccer stars of the late sixties and early seventies). Again, in Seoul, we have a tough draw. We face South Korea in our first match, China in the second and Bahrain in the third. But I am confident my boys will give off their best and do the country proud.

You spoke about a dearth of skillful players. Could anything be done to overcome this dearth?

Skill is something that is natural. Right now we do not seem to have such players in our country. I sincerely hope we can spot such players soon. But till the time such players are spotted, we have to pick the best we have and train them hard. Even by doing this, one can achieve fairly good results.

Pradip da, you were a member of the Indian side which last won the Asian Games Football title in 1962 at Jakarta. Could you for the benefit of readers recall that game?

That was an unforgettable final. The political situation that prevailed during that Asiad was so tense that the Indian side could not go out during the Games. South Korea whom we met in the finals had beaten us in the first round. But in the finals, we were a very committed lot. We were lucky too to have a coach like the late S.A. Rahim and at the end, we emerged 2-1 victors over South Korea to regain the title after 11 years.

You said that you were lucky to have a coach like Rahim. In what ways was Rahim an outstanding coach?

Late Rahim Saheb has been our most successful coach at the International level. Under him, we reached the semi-finals of the 1956 Melbourne Olympics and won the Asiad title in 1962 besides playing extremely well in the 1960 Rome Olympics. Rahim was a meticulous coach with a thorough knowledge of the game. Being a school teacher, he understood the psychology of the players well and could motivate them. He also possessed the rare preaching ability that could influence the dedicated, talented though generally uneducated, lower-middle-class players of those days. Lastly, he was a very strict disciplinarian.

DIANA EDULJEE– A STAR WOMEN'S CRICKETER

HINDUSTAN TIMES - 10 JANUARY 1987

Diana Eduljee, the 29-year-old Indian and Railway captain, has been a regular member of the Indian women's cricket team since the inaugural Test against Australia at Pune in 1975. In fact, this exciting all-rounder who is an aggressive right-hand bat and an outstanding left-arm spinner (the only bowler in the world to take 100 or more Test wickets) has missed only one Test in eleven years of her Test career. That Test was the first one against England last year when she had to drop out owing to a broken finger.

Diana was fortunate to have been brought up in a Railway colony in Bombay where tennis ball cricket matches used to be a regular feature. Initially these matches used to be played only by boys till Diana was old enough to join them. In 1971, a women's cricket club called ALBEES was formed and Diana along with her sister Behroze immediately joined it. Incidentally, Behroze, a left-arm medium pacer, also played Test cricket for India.

The year 1973 saw Diana make the Bombay side which participated in the first Nationals at Pune. She continued to successfully represent Bombay and West Zone till 1985. In 1985, the Railways side was formed and under Diana's captaincy the team won both the Nationals and the Rani Jhansi Trophy - the symbol for supremacy among zonal sides in India.

Diana's Test debut was against Australia at Pune in 1975. The Test was the first one to be played by Indian women. Her Test debut was quite remarkable in that she scored 48 not out and took 6 for 104. Diana has so far taken 114 Test wickets with the best performance of 7 for 76 against New Zealand at Lucknow in 1976. "I'll only retire when I reach 200 wickets," she added.

Asked about the best match of her career, Diana felt it was, without doubt, the fourth Test against the West Indies at Patna in 1976. It was India's first win in a Test. In that Test, India set only 55 for a win collapsed to 25 for 5 when Diana and Susan Itticheria got together. The two of them with some bold batting helped India to pull off a historic five-wicket win before a cheering 40,000 crowd. Diana had the honour of hitting the winning run.

About the present state of women's cricket in India, Diana felt that more tournaments should be organized. At present, women cricketers took part in just two tournaments and spent the rest of the time attending coaching camps. Diana felt that coaching camps were a waste of time and should be replaced by tournaments at different levels. She was pained to see the standard of university cricket (women's) going down and was of the opinion that this deterioration could be checked if school level cricket was properly organized.

When asked about the emergence of the Railways as a force in women's cricket, Diana said that it was mainly due to the efforts of the Railway Minister Madhav Rao Scindia. In 1985, Diana had requested Mr. Scindia to start a Railway women's cricket side and the green signal was given immediately. Diana started roping in players many of whom have played Test cricket for India. According to Diana, the main purpose behind all this is to provide promising youngsters with jobs and also to give something in return to those players who are needy and who have contributed their best to women's cricket for a number of years.

Regarding the sort of jobs and benefits given by the Railways to these players, Diana said, "The recruited cricketers are given clerical jobs and are placed in suitable grades according to their playing ability and academic qualifications." As regards incentives, Diana gave the example of Sandhya Aggarwal who got the world's highest Test score in England last year. Apart from two promotions, Sandhya was given Rs.25,000-partly by the Railways and the remaining from Mr. Scindia's Trust Fund.

"Isn't that sufficient incentive?" Diana asked.

SANDHYA AGGARWAL – A VERY SUCCESSFUL INDIAN WOMEN'S CRICKET OPENER

HINDUSTAN TIMES - 16 JANUARY 1987

In men's cricket, India has Sunil Gavaskar, an opening batsman who has broken almost all Test batting records. Among our women cricketers too we have an opener who has one world record to her credit – the highest individual Test score. She is 24-year-old Sandhya Aggarwal from Indore in Madhya Pradesh.

Sandhya was recently in Delhi to attend a camp organized by her employers, the Railways, in preparation for the ensuing National Women's Cricket Championship. For the record it is worth mentioning that in eight Tests to date, Sandhya has scored 879 runs at an average of 73.25. She has four Test centuries to her credit. In one-day cricket she has been reasonably successful with the highest score of 72 against England in the first One-Day at Leicester last year. I met Sandhya during the camp.

Do you come from a cricketing family?

You will be surprised to know that no one in my family barring me, of course, has played cricket.

Then how did you develop such a great interest in the game?

My interest in cricket developed by listening to radio commentaries. Slowly I started watching and then playing the game with the boys in our locality.

Have you been coached?

Not really. The only little coaching I have got was from former Test player S.Mustaq Ali during our university coaching camps.

Do you follow any practice schedule?

In Indore, we do not have many facilities for women's cricket. Despite that, I practise seven hours daily at a nearby club. This practice is broken up into two sessions.

When did you make your Test debut and how did you fare in it?

I was selected to play for India for the first time against Australia in the third Test Ahmedabad in 1984. I scored 71 in my only innings in that Test. In the next Test at Bombay- the last Test of that series, I scored 134 and 83. My 134 became the highest Test score by an Indian woman.

On your first tour to England last year you scored two centuries in the three Tests that were played. What would you attribute your success to?

I feel I succeeded in England first of all because Diana Eduljee, our captain, was a great source of encouragement and secondly because I concentrated hard and learned quickly from my mistakes.

Could you tell readers something about the wickets in England?

The wickets and the atmospheric conditions in England vary from place to place quite drastically. For example, some wickets are soft, some very green with patches and others quite hard too. Since there is a lot of late movement, one has to watch the ball till the last moment. The varied conditions really helped me to tighten my game. In short, my tour of England was a cricketing education.

What about the other things like food and accommodation?

The accommodation in most places was reasonably good but honestly, nothing compared to what we provide in India for touring cricketers. The vegetarians in the side did have problems regarding food.

How big were the crowds?

The crowds were reasonably good. On Saturdays and Sundays from about 3,000 to 4,000 people used to watch our matches.

You got your world record score of 190 against England in the third Test at Worcester last year. Could you recall that innings?

England batted first and declared their innings closed early on the second day after scoring 334 runs. We started off well being 100 for two but a little later we were 150 for 6. When Mani Mala Singhal joined me, we saw the day through and our side's score was 232 for six at the draw of stumps. The third day saw our team suffer three more losses and we were 316 for 9 with a day and a little more than three hours play left. I was on 160 at that stage when the last player Sujatha Sridhar joined me. Since the wicket was getting increasingly difficult, it was imperative that Sujatha and myself not only scored runs but also bat for quite a while. Fortunately, Sujatha batted sensibly and we put on 58 runs for the last wicket and left England with a little over a day to try and force a win. The game ended in a respectable draw. I was last out for 190 after batting for 9 hours and 45 minutes while Sujatha remained not out on 20.

When did you realize that you were near the world record and how did you finally achieve that distinction?

I was on 175 when my skipper Diana Eduljee sent me a message saying that the world record was 189 made by England's Betty Snowball against New Zealand at Christchurch in 1935 and that I ought to break it since I was so close to it. She also said that these opportunities do not come often. Thanks to Sujatha's support, I made it but after withstanding great pressure from the English team. When I was on 188, their star left-arm spinner Jill Macknway was brought on. They surrounded me with eight fielders close to the bat. To make matters worse, the first ball beat me badly. Fortunately, the next ball was short and I took a single to cover to become a holder of a world record.

Finally, what do you feel about women's cricket in India today?

There is a lot of talent available. However, encouragement and publicity are lacking. Our Test matches and other important tournaments should be given wide coverage. The highlights of our Tests and one-day games should be shown on television. Schools should have girls cricket teams and regular inter-school tournaments should be held. If all this is done I am certain our cricketers will hold their own at the international level.

B.S. CHANDRASEKHAR – ONE OF THE GREATEST LEG SPINNERS OF ALL TIME

HINDUSTAN TIMES - 23 MARCH 1987

"We may produce another Prasanna, Bedi or Venkat but we can never produce another Chandra," said G.R. Vishwanath to me about B.S. Chandrasekhar, one of the greatest leg-spinners India and the world has produced. In just 58 Tests, the 41-year-old Karnataka spin wizard took 242 wickets with an innings best of 8 for 79 in the first innings of the first Test against England at New Delhi, in 1972-73 and a match-best of 12 for 104 (6 for 52 in both innings) against Australia in the third Test at Melbourne in 1977-78. He took five or more wickets in an innings 16 times and ten or more wickets in a match twice. Chandra spoke to me about his bowling, career and about players he had played with and against.

Chandra, people have always referred to you as a freak bowler because you bowl with a polio-stricken right hand. What have you to say about it?

I was stricken by polio quite early. However, I did not allow it to interfere with my enthusiasm for the game. Of course, throwing with the right hand was difficult so I have always thrown with my left hand. I must clarify this misconception about my being a freak bowler. I was fully aware of what I wanted to bowl. I could, fortunately, bowl almost anything–legbreaks, googlies, top spinners and fast off breaks. Some of my deliveries possibly due to polio would come through really fast. But to say that I was a freak bowler is incorrect.

Which performance of yours would you rate as your most memorable one?

Three performances really come to mind. First of all was my 4 of 50 and 4 for 73 vs. Australia in the second Test at Bombay in 1964 – a Test which India won; secondly, my 7 for 157 and 4 for 78 vs. the West Indies in the first Test at Bombay in 1966-67 as the West Indies had a very powerful batting line – up and finally, my 6 for 38 in the second innings of the third Test at the Oval in 1971 against England which helped India to win a series in England for the first time. This performance helped me to reestablish my place in the Indian side.

In the late sixties and seventies you and the other three spinners (Prasanna, Bedi and Venkat) were helped greatly by some brilliant close-in fielders. Could you tell readers about them?

We were lucky to have superb close-in fielders like Solkar, Venkat, Abid Ali and Wadekar. Of these four fielders, Solkar deserves special mention. Solkar was a fielder who could make the impossible possible. He was very courageous and had wonderful anticipation. His very presence was an inspiration.

You have played under some of India's best captains. Whom would you rate the best?

Tiger Pataudi was the best captain of the lot. He could instill confidence in his team members and get the best out of them.

Chandra, you have bowled to some of the best batsmen all over the world. Who in your opinion is the best?

In my opinion, the late Ken Barrington of England is the best batsman I have bowled to. He had a sound defence and believed in tiring the bowlers before assuming control. He never gave bowlers a chance. In this assessment of mine, I am not considering the Indian batsmen.

In the 1967-68 Indian tour of Australia, you were sent back home. What went wrong?

Actually, things went wrong in England itself before the Australian tour. My ankles started giving trouble because of the soft English ground conditions. This ankle trouble upset me a lot on the hard Australian wickets, and so I had to return home.

Any disappointments?

Yes, I was most upset when I was left out of the 1971 tour of the West Indies. That is why I was determined to prove myself in England. Thank God I did so.

MANSUR ALI KHAN PATAUDI - A BRILLIANT BATSMAN AND GREAT CAPTAIN

SUNDAY HINDUSTAN TIMES - 12 APRIL 1987

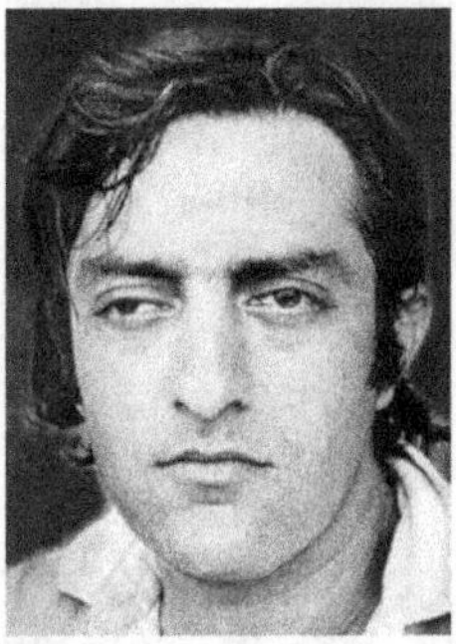

I met Mansur Ali Khan Pataudi at his residence in Delhi and the brilliant batsman and great captain spoke on the game and his contemporaries.

Do you feel that changes should be introduced in Test cricket to make it result-oriented?

Most certainly, yes. With the advent of limited-overs cricket, people have begun to expect results. They are, now, not prepared to sit through five days and watch Tests ending in draws. I honestly feel the time has come for the introduction of limited-overs Test cricket. To restrict, for example, the first innings of either side to 120 overs each and the second innings to 80 overs. This sort of a system will benefit everyone concerned, i.e., batsmen will get sufficient time to develop an innings, bowlers will get a fair opportunity to display their skills and the crowds are bound to return as all Tests will be decisive.

Limited-overs cricket has made such an impact. What have you to say on this kind of cricket?

Honestly, it is because of limited-overs cricket that the game is still surviving. People come in thousands to witness this kind of cricket. As far as the plus points are concerned: first of all, the running between the wickets has improved and secondly, the quality of fielding in Test cricket has really become much better due to this kind of cricket. But limited-overs cricket has its minus points too. **Only batsmen of the highest class can make the necessary adjustments in technique, concentration and general attitude, to remain really successful in Test cricket.** Limited-overs cricket, I feel, has also made bowlers more defensive. Most bowlers these days are tighter but less penetrative.

Sunil Gavaskar reached 10,000 runs in Test cricket in the Ahmedabad Test. Your comments.

I feel it is a remarkable achievement which only highlights Sunny's skill, dedication and powers of concentration as a batsman. But to me, it is Sunny's 34 Test centuries which I consider a greater achievement, as only Test cricketers will realize the great difference there is between scoring 99 and scoring 100. A player like Miandad of Pakistan, who has age in his favour, could, in the same number of Tests every year for the next six to seven years, break this 10,000 mark but it will take someone really exceptional to better 34 Test hundreds.

Tiger, going back to your playing days, which innings of your Test career would you rate as your best?

Three Tests in particular stand out. The first one was in 1964, in the second Test at Bombay, when we beat Australia. In that match I batted well in both innings to get scores of 86 and 53. But the knocks which I would rate very highly are the ones vs. England at Leeds in 1967 and vs. Australia at Melbourne in 1967-68. In both Tests, the odds were against India and the morale, too, was sagging. It was my knocks in both these Tests that restored confidence in our team. At Melbourne, with virtually one fit leg. I scored 75 and 85 while at Headingley, Leeds, when our team had given up all hope, being 386 runs behind on the first innings, I got 148 in our second innings score of 510. In the first innings, I scored 64 out of 164.

Whom would you rate the best fast bowler you played against in Tests?

Without a doubt, Andy Roberts of the West Indies. Roberts was really quick. He also bowled a very good bouncer. To make matters worse for the batsman, he was not only very accurate but also possessed great variety.

While on the topic of fast bowling, how do you evaluate Kapil Dev?

Kapil cannot be classified as a fast bowler, as Imran is. He is not quick enough to force a batsman on to his backfoot. Kapil's success has proved one thing – that is, you do not need to be a fast bowler to be successful in Tests. He has proved that if you are medium-fast but possess fine control and mastery over swing, particularly over the outswinger, you can be a successful bowler. His 300 plus Test wickets is a remarkable feat.

Could you give your assessment of the four great spinners who played under you?

Chandra was a unique bowler. He could either be a match-winner or a very expensive proposition. Fortunately, we got along well and he did prove quite successful under my tenure as captain.

Bishen was a great left-arm spinner – perfect control, perfect loop and sharp spin. The only drawback about his bowling was that at times he tended to be more generous with runs than he should have been.

Prasanna was the type who would willingly listen to what you told him. A great off-spinner, who would willingly bowl in any situation.

Venkat was the quickish type of off-spinner. He started his Test career with success but had a lean patch midway as he suddenly started flighting the ball – a style that never suited him all. Later, when he reverted to his normal style he achieved success once again. He was a good thinker. My biggest regret about Venkat was that he never realized his potential as a batsman. He could have become a really good all-rounder.

You have played with and against cricketers from Bombay. What is so special about them?

Cricket in Bombay is of a very tough variety. Bombay cricketers are taught from the early stages not to throw away their wickets. The great quality about Bombay cricketers is their extra determination and that they are not overawed by the opposition.

Certain countries have started having professional team managers. What do you feel about it?

First of all, it is difficult to choose the right kind of professional manager. The wrong manager can do more harm than good. I am, somehow, not in favour of this system.

Your comments regarding the present cricket scene?

I feel that there is too much Test cricket these days. This is killing public interest. Domestic cricket should be given its due importance and Test cricket should not be allowed to clash with domestic matches.

V.K. RAMASWAMY– ONE OF THE FIRST TWO NEUTRAL TEST UMPIRES

HINDUSTAN TIMES - 13 APRIL 1987

Forty-two-year-old Vrinchipuram Krishnamurthy Ramaswamy of Hyderabad is one of India's leading Test umpires today. V.K. Ramaswamy, as he is better known, made his Test debut as an umpire in the fourth Test between India and England at Madras on 13 January 1985. Last year, he was one of the neutral umpires for the Test series between West Indies and Pakistan in Pakistan. This season, he umpired six of the eleven Tests that were played in India. In a chat with me, Ramaswamy spoke on the India-Pakistan fifth Test at Bangalore in which he was one of the umpires, his experiences as a neutral umpire, his career and what it takes to become a good umpire.

Could you tell readers about your experience at the Bangalore Test?

The Bangalore Test has been the most difficult one of my career to date. It was a wicket where it was impossible for a bowler to bowl a straight ball. The ball turned sharply, gathered pace all of a sudden and at times jumped awkwardly. On such a wicket, whenever I was in doubt, I, without the least hesitation, gave the benefit of the doubt to the batsman.

Certain decisions of your in that Test were questioned as being incorrect. What have you to say?

The only thing I can say is that it was a very difficult wicket for one to umpire on. However, I must add that whatever decision I gave was given after great thought and only when I was absolutely convinced. You must remember mistakes can even be made by the best.

You were selected as a neutral umpire in the Pakistan-West Indies Test series in Pakistan last year. What were your experiences there?

P D Reporter and I (both from India) became Test cricket's first two neutral umpires in the second Test of the series at Lahore on 7-9 November 1986. The wickets in Pakistan during the two Tests we umpired were also bad. Despite that, there was less dissatisfaction among the players as the decisions we gave were not disputed. Right or wrong, the decisions were accepted without a murmur. From the personal point of view, I felt quite thrilled and honoured at being selected as a neutral umpire, and that too in a Test match.

As an experienced umpire, what do you feel are the qualities a good umpire should possess?

In my opinion, any good umpire should be dedicated, knowledgeable, possess powers of concentration, and lastly be keen on match practice.

Do you feel umpires in India lack match practice?

Not quite. In a number of big cities the local season starts from May/June and spreads till September. As a result, umpires get match practice before the big matches start. But this depends on which city one is based in.

Do big and noisy crowds affect an umpire's performance?

Yes, to an extent it does. Umpiring in these conditions requires a lot more of concentration. This is so because at times a few snicks are missed.

Finally, would you like to say anything from the point of view of umpires in India?

I feel umpires need more understanding and recognition. I feel organizations employing Test umpires should give them the same facilities and recognition as given to Test cricketers working with them.

MOHINDER LAL – SCORER OF HOCKEY GOLD MEDAL WINNING GOAL IN 1964 OLYMPICS

HINDUSTAN TIMES - 22 APRIL 1987

The Real Club de Polo de Barcelona (Spain) played an exhibition hockey match in Delhi against the IFFCO XI. What struck one most about the Spanish team was that their coach was Mohinder Lal, a former India Olympian. 51-year-old Mohinder Lal, a fine half back in his hey day, is best remembered for converting the penalty stroke against Pakistan in the finals of the 1964 Tokyo Olympics which won India the Olympic gold after a gap of eight years. I met Mohinder Lal at the Shivaji Stadium and spoke to him about his career both as a player and a coach and Indian Hockey too.

Before I ask you anything else, I would like you to tell our readers about that winning goal you scored in Tokyo?

I cannot forget that moment. The penalty stroke was awarded as a penalty corner taken by our side struck a Pakistan defender on his foot. Much to the relief of the entire side and myself, I converted it. In that tournament I converted all the three strokes I took so I was not nervous at all. This goal of mine gave us the gold which had eluded us in the 1960 Rome Olympics.

When did you qualify as a coach?

In 1963, I did a nine months coaching diploma from the National Institute of Sports at Patiala.

When did you take to coaching?

While captaining the Northern Railway side, I would, on occasions, give tips as a coach. But I started full time coaching when I went to Spain in 1968.

What made you choose Spain?

I went to Spain in 1968 for treatment of my heart problem which was due to overexertion. It was while I was there, I got this offer to coach. I have been in Barcelona since then.

Could you tell our readers about the club where you coach?

The club is basically for Polo but it also encourages hockey. It is one of the richest clubs in Europe. It has three hockey grounds – one natural grass, one artificial surface and one all weather.

What other coaching assignments did you take up in Spain?

I have coached the Spanish Junior National side two or three times in the late seventies. In 1983, I was the coach of the Spanish Senior Women's side which finished second in the Inter-Continental Championship in Malaysia.

You were at London during the World Cup Hockey Tournament last year. What do you feel is wrong with Indian Hockey?

Technically, I feel India is still one of the best in the world. What we need to change is our attitude. For example, we still feel we are the best in the world dreaming about our glorious past. We are yet to accept and understand reality. Again, I feel we must try to get a good foreign coach for our national team. We do not need a foreign coach to teach us hockey but we certainly need one to change the mental attitude of our players. Our players lack team spirit and a killer instinct. A foreign coach will be able to instill these qualities in our players.

Finally, you were an excellent player and also have years of coaching experience behind you. Why do you not coach our National side?

Who does not want to coach his or her National side? The fact is I have never been asked to do so.

1996-1999

S. Vishwanath, Charles Cornelius, Ajitpal Singh, Ashok Kumar, T.A.P. Sekar, Roger Binny, Purnima Rau, Manuel Aaron, S. Vijayalakshmi, Praveen Amre, Kamlesh Mehta and M.L. Jaisimha

SADANAND VISHWANATH – A TALENTED WICKET-KEEPER AND CAPABLE UMPIRE

ENGLISH RAJASTHAN PATRIKA SUNDAY 15 DECEMBER 1996

The years 1984 and 1985 saw the arrival of Sadanand Vishwanath, a 22-year-old Karnataka wicket keeper, who not only made the Indian side but also literally had the cricketing world at his feet in the Benson and Hedges World Series Championships at Australia in 1985 which India won. In fact, skipper Sunil Gavaskar said,"One of the main reasons for India winning the B & H World Cup was the presence of Sadanand Vishwanath."Sadanand was in the Pink City recently to umpire a Ranji Trophy match and he spoke to me on his cricket career-past and present.

When did you take to umpiring?

I passed the All India Umpiring exam held at Hyderabad in 1994 for players. Test players have to umpire eight first-class matches before they become eligible to officiate International matches. So far, I have umpired six games including a few Ranji games and the 1995 Vizzy trophy final.

Karnataka seems to be dominating the Indian Cricket scene at present. What would you attribute this to?

I am thrilled that so many Karnataka players are in the Indian squad. The reasons for this are first of all peer pressure, secondly trying to keep a tradition alive and lastly the great encouragement being given to talent from the districts. By peer pressure, I mean that once Kumble and Srinath made the Indian side, the other players in the Karnataka side began to feel that if Anil and Javagal could make it, so can we. Again in 1976, Karnataka had G.R.

Vishwanath, Brijesh Patel, Kirmani, Prasanna, Chandrasekhar and Sudhakar Rao in the Indian side that toured New Zealand and the West Indies. Vishwanath, Prasanna and Chandrasekhar were greats of Indian Cricket. The MRF pace academy in Chennai, too, has been a great help to budding pacemen.

Apart from umpiring, how are you contributing to the improvement of cricket in Karnataka?

I have now taken to coaching youngsters. For the last two seasons,I have been conducting summer camps for the poorer children in the state who wish to learn the game and do well in it. I feel the hunger to succeed is most in the economically poor people.

You achieved so much at an early age. Who inspired and helped you to achieve all that you did?_

I owe almost everything to the encouragement given by my father and mother. Qualities like working hard, fighting against odds and being sincere were inculcated in me by my mother. When I was young, she presented me with a book on wicket-keeping by Alan Knott. This book served as an inspiration. My coach in the early days- Mr.Tarapore also helped me a lot.

Ravi Shastri was your skipper on quite a few junior level International tours. What are your memories of Ravi and those tours?

Ravi Shastri was and is an intelligent person who was a born leader. Shastri, who had got his baptism at the highest level much before my colleagues and me, helped and guided us a lot on those tours. He helped us to settle down easily and also perform to the best of our capabilities. Quite a few of us developed under his leadership. In fact, he could easily be called the leader of the youth brigade.

Talking about the under-19 and under-25 National sides and the international tours, I cannot help but remember 1984 under-25 tour to Zimbabwe. In that side, which was led by Ravi Shastri, we also had Srikkant, Siddhu, Prabakhar, Maninder Singh and Lalchand Rajput. I was the only wicket-keeper on the tour and I had 31 victims in 10 matches. The Zimbabweans were most impressed by my keeping.

Sadanand, even to this day we all remember your tremendous performance in the Benson and Hedges World Championship in Australia in 1985. What were your feelings on that tour?

It was my first tour abroad with the senior Indian side. That was the greatest period of my cricketing career. On that tour, I felt that it was a golden opportunity for me to establish myself as the country's number one keeper. Again, my mother to whom I owe almost everything was not well. I felt that for her sake I must do my best. Fortunately,God was with me and I justified my presence with some highly motivating performances. The performances were motivating as I not only kept well but also pepped-up my team-mates and lifted their sagging spirits.

What would you say were the reasons for India winning that tournament?

The Indian side for the Benson and Hedges World Series Championships was an excellent blend of youth and experience. It was a real brain-wave to have kept in mind the large grounds in Australia and selected leg-spinner L. Sivaramakrishnan. Siva proved to be a great success. We were led by the analytical, astute cricketing brain of Sunil Gavaskar who also showed on that tour that he was a master in the art of man-management. He inspired everyone and got the best out of all the players. The team spirit was very high. The whole team played well with each player performing for the side whenever required. Except the final where Pakistan lost nine wickets, all other sides that played us were bowled out.

How did you reach the senior level in the International scene so quickly?

The former Indian wicket-keeper Syed Kirmani who was nearly 11 ½ years older than I was, also came from Karnataka. It became my deepest desire to take over as India'swicketkeeper from him. When young,i.e. as an 18-year-old, I was not only able to represent Karnataka but also South Zone. In my Duleep Trophy debut, I had seven victims including six in an innings against Central Zone at Kanpur. Kirmani going abroad to represent the country or playing for India in Tests at home provided me with opportunities at the

Ranji and Duleep levels. My determination and talent too helped me to capitalize on those breaks and reach the International level by the time I was barely 22. I was 22 ½ when I went to Australia for the B & H World Series. I was also the Indian wicketkeeper during the Rothman's Four Nation trophy tournament at Sharjah, which India won defeating Pakistan and Australia.

In 1985 you also made your Test debut in Sri Lanka. Tell us about that tour.

That tour was probably the only one India has embarked on before the start of the Indian Cricket season – as early as August. It was basically a political tour. The umpiring was poor and the team did not play too well. In the three Tests I played I kept quite well to finish with 11 catches. Unfortunately, I never played another Test for India after this series.

What would you say were the reasons for your not consolidating on your early successes?

The tragedy of my career was that in 1985 when I had established myself as the best wicket keeper in the country, I still could not consider myself a certainty in the Karnataka side as the then veteran Kirmani kept on insisting that he should be Karnataka's keeper rather than permitting me to gracefully take over. My state officials and the South Zone selectors never played me on crucial occasions and I kept on losing opportunities of coming back into the Indian side especially for Tests. Mind you till the 1988-89 season when I finally decided that it was time I gave up the fight, I was in terrific form both behind the wickets and as a batsman. I also could not consider leaving Karnataka and playing for another state due to family reasons. In the final analysis I suppose it was just my fate.

Finally, what are your future plans?

Firstly I am looking forward to my benefit match. Once that is through, I shall concentrate on my coaching and umpiring because cricket to me is life.

CHARLES CORNELIUS – A DEPENDABLE GOAL-KEEPER

ENGLISH RAJASTHAN PATRIKA SUNDAY 12 JANUARY 1997

Fifty-five-year-old Charles Cornelius, an officer with the Sports Authority of India in Chennai, was one of the most reliable goal-keepers India has had in the last twenty-five years. I was fortunate to talk to this unassuming, helpful veteran about his career and his life in Chennai.

You played for Punjab throughout your career. Which state are you actually from?

Yes. I played for Punjab throughout my hockey career. However, I am basically a

Tamilian who studied upto the second standard in Madras before moving to Punjab.

Who suggested that you take up goal-keeping?

It was the great Udham Singh who first suggested that I become a goal-keeper.

Did you model yourself on any one?

Yes, Christie, the former Indian goalie.

When did you make your debut for Punjab and for how many years did you represent the state?

I made my debut for Punjab in 1963-64. I continued to represent my state until 1974.

When did you make your debut for India in a major international tournament?

The first major international tournament in which I represented India was the 1970 Asian Games.

Till when did you continue to represent India?

I continued to represent India till 1973-the 1971 and 1973 World Cups at Barcelona and Amsterdam and the 1972 Munich Olympics. I was selected for the 1974 Asian Games but a week before the Asiad I was accidentally injured in my leg during the training. Hence I could not go. Again, I was also selected for the 1975 World Cup side without the selectors being aware of my physical condition. In fact, my name was in the papers but I was confined to bed because of injury.

How did your leg get injured and how was it cured?

During the training a week before the 1974 Asiad I accidentally collided with an attacker. The injury in my leg took a very serious turn. Honestly, I really had a very difficult time from 1974 till 1976. In 1976, a sports lover after reading about my plight sent me to London to have an operation. The operation was successful and I was cured. Unfortunately, I had to leave the game after that.

In your international career, who are the forwards from other countries who impressed you the most?

Azad Malik of Pakistan was the trickiest forward I have come across. He was a master of the sliced shot which make players move the wrong way. Ric Charlesworth of Australia was also a superb forward.

Which international match do you have fondest memories of?

The match was against Pakistan in the 1973 World Cup. Pakistan's full back Tanvir Dar had said before the game that Pakistan would crush India. The match was on a Friday—an auspicious day for Pakistan and so our boys were tense. However, I had other ideas. I told my team-mates that Friday is a good day for Christians and I took the team to a church. I had a brilliant match and India won 1-0. The next day's papers had headings of 'Charles Saves India.'

Which was your saddest moment in International Hockey?

Without a doubt, the final of the 1973 World Cup tournament. We were leading 2-0 against Holland. We then scored two more genuine goals which were strangely disallowed. Holland then equalized and at full-time, the score was 2-2. In the sudden death, we got a penalty stroke which we missed. Had we scored we would have won. Finally, we lost 4-5 in the tie-breaker and finished runner-up.

Is stopping penalty strokes a matter of luck or technique?

To be honest luck plays a very big role as most often the ball is stroked to the right of the goalie. There are three methods to be followed when trying to save a stroke. First is to see the ball only, secondly-to see the action of the player only and thirdly, to take one side.

Finally what are the qualities one must possess to become a top-class goalie?

First of all the goalie must position himself perfectly,i.e. the legs must be correctly balanced and in a position of constant readiness. The goalie must have good anticipation and must know how to cover the angle of the ball. Goalies also must not only know when to advance but also to stop the ball properly and clear it away intelligently. A goalie must also kick well with both legs, stop aeriel balls and guide the defence from his position. The last point I would like to mention is a cool temperament - that is not to get over-awed by the big occasion and crack under pressure.

AJITPAL SINGH - CAPTAIN OF THE 1975 WORLD CUP WINNING INDIAN HOCKEY TEAM

ENGLISH RAJASTHAN PATRIKA
SUNDAY 2 FEBRUARY 1997

Forty-nine-year-old Ajitpal Singh was one of the finest centre-halves Indian Hockey has produced. The soft-spoken, cultured Ajitpal was in Chennai for the Champions Trophy. I met Ajitpal and he spoke to me about his career and hockey in general.

When and how did you start playing hockey?

I come from a village in Punjab called Sansarpur. This village has produced atleast twelve Olympians. So, in our village nearly all the children played hockey. Like the other children, I too, took to the game at an early age.

When did you first start playing competitive hockey at a higher level?

In the season 1964-65, I was selected to represent the All India Varsity team. In 1965, I made it to the Punjab state side. The Punjab side in those days used to be almost the Indian side. I continued to represent Punjab till 1984.

When did you first represent India and till when?

The first time I was selected to play for India was in 1966 when the Indian side toured Japan. I continued to regularly represent India till the 1976 Montreal Olympics. I represented India once later in the 1980 Champions Trophy at Karachi.

Could you tell readers about the main tournaments in which you represented the country?

I have represented India in three Olympics- 1968 at Mexico, 1972 at Munich and 1976 at Montreal, two Asiads 1970 at Bangkok and 1974 at Tehran; three World Cups tournaments-1971 at Barcelona, 1973 at Amsterdam and 1975 at Kuala Lumpur and the Champions Trophy tournament in 1980 at Karachi.

When did you captain India for the first time and which are the major tournaments where you have led India?

The first time I captained India was in 1971 at the Pesta Sukan tournament. I have had the honour of captaining India in the 1976 Olympics at Montreal, the 1971 World Cup at Barcelona and 1975 World Cup at Kuala Lumpur and the 1974 Asiad at Tehran.

You were the captain of the Indian side which won the 1975 World Cup at Kuala Lumpur and a member of the side which won the silver medal in the 1973 World Cup at Amsterdam. Could you tell readers about those two tournaments?

The 1975 win in the World Cup at Kuala Lumpur was a great moment for all of us. The team was a balanced one and the deep defence particularly was good. However, according to me the 1973 side was probably the best Indian team I have been a member of. We were unlucky to lose in the final to Holland.

Who is the best forward you have come across in International hockey?

The Pakistan forward line in 1973-74 was brilliant, Pakistan had four world-class forwards at that time- Islauddin, Abdul Rashid, Shahnaz and Samiullah. They were the best forwards I have played against.

What are the qualities that one needs to possess to become a good centre-half?

To be a good centre-half one must, first of all, possess a sharp hockey brain which enables one to anticipate and intercept; secondly, possess total skills; thirdly be superbly fit and lastly be dedicated.

What has been the impact of astro-turf in hockey?

The biggest plus-point about astro-turf is that the matches can be held in very wet weather as in the Champions Trophy at Chennai.

The game has become much faster. Again, players have to be much fitter. Basic skills of players have to be perfect if a team wishes to be successful.

What has been the impact of the new rules on the game?

The removal of the off-side rule has been the biggest change. The game has really opened up resulting in more field goals. The removal of the off-side rule has resulted in less pressure on the umpires as, whether goals scored were off-side or not, have created controversies in the past.

ASHOK KUMAR – A BRILLIANT FORWARD AND SON OF DHYAN CHAND

ENGLISH RAJASTHAN PATRIKA SUNDAY 2 FEBRUARY 1997

The late Dhyan Chand and hockey are synonymous. One of his sons – 47-year-old Ashok Kumar played for India with distinction and was widely regarded the world over as a very shrewd inside forward. Ashok was in Chennai for the Champions Trophy. I met him and we spoke about his career and hockey in general.

Did being the son of the great Dhyan Chand affect you?

Being the son of an all-time hockey great had both its advantages and disadvantages. The main advantage was a relatively easy entry. The biggest disadvantage was the expectations were very high and unnecessary and unfair comparisons used to be made. Fortunately I was myself good and I am happy that now long after retirement I am known as Ashok Kumar.

When did you first start playing competitive hockey?

I started playing serious competitive hockey in 1967 when I started playing inter-college matches. In 1969 I was selected for the Combined Universities side. My career really opened up when I joined Mohun Bagan Club, Calcutta in 1970. I continued to play in Calcutta for Mohun Bagan till 1972.

Was there any senior forward who had a great impact on you?

Without doubt, Inambhai (Inam-ur-Rehman). He was a genius-very skillful and a good scorer. Pity he never played more for India.

When did you first represent India and till when?

I first represented India in the 1970 Asiad in Bangkok. I continued to regularly represent India till the 1978 World Cup at Buenos Aires in Argentina.

Could you tell readers which are the main tournaments in which you represented India?

I have represented India in two Olympics – 1972 at Munich and 1976 at Montreal; four World Cups-1971 at Barcelona, 1973 at Amsterdam, 1975 at Kuala Lumpur where we won and 1978 at Buenos Aires; and three Asiads – 1970 at Bangkok, 1974 at Tehran and 1978 at Bangkok.

In which tournament did you perform outstandingly well?

My best tournament was the 1971 World Cup at Barcelona. However, I also played extremely well in the 1973 and 1975 World Cups at Amsterdam and Kuala Lumpur respectively and the 1972 Munich Olympics.

Which is the best Indian side you have played for?

True, we won the World Cup in 1975 but in my opinion, the 1973 World Cup side was the best Indian team I have ever played in. Not only did the team have plenty of class but it was also perhaps the fittest to play for India. We were trained by Jagmohan Singh, an athletics coach at NIS, Patiala. He made us have strenuous workoutsand we were really the better for it. In 1973, we were most unfortunate to lose in the final to Holland, in the tie-breaker.

Talking about fitness programmes, the present Indian side attended a workshop on yoga before the Champions Trophy. How beneficial is Yoga for hockey players?

We also had a few sessions of yoga in 1973. To be frank, yoga is of little use for hockey players as it does not help where speedy work is involved.

Who were the outstanding defenders in your time?

In India, we had two outstanding fullbacks in the late Surjit Singh and Michael Kindo. Ajitpal was also a great centre-half.

Of the defenders from other countries I rate Munnawar Zaman of Pakistan and Michael Peter of Germany very highly.

What must India do to become a force in International hockey?

We must go for players who are in the age group of 18-22 years. Now is the time to do it as the next Olympic Games is nearly three and a half years away. We must have a squad of 25 players who have the basic talent. These players should be left with a coach and a physical trainer. The coach's job will be to form a cohesive unit while the physical trainer's job will be to ensure that the boys are fit. In a huge country like India I am sure the talent is there.

You have played both as an inside right and as an inside left with distinction. Could you tell readers what qualities are required to be successful as an inside right and as an inside left?

The inside-right is the planner. He has to be a quick thinker and anticipate situations quickly. He has to ensure that the inside left and the center-forward get opportunities to exploit the no off-side rule.

The inside-left also has to be skillful but he is more of a scorer. He has to intercept the crosses from the right and convert them. Coordination between him, the centre-forward and the centre-half is a must. Each position is important and success will only come if we bear in mind that hockey is a team game.

T.A.P. SEKAR – CHIEF COACH AT MRF PACE ACADEMY

ENGLISH RAJASTHAN PATRIKA
SUNDAY 9 FEBRUARY 1997

On a recent visit to Chennai, I was fortunate to visit the MRF Pace Foundation and meet its chief coach- T.A.P. Sekar. 40-year-old Tirumalai Anantha Pillai Sekar is a former Indian Test paceman who represented the country in two Tests against Pakistan in Pakistan in 1982-83 and four one-day internationals. In his Test debut, he was unfortunate to have had three catches of his bowling dropped off batsmen like Mudassar Nazar and Javed Miandad who were both in terrific form that season. Sekar was a genuinely quick bowler with a splendid physique who was most unlucky not to have represented India on more occasions. In 1995, Sekar passed the Level 3 Cricket Coaching diploma awarded by the Australian Cricket Board. This diploma is the highest coaching diploma one can earn in cricket.

When did the MRF Pace Foundation get underway?

The Foundation was started in 1987. Initially, we did have a few problems. The training used to be carried out six days a week. As a result the trainees became very stale and tired.

How were things set right?

The programme and the schedule were so restructured so as to avoid fatigue and monotony. Now,all the aspects of training – nets, weight training, swimming and sprinting are all done thrice a week. The trainees also have to practise long-distance running. During the day, different classes on mental psychology, spoken English, public speaking and handling of the press are held. Academics is also looked after.

How are the trainees selected?

First of all, we write to each State Association asking them to advertise the open selections we would be holding. The selections are held over a period of 2 to 3 days. Usually we go for bowlers with the potential to make it big. We do give opportunities to those pacemen who have represented their states at the under-16 or under-19 levels, if we feel they have it in them to go far.

How many trainees do you finally take and for how long?

15 trainees from our country-wide search are short-listed and kept for a year on probation. We have different types of trainees who attend our Foundation. The youngest of them who are around 16 years of age are usually kept for two to three years. By that time we are clear whether they would make it or not. We also have trainees for short and very short durations. Those coming for very short durations usually come when Dennis Lillee is around. They are usually the kind of pacemen who have either made it to Test level or about to do so.

What is Dennis Lillee's role in the MRF Pace Foundation?

Dennis Lillee is the main person-cricket wise-in this Foundation. He visits the Foundation thrice a year for a period of two weeks at a time. In his first two visits,i.e. in June and August/September, he usually teaches, guides and suggests remedial measures. During his third visit in February/March he reviews the progress of the trainees so that they can correct themselves. I am in regular touch with Lillee too. I ensure that videos-tapes of the trainees are regularly sent to him. On his part, he will send his observations and remarks on the trainees to me.

What facilities are the trainees given?

Everything the trainees need is taken care of. The trainees are paid Rs. 500 as out of pocket expenses. Again, for trainees academically inclined, private tuitions are arranged.

When was the MRF Pace Foundation thrown open to other countries?

In 1992, the Foundation was thrown open to other countries. The Foundation has become a training-cum-finishing school for overseas Test pacemen and some Indian bowlers too. These pacemen would make it a point to visit the Foundation when Lillee was visiting, pick up tips, make corrections and then put to practical use all that was learnt.

Who are the international pacemen who have benefitted from the Foundation?

In India, the present Indian pace attack of Srinath, Prasad, Johnson and Ganesh have spent time at the Foundation. Sri Lanka's two best pacemen-ChamindaVaas and Sajeewa De Silva have learnt a lot here too.Australia's Glen McGrath also spent a month at the Foundation.

Finally, apart from Lillee are there any other former stars who help out at the Foundation?

Lillee ensures that former Australian stars, some of whom are closely associated with the Australian Cricket Academy, keep visiting the Foundation. The Chappell brothers – Ian and Greg, Rodney Marsh, Jeff Thompson, Graham McKenzie and even Joel Garner of the West Indies have visited the Foundation and passed on useful tips to the trainees.

ROGER BINNY – A MOST USEFUL ALL-ROUNDER

ENGLISH RAJASTHAN PATRIKA
SUNDAY 23 FEBRUARY 1997

The manager of the Karnataka cricket side which won the Irani Trophy in 1996 with an almost half-strength side was Roger Binny, the former Indian all-rounder. Binny, who played for India from 1979 till 1987, was a batsman who displayed great courage and common sense in any position from opener to lower down in the order. He was also not only an intelligent new ball bowler but also a good fielder.

I met Binny in Chennai when he had come as the manager of the Karnataka side and spoke to him about the great moments of his career and cricket in general.

As the manager of the Karnataka side and a former Indian opening bowler yourself, you must be delighted that at present the entire Indian pace attack is from Karnataka. What would you attribute this to?

At the very outset, I would like to say that if our younger cricketers in Karnataka and other parts of the country are taking to fast bowling the main credit for it must go to Kapil Dev. He has been the inspiration. The different pace academies – MRF Pace Foundation in Chennai, in particular, have also played quite a role.

In Karnataka, the basic feeling has been if Anil and Javagal can make it then so can we. It was Prasad, Rahul Dravid and Sunil Joshi first and now Johnson and Ganesh. I am confident Joshi will return to the Indian side as he is a keen learner and a fighter.

Personally, I am thrilled that Karnataka has six players in the Indian squad but at times I feel unhappy when they are not available for Ranji Trophy games.

What is your opinion about Johnson and Ganesh?

Johnson is quick. He has the pace but will have to bowl a fuller length if he is to be successful at Test level. Ganesh is younger than Johnson. He is not as quick as Johnson but he is an excellent mover of the ball. His control over length and direction is also good.

What is your opinion on our domestic cricket?

The main problem with our domestic cricket is that the wickets are totally in favour of the batsmen. It is therefore very difficult to assess the true worth of our batsmen. The wickets must be so prepared so as to give bowlers a fair chance too.

Why is it that many cricketers fail to succeed at the international level?

At the highest level of cricket, the slightest loophole in technique will be ruthlessly exploited so technical expertise is a must. Apart from technical competence, I feel that to be a success at Test level, a player must have a cool temperament, courage and be able to grab the slightest opportunity that comes one's way.

Among the batsmen you have bowled to in international cricket, who in your opinion was the best?

Without a doubt, the best batsman I have bowled to in international cricket was Vivian Richards of the West Indies. Richards was a devastating stroke-maker who attacked all the time. Greg Chappell of Australia was also a superb player.

Could you tell readers about Sunil Gavaskar and Gundappa Vishwanath- two of our batting legends whom you played with?

Gavaskar was a perfectionist. Once he settled in there was little or no chance of getting him out. For him batting was an obsession and he loved to get huge scores. Vishwanath was a delightful stroke maker. He possessed the gift of making the most hostile bowling on a difficult pitch look easy. He was a true artist.

Finally, you were a member of three very successful Indian sides abroad- 1983 World Cup in England, 1985 WSC tournament in

Australia and 1986 vs. England in England. Please tell readers about these sides?

The Indian side that won the 1983 World Cup in England was a good all-round side which fielded very well. Kapil's catch of Richards in the final still comes back to mind. The turning point of that tournament was our win against Zimbabwe made possible by Kapil Dev's fabulous innings.

The 1985 WSC tournament in Australia which we won was an extremely tough limited-overs tournament. It was really a master-stroke to have had Sivaramakrishnan-the legspinner from Tamil Nadu in the team. Siva bowled magnificently and put a lot of pressure on the batsmen who found it difficult to attack him on the big grounds. The 1985 side, which was again a good all-round side, was astutely led by Sunil Gavaskar.

We convincingly defeated England in England in 1986. I had a good match in the Test at Headingley where there is a lot of movement of the seam. Our team batted well-Vengsarkar in particular-being outstanding. All the bowlers-pace and spin-bowled well and we fielded well too. We really played well on that tour.

PURNIMA RAU – A TALENTED, DETERMINED AND DEDICATED CRICKETER

ENGLISH RAJASTHAN PATRIKA
SUNDAY 25 MAY 1997

In 1995, the Indian women's cricket side won the Centenary Cup tournament in New Zealand in a most convincing manner. The team was led by Purnima Rau, the Hyderabad all-rounder. Purnima is one of India's leading women cricketers at present. After working for the Railways, she joined Air India in Mumbai this year. I met Purnima in Mumbai and spoke to her about her life, her cricketing career and women's cricket in India.

Purnima, when and how did you take to cricket?

I developed an interest in cricket during my school days. I used to play with a tennis ball then. My family too was keen on sports.

Have you been coached?

Not really in the early stages. But later on, yes. I owe a lot to M.G. Sampath Kumar my coach in Hyderabad. Not only did he correct my defects, but he also provided me with the opportunity of practising with the men's players of the Hyderabad Ranji Trophy side.

What role has your family played in your pursuing your cricket career?

When I started my career my parents provided me with all the encouragement Later on when I got married, my late husband Squadron leader Narsing Rao encouraged me to play the game even at the highest level. My in-laws have always been most supportive of me. When my husband was alive they were very supportive. After my husband's death, they have been a tower of strength encouraging me to play as much as possible.

Could you tell readers about your career before you made the Indian side?

In 1985, I started playing cricket seriously when I joined Osmania University. I also represented South Zone University from 1986-88. In 1985, I also made my debut for Hyderabad.

How was your debut for Hyderabad?

It was a great one as I scored a hundred against Jammu and Kashmir at Lucknow.

When did you make your debut for India in international cricket?

I made my international debut against the West Indies during the 1993 World Cup in England. The following year in 1994, I led the Indian side against Australia.

Your greatest moment as captain of India must surely have been the Centenary Cup tournament in New Zealand in 1995 when India won the tournament. Please tell readers about the tournament and the impact the win had on women's cricket in India?

The triumph in New Zealand totally transformed the woman cricketer's status in our country People really started taking our performances seriously and the way for job opportunities for women cricketers was paved.

It also improved the team's standing internationally since we had beaten two of the best teams-Australia and New Zealand on the way to our title triumph. And now we are among the top contenders to win this year's World Cup to be held in India.

For me, the final was a memorable one. I scored 48 runs and took three wickets. We were helped by an excellent opening spell by Smita Harikrishna who conceded only 18 runs off ten overs.

I understand you spent some time in England last year playing cricket. What was your experience like?

Yes, you are correct. I spent 3 ½ months playing for a club called Gunnersbury in Middlesex. I did get to play on wickets and conditions which helped the medium pacers who move the ball. However, the standard was not much. My stay in England also helped me as a person.

The World Cup will be held in India this year. Could you tell readers about the Indian team's preparations?

Our build- up for the World Cup has already begun with 30- odd probables attending the first three-week training camp at Calcutta recently. We are scheduled to have more such camps before the final side is announced.

How helpful are these camps?

I do remember the camp we had before the New Zealand tour. Camps really help us to improve our fitness and fielding.

How do you rate the present Indian side keeping in mind the World Cup?

Our spinners rank among the world's best and so does our batting line-up. It is only in the pace department that our rivals hold an edge over us and that too because of our conditions, do not really help quicker bowlers. I will never forget Smita Harikrishna's tight opening spell in the final of the Centenary Cup in 1995. Therefore I am confident that our medium pacers too will not let us down.

MANUEL AARON – FORMER CHESS STAR AND REPUTED CHESS CRITIC

ENGLISH RAJASTHAN PATRIKA
SUNDAY 12 OCTOBER 1997

In the sixties and seventies, Indian chess could only boast of very few good men's players. Manuel Aaron of Tamil Nadu was probably the best of the lot. The recently concluded Asian Junior Chess Competition which was held in Jaipur provided me with the opportunity of meeting and speaking to the 62-year-old Manuel Aaron who had come to cover the event as a journalist. Aaron retired from the banking industry a couple of years ago.

When did you start reporting on chess?

Actually chess for me is a way of life. It is difficult for me to be away from chess. So I started writing on chess even when I was playing. That was twenty years ago.

For the benefit of readers, could you mention about your achievements in competitive chess?

First of all I wish to state that I have been National Champion nine times – 1959, 1961, 1969, 1971, 1972, 1973, 1974, 1976 and 1981. It must be mentioned that till 1971, the Nationals used to be held once in two years. I have also participated in three Chess Olympiads – 1960 at Leipzig in Germany, 1962 at Warna in Bulgaria and 1964 at Tel Aviv in Israel. I have also participated in the Asian Team Championships twice – 1977 at Auckland in New Zealand and 1981 at Hangzhou in China. These are the main competitions I have participated in.

Who were the other outstanding players in the National scene during your time?

During my time in India we had only one outstanding player. He was Nasir Ali of U.P. The title clashes at home would inevitably be between him and me. In the international scene, the outstanding player in my time was Bobby Fischer.

Please tell readers about Chess in your time.

Chess was not so popular in our time. International exposure was limited. Again, chess literature was very limited. Of course, video recordings and computers were also not available to us then. You may not believe that for the first Chess Olympiad in 1956 the Indian players had to buy their own tickets.

What about Chess today in our country?

Things are much better now in our country particularly since 1987 when Vishwanathan Anand made it big. Since then there has been a chess boom in India. At present, we have a number of talented players. These players do have the advantage of international exposure, and of course, the benefit of video recordings, a lot of reading material on the game and the facility of computers. Unfortunately, in quite a few states the game is not properly organized.

India now has three Grandmasters-Vishwanathan Anand, Dibyendu Barua and Pravin Thipsay. Please comment on their styles of play.

Vishwanathan Anand has really done India proud at the international level. Because of his achievements, a lot more youngsters in India will try to emulate him. Anand is a wonderful attacking player with speed as his forte. **Dibyendu Barua** has reached great heights despite not coming from an affluent background. He has great talent and is basically an excellent defensive player. Finally, **Pravin Thipsay** has great talent. He is an all-round player who plays both an excellent attacking and defensive game.

Your son Arvind, also writes on chess. Was he a chess player too?

Yes, Arvind has played the game too. He was the National Sub-junior Champion in 1978. He now runs a magazine on chess and is the chess correspondent of the Hindu in Madras. He also deals in chess books.

How were your achievements in Chess recognized?

In 1962, I won the Arjuna Award for Chess. However, awards do not appeal to me as much as the satisfaction I derive by being associated with the game in any manner.

Finally what are the requisites a person should possess to become a successful chess player?

I feel the first basic requisite is to be born in an affluent family particularly in our country. If one is born rich, then one can concentrate on chess and not bother about other things. Again, one must have an analytical mind, be able to observe and capitalize on opportunities and ofcourse possess qualities like determination, character and patience. I am certain if one has all these qualities one can achieve greatness in the game.

S. VIJAYALAKSHMI – A QUALITY YOUNG CHESS PLAYER

ENGLISH RAJASTHAN PATRIKA
SUNDAY 26 OCTOBER 1997

India's highest ranked women's chess player S. Vijayalakshmi was in Jaipur recently to participate in the Asian Junior Chess championship. 18-year-old Vijayalakshmi finished runner-up in the tournament. I met her during the tournament and spoke to her about her chess career in particular and chess in India and abroad in general.

When and how did you take to chess?

I started playing chess when I was barely 3 ½ years old. My father, A.S. Subbaraman, is a very sports-minded person. He was very keen that his children – we are three sisters-must make a name in a sport. We all found chess the most convenient sport so all of us in the family spend most of our time playing chess only.

Has any other sister of yours made some mark in chess?

Yes, my younger sister Meenakshi is an international player too while Bhanupriya, my youngest sister is also very talented.

Who has been your coach?

My father has been and will continue to be my coach. The biggest quality he possesses is that he understands me well and helps me psychologically particularly when it comes to tackling difficult situations. In this context, I would like to make special mention of the role my family has played in my progress as a chess player. My father has helped in my game while my mother has looked after all my needs. Finally, my sisters have provided me with practice opportunities at home. All my achievements belong to them rather than myself.

Could you tell readers about your major achievements in your career so far?

The year 1995 was a big year for me. That year I won all the National titles-under-16, under-18, under-20, Women's B (qualifying tournament for Women's A) and Women's A (the top 16 in the country play). I also participated in the Asian Zonal Chess Championship held in Chennai and finished runner-up. In December 1996, I won the women's title in the Commonwealth Chess Championship held in Calcutta. This year too I have been quite successful. In July I took part in the World Juniors Championship at Zagen in Poland and finished seventh (tied for fifth place) out of a field of 60 which included a number of WGMS. In August, I won the Asian Zonal Chess Championship at Tehran in Iran.

Has Chess affected your studies?

In my case, unfortunately, chess has affected my studies. To concentrate on chess, I am doing my graduation through correspondence. Chess as a game calls for a lot of time because it involves a lot of study and practice. I love studies and hence feel sad at times that Chess has prevented me from studying more.

How do the facilities for chess players in India and abroad differ?

Chess is an individual game. It does help to come from an affluent family. What young players in India need is to get good sponsorship. If this happens I am certain we can reach greater heights.

Some countries abroad provide greater facilities for their chess players because in those countries there is an established chess culture. In Russia, for example, talent is spotted early. The promising ones join chess schools where the young ones not only specialize in chess but are also taught Science and Maths so that they can also go in for careers. In those countries, the Government helps its players in every possible way.

What makes Chess such a fascinating game?

Chess is an intellectual pastime. It is a game which can be played at any time and there is no age limit. The biggest thing is that this is one game where women can equal men.

Finally, you like Vishwanathan Anand, come from Tamil Nadu. What impact has Anand's achievements had on you?

Anand has achieved in chess at the international level what no other Indian had done before. His was a pioneering effort. His achievement has been a source of inspiration not only to me but also to the chess-loving youngsters from all parts of India.

PRAVEEN AMRE – A CRICKET TALENT NOT DULY RECOGNISED

ENGLISH RAJASTHAN PATRIKA
SUNDAY 9 NOVEMBER 1997

One of the most unlucky players in contemporary Indian Test Cricket has been 29-year-old Praveen Amre currently playing for Rajasthan in the Ranji Trophy. Despite having a Test average of 42.50 in eleven Tests inclusive of a brilliant 103 on debut versus South Africa at Durban against the likes of Donald, Schultz, McMillan and Mervyn Pringle and always being among the runs in domestic cricket, Amre is out of the Indian side. Praveen Amre, was also a most useful one day player for India. I met Praveen recently and spoke to him about his early days and his career.

How and when did you take to cricket?

I took to cricket at the age of ten as I lived near Shivaji Park – the home of cricket in Mumbai. I studied in Vidhyasharam School which has also produced players like Tendulkar and Kambli. We all had the same coach – Ramakant Achrekar.

Could you tell readers about Achrekar?

Achrekar Sir is 65 years of age. He has been my friend, philosopher and guide. He helps me make all my major cricketing decisions. He is a man totally devoted to the game. He is a person who will do anything possible for one with talent, keen on becoming a cricketer. I have even seen him provide kit and other accessories to young, talented but poor boys desperately keen on making it big as cricketers.

What were his coaching methods?

Achrekar Sir believes in a practical method of coaching. He is of the opinion that only in matches are the skills and temperament of players really put to the test. Therefore he used to make us play matches almost every day after school hours – even if it meant the playing of an innings on a particular day. While the matches were on, he would be sitting quietly with a diary in hand noting down the mistakes committed by the different trainees. At the end of the day, he would call all the trainees. Then he would tell each one of them about the mistakes made and how to rectify them. This would be done in front of all the trainees so that all could learn at the same time.

You played all your early cricket in Mumbai. Please tell readers about cricket in Mumbai.

Cricket in Mumbai is very competitive. Unless you have an extraordinary ability like Sachin Tendulkar, one has to normally come through the grind. The competition starts at the school level- the under-15 and under-19 stages. At one time, it was easier for a player to get an Indian cap than get a Mumbai one.

Why then did you leave Mumbai?

After I had represented Mumbai in only one match in the Ranji Trophy in 1986-87, my coach Achrekar Sir suggested I leave Mumbai as at that time there was no place for me in the first eleven. He told me that I should join a Ranji side where I could be a regular first eleven player. So I joined the Railways the following season. While representing the Railways, I even made my debut for India in one-day internationals and Tests.

In domestic cricket, which feat of yours do you cherish the most?

I am one of those very few Indian cricketers who has scored a double century each in Ranji, Duleep and Irani Trophy games. Of course, I have been consistently doing well in the domestic circuit.

You are only one of the ten Indian players to date to have scored a century on Test debut and in fact, only one of the four to achieve this distinction abroad. Please recall that innings.

My Test debut was against South Africa in the first Test at Durban in 1992-93. When I came in to bat, India was deep in trouble at 38 for 4. Though I managed to remain at one end, the struggle continued and we were 146 for 7 when Kiran More joined me. On a wicket that helped the pacemen and against bowlers of the calibre of Alan Donald, Schultz, McMillan and Mervyn Pringle, we fought it out and put on 101 runs for the eighth wicket. This partnership enabled India to get the first innings lead and I scored 103 in the side's score of 277.I wish to add that in the last one-dayer in East London, I scored 84 not out and also won the Man of the Match award. So, all in all, it was not a bad debut tour for me.

Why is it that despite such a brilliant start to you Test career, you could not consolidate your position in the Indian side?

I would say it is probably fate as for some reason or the other, I was always made to feel I was on trial. For the past few years I have been getting runs consistently yet that important recall has not come. I am certain that if that recall comes. I will definitely prove myself.

Finally, in your international career, which fast bowler impressed you the most?

Without a doubt, it is Alan Donald. Alan Donald was generally quick. However, his ability to produce that extra fast one surprised the best. Apart from the pace he generated, Donald could move the ball most sharply.

KAMLESH MEHTA – FORMER NATIONAL TABLE TENNIS CHAMPION AND INTERNATIONAL

ENGLISH RAJASTHAN PATRIKA SUNDAY 26 APRIL 1998

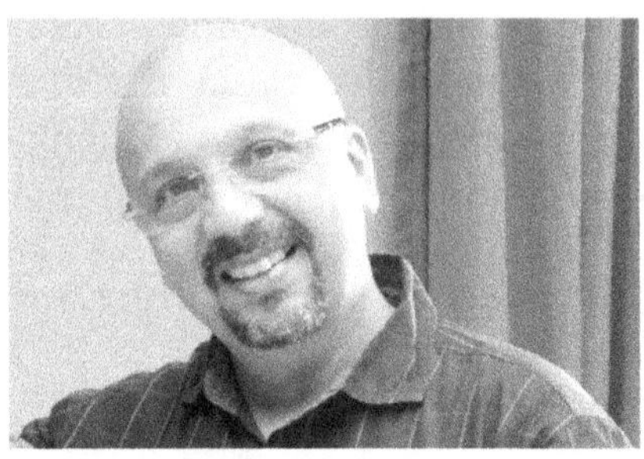

Eight times men's table tennis national champion Kamlesh Mehta, was a very fine player. Kamlesh and his wife Monalisa – a former women's national champion in table tennis know almost everything there is to know about table tennis at the national scene. They have also had plenty of exposure in the international scene too. Both are Arjuna awardees. I met Kamlesh recently and spoke to him about his career and table tennis in India and abroad.

When and how did you take to table tennis?

My parents were keenly interested in sports. It was mainly because of their interest and encouragement that I took to table tennis. I started playing at Matunga Gymkhana at the age of 10. I have also played for the P.J. Hindu Gymkhana. Both of these places are in Mumbai.

Have you been coached?

I have not really been coached. But I have been fortunate to have received guidance and suggestions from players like Bomi Amalsadvala and Ratish Chachad.

Could you give readers an idea of your practice schedule?

I used to practise regularly throughout the year. Physical fitness plays a great part in the success of a player. In the mornings, I would exercise for 40 minutes and then practise for about 1 ½ to 2 hours. Again in the evenings, I would practise for about 2 ½ to 3 hours. I would also play in as many competitions as possible.

You have been eight times National champion. Could you for the benefit of readers mention the years?

I won the men's title (singles) in the National Table Tennis championship for the first time in 1982. After that I won titles from 1984 to 1987 and again in 1990, 1991, and 1994. I was also thrice runners-up in 1981, 1983 and 1989.

In which major international tournaments have you represented India?

The World Championships are held every alternate year. I participated in all World Championships from 1981 till 1993. Table Tennis was introduced in the Olympics for the first time in 1988 at Seoul. I have represented India in two Olympics -1988 in Seoul and 1992 at Barcelona in Spain. My best moment came in the 1992 Olympics when I defeated Lu Lin-a Chinese player. Of course, I have represented India in other competitions but these were the main ones.

Could you mention some outstanding players you have seen in action?

I have seen a number of very good players in action during my career. Of the lot, three players stand out. They are Gio Yeh Hua of China, Tibor Klampar of Hungary and Jan Ove Waldner of Sweden – the current World champion. Gio Yeh Hua used a pen holder grip. He possessed a majestic style. Tibor Klampar was a genius. He played both original and brilliant strokes. Jan Ove Waldner is both a good all-round player and one who possesses a most attractive style of play. He has won all possible titles in the world.

Some of the European countries are probably the best in the world. Why is that so?

The structure of table tennis in these European countries is very broad-based in the sense that there are a number of children playing the game at the school level – the level at which talent is spotted and can be nurtured. Again the players keen in taking up table tennis as a career have access to excellent professional coaching. Even the basic kit and playing facilities are easily available. Here

I must mention that it is possible to live on table tennis in those countries. A professional table tennis league is held throughout the year among clubs from quite a few European countries. All these clubs have sponsors.

Could you tell readers about the European style of play?

The European players are basically attacking players. It was the European players who introduced attacking double flanks-both forehand and backhand.

How are the Chinese players so good?

The system that is followed in China is very different from what we are used to. In China, everything is looked after by the State. Professional coaches are available at all levels – schools, colleges, universities and the national level. These coaches are excellent players who possess the gift of passing on their knowledge to their wards. Their job is to coach and they are paid for it. The players with talent are spotted early. The job of the players is only to play. Everything is looked after by the Government – education and family for example. Once their playing days are over they are given jobs as coaches.

Could you tell readers something about the Chinese style of play?

The Chinese players are perfectionists. Quite a few of them are changing from the pen-holder grip to the shake-hand grip. The Chinese have both exceptionally good attacking and defensive players.

Why is it that India has not been able to reach the same heights as the leading table tennis playing nations?

Some of the main reasons for India not reaching very high levels are as follows. First of all, unlike the top table tennis playing countries, we do not have the physical fitness culture. In those countries even the elderly people are very conscious about their fitness. Secondly, the basic infrastructure in our country needs a lot of improvement. We do not have many proper stadia and good coaches. Our youngsters and up and coming players lack professional coaching at the various levels to the top. Again, in India equipment and the good kit is not easily available. Finally, our players generally lack a professional attitude.

What ought to be done to improve the situation?

First of all, our youngsters must easily get kit and equipment. The authorities must identify good, young players. After that, good coaches who are sincere must be given responsibility. The promising youngsters must be put under good coaches for a period of atleast two years. Something ought to be done about the tenth and twelfth class Board exams. These exams come between the ages of 15 to 17 – a time when youngsters are nearing their peak. Because of these exams we do tend to lose a lot of our prospective stars. Sports must be given nearly equal importance in our curriculum if we are to have more good players.Again, our top players must be given international exposure – both by playing against top stars and watching them too. Finally, we must try to improve gradually over a period of time. Only then can we make real progress.

M.L. JAISIMHA – A GIFTED CRICKETER AND A GREAT HUMAN BEING

THE STATESMAN (DELHI) – 20 AND 21 JULY1999

The passing away of M.L. Jaisimha, the former Indian Test cricketer from Hyderabad, pained me immensely as only about two and half months before I had spent nearly three hours with him at the Gymkhana grounds in Hyderabad where he was coaching the Hyderabad Ranji Trophy side. In those three hours, Jaisimha made me realize that not only was he a great human being but also a person who thoroughly enjoyed the game he knew inside out. Right from the time he made me have breakfast with him till the time he arranged for me to be dropped, Jaisimha not only enlightened me with his experiences but also gave useful and encouraging tips to the youngsters at the nets.

When leaving the place, I felt sorry that I had neither taped the conversation nor taken a photograph with him as it could be the last time I would be meeting him. Unfortunately, it was so but the pleasure of that meeting will remain with me till I live. It is not a surprise that the great Sunil Gavaskar considers him his hero.

How did you make it so big so young?

My father was keen on sports and encouraged me in every possible way to play games. So I played tennis, cricket and badminton. I represented Hyderabad Schools at the age of 13 and made the Hyderabad Ranji Trophy side at 15. My debut was against Andhra. My talent seemed to catch the eyes of the national selectors and at the age of 20 in 1959, I was selected to tour England with the Indian side.

Could you tell readers about that tour of England?

We were outplayed on that tour losing all the five Tests. The wickets were green and the conditions helped pace bowling. Unfortunately, our selectors went for a spin-oriented attack and the wickets blunted their effectiveness. Even such a fine leg-spinner like Subhas Gupte was only reasonably successful. England also had top class pacemen in Fred Trueman and Brian Statham. Trueman was very very quick while Statham was not only quick but also extremely accurate. Our pacemen (Ramakant) Desai and Surendranath also bowled well.

Our batting did not fare too well. Vijay Manjrekar, our best batsman, had a knee problem and did not play after the second Test. I made an unsuccessful debut at Lord's in the second Test.

In the series that followed against Australia, you played against some Australia greats. Tell us something about them.

Ray Lindwall, the great fast bowler was in that team. He was not quite at his best then. Neil Harvey, the left-hand batsman, was a top-class performer. He was a complete batsman who had all the strokes and most important of all used his feet well to the spinners. Wally Grout was a very good wicketkeeper. Finally, the two great bowling all-rounders – Alan Davidson and Richie Benaud. Davidson was a quickish left-arm bowler who could move the ball both ways. He was accurate too- a real match winner.

Benaud was a complete leg-spinner. On all types of wickets, he was even better than our Subhas Gupte. Benaud was tall, imparted sufficient spin, possessed excellent control and had a lot of variety. He was also an attacking bowler who had an excellent flipper. Benaud was also a thinking captain with great self-belief.

In 1962, you were a member of the Indian side that visited the West Indies and lost all five Tests. What went wrong there?

The wickets in the West Indies particularly at Jamaica and Barbados were not only quick but also had a lot of bounce. Our batsmen did not have first-hand experience of such conditions. Moreover, West Hall was at his fastest then. Hall was well supported by the great

Gary Sobers and the off-spin of Lance Gibbs.The West Indies batting with Sobers and (Rohan) Kanhai in its ranks was very strong. They were also brilliantly led by the late Sir Frank Worrell. Worrell was a great leader in every sense. On the tour, our captain Nari Contractor was seriously felled by a Griffith bouncer. All in all, it was a forgettable trip.

Could you tell readers about your sudden recall to the Indian side in the third Test at Brisbane in 1968 and your knocks of 74 and 101 in that Test?

Before I come to that I wish to make it clear that on that tour I was not a replacement for the injured leg-spinner B.S. Chandrasekhar but a full-fledged batting re-enforcement. Three or four days before the Test, I got a telephone call from Mr. S Sriraman of the BCCI. At first I thought it was Sriraman, my vice-captain in college as I had at that stage decided to give up the game. On clarifying the identity of the caller, I learnt it was actually Mr. S Sriraman of the BCCI asking me to proceed immediately to Australia to be in time for the Test.

I borrowed pads and a bat from P R Man Singh and an old cricket bag and a pair of old cricket shoes from a friend. I arrived in Australia two days before the Test.

It rained the next day and so I could not have any practice at all as there was no indoor practice facility in Brisbane. We fielded first on a wicket which proved to be a decent batting track. In the first innings, I got 74 while in the second innings I got 101.

In the second innings we were well on the way to reaching the victory target of 395. We were 310 for five at one stage with Chandu Borde and myself going strong. We had already put on 119 runs. At that stage Borde, who was suffering from a muscle pull, unfortunately, got out. We then lost Nadkarni, Prasanna and Bedi quickly.

Despite these losses, last man Umesh Kulkarni batted sensibly and we had put on 22 runs for the last wicket. At the stage, Cowper was bowling the sixth ball of his 40th over. I got a rank long hop which I was getting ready to hit for a six but suddenly I realized that I needed to take a single to keep the strike after letting Umesh face a ball (Australia had eight-ball overs then). Believe it or not I ended up patting the ball into Gleeson's hands at a close-in position. **What should have been a great win ended in a sad defeat with my dismissal.**

Sunil Gavaskar speaks so much about the impact you made on him. Tell us how you found the debutant Sunil on the 1971 tour of the West Indies?

At that age too, Gavaskar was not only intelligent but also a ready learner who never hesitated to take advice from seniors. He was very focussed with his priorities absolutely clear. Initially, he was a very attacking player but he quickly realized that to succeed at Test level one had to graft for runs.

Despite your great talent, why did you not have a longer and more successful career?

Yes. You are correct. I generally had a devil-may-care attitude to the game which was not helped by the fact that in those days Tests played by India were few and far between. My general casualness was responsible for my not forcing my way into the Indian team for England in 1967, the original squad to Australia in 1967-68 and again the team that toured England in 1971.Yes, with a more serious approach, I could have scored another 1,000 more Test runs with at least four or five more Test hundreds.

Mansur Ali Khan Pataudi and Ajit Wadekar captained you when you were a more mature and experienced cricketer. How would you rate them?

Tiger (Pataudi) had a tough baptism as India's captain in the West Indies in 1962. He really matured as a captain in the 1968 tour of New Zealand. Tiger changed the thinking of Indian Test cricketers – bringing about an attacking approach. He lifted the standard of Indian fielding by personal example. His early English cricketing education helped him a lot.

Wadekar was less flamboyant as a skipper. He would go for a win only if he was absolutely sure. He did not hesitate to consult others. For example on the 1971 West Indies tour he asked me to give suggestions. On those historic tours of the West Indies and England in 1971, Wadekar took calculated moves that clicked and helped India to achieve glory.

You played a lot of cricket with and against those four outstanding spinners – Prasanna, Bedi, Chandrasekhar and Venkataraghavan. Please give us your observations on each one of them.

Prasanna was a remarkable off spin bowler. He was a master of flight who also had the great ability of controlling the amount of spin to be imparted. He also possessed an excellent drifter. He was a thinking bowler.

Bedi was a classic left-arm spinner bowler with a beautiful action. Like Prasanna he was a master of flight and also had the great ability of controlling the amount of spin to be imparted. He also possessed a beautiful arm ball.

Chandrasekhar was a unique leg-spinner who was quick off the wicket and through the air. At times he could bowl slower if required. He was most often quite unplayable.

Venkataraghavan was also a top class off spinner who was very tall and so able to extract a lot of bounce. He would hit the deck and on helpful wickets he was dangerous. Again, he was a tight bowler who would block one end up.

Finally, Salim Durrani, the talented left-hand batsman and left-arm spinner was your contemporary. Could you tell readers about him?

Salim was an outstanding cricketer who could win a match either with the bat or ball. He was one of the most talented cricketers the country has produced. However, he was temperamental and wayward and difficult to handle. This resulted in Salim not being able to contribute more as a player to the country.

2002-2006

Ashwini Kumar, Indu Puri, Mamta Kharab, Tarak Sinha, Mithali Raj, Aakash Chopra, Shikhar Dhawan, Eknath Solkar, Balbir Singh(Sr), Harbinder Singh, Anju Jain, Gautam Gambhir, Anshuman Gaekwad and Jhulan Goswami

ASHWINI KUMAR – A GREAT SPORTS ADMINISTRATOR (ESPECIALLY HOCKEY)

WOMAN'S ERA – JULY (SECOND) 2002

82-year-old Ashwini Kumar is a versatile person. A brilliant police officer, an able sports administrator and a connoisseur of music – all rolled into one. The brilliant and extra- ordinarily talented octogenarian, who retired as the Director General of the Border Security Force in 1978, has been one of the most distinguished sports officials India has produced.

Ashwini Kumar has been President, Indian Hockey Federation and Vice-President, International Olympic Committee. He was also in charge of Security for Olympic Games from 1980 in Moscow to 2000 in Sydney. I met Ashwini Kumar who has had four open-heart surgeries, at his Delhi residence and spoke to him on his career as a sports administrator with a view to finding out how India can become a top sporting nation.

What enabled you to be a successful sports administrator?

There were a number of qualities in me that enabled me to be successful in sports administration. First of all, I had been a very good sportsman in my younger days. I excelled in hockey, athletics and boxing. As a hockey player, despite the outstanding players present at that time, I might have made the national team. Secondly, my education and my family background helped me a lot. These things helped me to select the right players and help them develop.

To be honest, I was among the first few people in the country who believed that players needed security and patronage. Realizing that, I went about recruiting the best possible talent in different games for the Punjab Police. As a policy, we decided that Indian players would be recruited at the level of inspectors, state-level players as sub-inspectors and promising youngsters as head constables. Of course, if they were educated, they would be placed in higher scales. It was because of this that Punjab had the best hockey and athletics sides in the country. Of course, Punjab was very good in other games, too.

I recruited the great Balbir Singh (Sr) straight from the college. He started as a fullback. But seeing his speed, his scoring ability and dash, I made him play at the centre forward position where he made a name for himself. Udham Singh, another great, was the other player of that time to be groomed by me. I would like to mention here that Balbir made the side to the 1948 London Olympics in fortuitous circumstances. For that Olympics, Udham Singh was the original centre forward. However, just before the team left, Udham fractured his hand and Balbir replaced him. Balbir played so well that on his return to the team, Udham had to shift to the inside left position where he served India with great distinction. Ajitpal Singh was another player I spotted at the school level when he was 13 or 14 years old. I then recruited him at 18.

Apart from all that you have mentioned, what else did you do to make Punjab so good at sports?

I saw to it that a lot of competitions were held at the school and college levels. The talent that was spotted, used to be properly groomed and given the best possible exposure. Players' personal problems were taken care of, too.

Please tell readers about your association with the International Olympic Committee.

I have been a Vice-President of the International Olympic Committee (IOC)-the first Asian to achieve this distinction. From the 1980 Olympics at Moscow until the 2000 Olympics at Sydney, I have been in charge of the security of the Olympic Games. Until the time I became a member of the IOC, sports to me meant regional, national and international competitions and little else. The IOC exposed me to the Olympics. It taught me to blend sport with education and culture. Participation in sports acquired a new meaning and purpose.

You have been closely associated with Indian sports for a number of years. Please highlight what is wrong with Indian sports.

The 20thcentury has been a witness to our fall in the sports arena. Having spent years looking after the affairs of Indian sports at the highest level, I can say with candour that we have been hopelessly left behind in our quest for sporting excellence. The fault lies in ourselves in as much as our priority for sports has been very low. There are three major inadequacies in our set-up – no planning, absence of developmental programmes and no proper coaching and grooming at both the grassroots and elite levels.

By elite level, I mean children in the age group of 10 to 13 who can make it to the international grade. These children need to be given special training, diet and competitive exposure of a higher kind.

Again, we lack scientific and medical support. For example, to know the endurance capacity of a player, it is necessary to know the rate of oxygen replaced in a body. These studies are lacking. We also lack qualified coaches with a missionary zeal, equipment and facilities. Equipment must be made more easily available if a greater number of players are to participate.

When talking of facilities, I mean the availability of courts, grounds and courses for the general public at most moderate rates. Finally, competitive opportunities are limited and apart from having a poor athletic culture, our national sports policy is vague, confused and lacks financial backing. Unless money is put in, we cannot expect to win gold medals or achieve big success in international competitions. The countries that are doing well in sports are economically well-to-do.

What must we do to improve the present state?

What we need today are playgrounds of any dimension in every school in our country. A vast majority of schools do not have them. We must also introduce sports as a subject available for study in every school and college. Every state should have an Institute for Physical Education. Sports should be made a Central subject, since as a State subject, it has not received the kind of attention it should have. Basically, what is urgently required is a Central Institute for Sports Research and Biotechnology. We must also take the help of experienced foreign sports advisers who could lay down the essentials for a meaningful sports policy. Our Government must also properly and purposefully put in more money into sports. Only if these things are in place, can we dream of excellence in sports.

INDU PURI – FORMER NATIONAL WOMEN'S T.T. CHAMPION AND INTERNATIONAL

WOMAN'S ERA – SEPTEMBER (FIRST) 2002

Two Indian women's table tennis players have been an inspiration to many of their ilk in our country. They are Kaity Khodaji (Chargeman) and Indu Puri. Kaity was a pioneer in the sense that she was the one who ensured that Indian women got opportunities to play abroad. Indu Puri is a kind of a legend, for her achievements in the game have yet to be surpassed by any Indian woman. I spoke to the 48-year-old Indu Puri, an Arjuna Award winner, at her South Delhi residence about Table Tennis and her association with the game.

What ails Indian table tennis?

Just as in all walks of life, in table tennis too, mediocrity is encouraged. There is too much of politics and favouritism, resulting in poor selection and other problems. The best, at times, are left out. Self-interest gets the better of national interest, resulting in poor performance by such a big nation. In Indian women's table tennis today, we lack one top class player whom we can bank on. We do have 8-10 players of the same level, but no one to bank on.

When did you first represent your state at the Nationals?

I made my debut at the senior level for Bengal in 1969 at the age of 16. It was a case of playing at the senior level straight away.

Tell us about your performances at the national level.

I represented Bengal till 1975. From 1976 till 1980, I represented the Railways and from 1981 till 1984, I represented Delhi and the Union Bank (institutional sides participated in the Nationals). I was National Champion a record eight times-in 1972, 1975 and 1979-1984. This feat is yet to be equalled. In 1982-1984, I won the triple crown-singles, doubles and mixed doubles titles. This feat too is yet to be equalled. I would like to mention here that I joined the Railways in 1976 and Union Bank in 1981 (playing for Delhi for a year or two). I moved to Delhi in 1978.

How is it that other nations do so much better than India?

I would like to classify other countries into **capitalistic** and **communist**. In **capitalist countries**, they have the club system. Each town or city has 30 to 40 clubs which encourage different games. Each game has a separate coach. The base is very wide. Regular competitions take place among the clubs. This is how a lot of players come up. Again, a lot of former players return to the game as coaches because the remuneration is good.

In **communist countries**, the State looks after everything. The coaches pick talent at a very early age. Talent, once spotted, is systematically groomed. Every aspect of the player is looked after by the State. So, the talented players have only to concentrate on their game. Even in these countries, former players return as coaches. In India, on the other hand, because of the low remuneration, very few former players take to full-time coaching.

What about your achievements at the international level?

I first represented India at the school level in the Asian School Championship at Singapore in 1970.

At the senior level, I first played for India in the Commonwealth Games at Cardiff, UK, in 1973 where I won a bronze medal. I also won a bronze medal at the Afro-Asian Games at Beijing, China that year. Since then I have regularly won medals in both these competitions till 1985. I have represented India in the Asian championship six times in 1974, 1976, 1978, 1980, 1982 and 1984 and my best performance in this championship was to win a bronze medal in 1978 at Kuala Lumpur, Malaysia. I have had the honour of representing India in the World Championship six times – in 1973, 1975, 1977, 1979, 1981 and 1983.

What has been your contribution to the game after having given it up at the really competitive level?

In 1986, I was coach of the Indian team at the Junior Asian championship at Nagoya, Japan. In 1988, I was coach of the Indian side that participated in the Asian championship at Nigata, Japan, and the Seoul Olympics. I won silver medals in the World Veterans Championship in Vancouver, Canada in 2000. Despite my very heavy schedule at the Union Bank of India, I still manage to coach youngsters in a nearby school on Saturday evenings and Sunday mornings.

What have been the highest ranking achieved by you?

I was ranked No.2 in the Commonwealth in 1982, 8th in Asia the same year and 63rd in the World in 1985.

Could you mention your outstanding moments at the international level?

My first memorable moment came in 1978 at the Asian Championship at Kuala Lumpur when I defeated the reigning World Champion Pak Yung Sun of North Korea.

The next great occasion was in 1979 in Pyongyang, North Korea, when I was instrumental in helping India get promoted to category I – the top 16 teams in the world.

What made you the champion you were – at least by Indian standards?

To achieve success in any walk of life, one must have a one-track mind. One must be totally dedicated. There has to be *tapasya.* I used to follow a very strict programme of physical fitness and practice. I also ensured that my hours of sleep were fixed and there were no distractions of any kind.

Could you not have achieved more at the international level?

Yes, the feeling of not having achieved more does come when one reflects. I was never made aware of the levels I could reach. Again, considering the lack of facilities and equipment one had to cope with, the absence of a really good coach and the lack of regular international exposure, I feel I did quite well at the international level.

Finally, what qualities must a youngster have and develop to become a top-notch table tennis player?

A youngster to be a top-notch table tennis player must have great concentration, the ability to fight back when down, anticipation, quick reflexes and of course a very flexible body. Lastly, I strongly feel that only if a youngster takes the game as *tapasya*-total dedication and devotion- will he or she be very successful and reach the top.

MAMTA KHARAB–INDIAN WOMEN'S HOCKEY STAR AT 2002 MANCHESTER CWG

ALIVE – OCTOBER 2002

The star of the Indian women's hockey team, which won the gold medal for the first time in the Commonwealth Games at Manchester in England, was 20- year old Mamta Kharab. The shy, simple, yet hugely talented, left-forward scored the winning goal against New Zealand to take India to the final. In the final against host England, Mamta once again showed great opportunism by scoring the golden goal just before the half-time whistle of the first half of extra time. Mamta Kharab's presence proved very ***kharab*** for India's opponent! I met Mamta at her Rohtak residence soon after her return from Manchester and spoke to her about the Commonwealth Games and her career to date.

How did you take to playing hockey?

Hockey has been in my family, My two elder sisters – Poonam and Sushma – are good players. It was because of them I developed a great interest in the game. Sushma still plays with me for the Western Railway in Mumbai.

Have you been coached?

My sisters helped me a lot in the early stages. In Rohtak, I was fortunate to learn the basics of hockey from Murti Devi and Bhoop Singh. They coached me from 1993 to 1996. Even now, if I need any tips, they help me out. Other national coaches have guided me too.

How did you manage to catch the eyes of the selectors?

In 1996, I decided to join the Sports School in Chandigarh, which turned out to be a very good decision for me. I learnt a lot there and developed my talents. In 1999, I was recruited by the Western

Railway in Mumbai and have been playing for them since then. The Railways has a very powerful team. This enabled me to make it to the national team – first at the junior level and then at the senior level.

How has been your international career to date?

I made my debut for India at the junior level in a four-nation tournament in the USA in 1999. The four nations were USA, England, Chile and India. The Indian side won the title. The following year, I was a member of the Indian team which won a bronze medal in the junior Asia Cup at Hongkong. I have also captained the Indian team that participated in the junior World Cup at Buenos Aires in 2001.

At the senior level, I first participated in the World Cup qualifiers in France in 2001. I then represented India in a four-nation tournament in England. The next tournament I took part in was the Champion Challenge trophy in Johannesburg, where we won the bronze medal. This was followed by the World Cup final place qualifier against the USA in England. This was a three-test series, where we drew two matches and lost one. As a result, we failed to make it to the World Cup. After this, was the Commonwealth Games at Manchester in England.

Tell us about your experience as captain of the Indian junior team in the World Cup in Argentina?

The experience in Argentina resulted in me and other youngsters not fearing the European teams any more. In that tournament, we conceded only two goals in 7 matches (winning 5, drawing 1 and losing 1). Despite playing well, we finished 9th because of the format. The experience however, made us more confident in taking on any opponent. It also made us fighters, when the chips are down.

What brought about such gutsy performances particularly in the knock-out matches of the Commonwealth Games in 2002?

Our first knock-out match was against South Africa. This was a match which I will probably never forget for the rest of my life! In this match, India was trailing 0-3 at half-time as we caved in under the opponents' attacks. In the second half, our team found its rhythm and took control of the game with a fine blend of defence and attack. We not only levelled 3-3 but also scored the winning golden goal in the 7th minute of extra time through Jyoti Kullu, our speedy and skillful centre-forward. It was an incredible win. Basically, we had decided to give our very best in the knock-out matches.

Our semi-final was against New Zealand, who had defeated us 3-1 in a league match. In the semi-final, we did our best to learn from the mistakes we had committed in the league match. In this game, we conceded an early lead but fought back to level 1-1 at the end of the first half and then scored the winning goal in the 62nd minute. Jyoti Kullu scored the equalizer, while I had the honour of scoring the match-winner. We faced poor umpiring in this match and were even deprived of a penalty stroke in the 58th minute by the England umpire, who opined that Jyoti Kullu had taken too long to convert it. The Kiwis could not withstand the constant pressure we put on their defence and we won 2-1.

The final against England was a hard-fought match. Having drawn with England in the league-stage we changed our tactics in the final. In the final, our game plan was to bottle up England's star forward Jane Smith. Sangai Chanu was assigned the job and we played with three forwards. I played in the right wing instead of the usual left. Kanti Baa, an excellent tackler, played the first 20 minutes and all this worked at the end. We took a 2-0 lead only to see England draw level 2-2. Sita Gosain and I scored the two goals. The two teams were 2-2 at the end of the regulation time. Just as the first half of extra time was about to end, I managed to score the golden goal which gave us a 3-2 win. Strangely, the umpire disallowed the goal, saying that the hooter to signal the end of the half had gone before the ball entered the goal. However, the tournament director turned down the decision and India was awarded the game and the gold medal too.

It was the greatest moment of our lives as this was the first time our Women's Hockey team had won any medal in the Commonwealth Games – and we had landed with gold!

TARAK SINHA - A LIFE DEVOTED TO CRICKET

ALIVE – NOVEMBER 2002.

Think of cricket coaches and the name of Tarak Sinha will immediately come to one's mind. Sinha has produced a number of international players - Surinder Khanna, the Indian wicket-keeper batsman to Ashish Nehra, India's present left arm medium-fast bowler. His most outstanding trainee to date has been all-rounder Manoj Prabhakar. I met the legendary coach at his South Delhi residence and spoke to him about his life and coaching career.

Are you a bachelor?

No. I was married in 1982. Unfortunately, within 10 months of marriage I lost my wife. I did not marry again as I decided to devote all my time to cricket coaching.

What level of cricket have you played?

I played school and college-level cricket in Delhi as a wicket-keeper batsman. Incidentally, I am a Bengali who has been born and brought up in Delhi.

When did you take to coaching?

I started my own Sonnet club in 1969.I felt such a club would provide children from middle-class background with an opportunity to learn the basics of the game and play it too. Initially, l did the role of a player-cum-coach. Our base was the Birla School at Kamla Nagar.

Why did you select the name 'Sonnet?'

I was keen to give my club a unique name. So, I chose the name Sonnet which is a special kind of poem.

Do you have any permanent ground for your club?

No. Despite all the success the club has achieved all these years, we have not been able to get a permanent practice area for ourselves. Over the years, we have shifted from Birla School, Roshanara Bagh, Ajmal Khan Park, Rajdhani College, DCM Ground, to Ashok Vihar and now to Venkateshwara College. We have a five-year agreement with Venkateshwara College.

***When you started your coaching, you must have* faced problems. How did you overcome them?**

In the beginning, children were reluctant to join. However, gradually local children from Kamla Nagar and Shakti Nagar came to me for coaching. We had problems getting equipment. In this regard, we are very grateful to the late D.V. Jain of Jain Sports who helped us by giving us old sports equipment at moderate prices.

When did you take to full-time coaching?

It took me two years to start full-time coaching. During this period, I used to watch the methods followed by other coaches and also did a lot of personal reading of the best coaching manuals.

What are your coaching methods?

As a coach, I believe in giving individual coaching as against coaching in groups. When I get children I usually get them at 13 to 14 years of age. I first see if they have the cricketing sense. This is a must for any child aspiring to be a cricketer. The two main things which I look for in budding cricketers are natural talent and the capacity to work hard. I keep assessing their progress after fixed periods of time. Discipline is maintained at all cost.

Who are the outstanding players you have produced so far?

The players I have trained so far are – Surinder Khanna, K.P. Bhaskar (most unlucky not to have played for India) Manoj Prabhakar, Randhir Singh, Raman Lamba, Sanjeev Sharma, Atul Wassan and Ajay Sharma.

Why is it that even though all these players had a lot of talent, only Manoj Prabhakar played for India over a period of time with success?

This is really a good question. All the players I have mentioned have middle-class backgrounds. Unfortunately, the problem with players coming from this background is that they do not make persistent efforts to improve their careers. A little bit of success makes them complacent. The exception was Prabhakar. He was a fighter to the core. He was a hard worker who possessed the required amount of aggression. Despite his average build, he achieved great success as a medium pacer. Prabhakar was a thinking cricketer who was determined to do well at the international level.

What has been your record as a college-level coach?

I have had great success as a college-level coach. I started coaching P.G.D.A. V College and they became champions ending the supremacy of Hindu College and St. Stephen's. Then I coached Rajdhani College and they too became champions.

The Board of Control for Cricket in India had appointed you as state coach for Delhi. How had you performed in that assignment?

I had been appointed by the BCCI in the mid-eighties as Delhi's coach for a period of two years. However, I left after one year. In that period, Delhi had become champions at all levels - under-16, under-19, under-22 and Ranji Trophy.

This year you have taken up the Indian women's cricket side. How have you found the experience?

I coach the Indian women's cricket team on an honorary basis. I am enjoying it as there is a lot of talent. Moreover, the girls are keen learners.My first assignment was when England toured India early this year. The Test was drawn-but we won the one-day series 5-0. A new team was selected for the series against England. After that I went with the Indian side to South Africa. In South Africa we lost the one-day series 1-2 as our players were not familiar with the Duckworth-Lewis system. However, we won the Test match at Cape Town by 10 wickets. Our girls played splendidly on that tour.The last assignment was India's recent tour of England. In the triangular series which had New Zealand as the third side, we did not do well as we had not yet got used to the conditions, especially the weather. In the Test series, the first Test was washed out while the second one ended in a creditable draw.

What are the characteristics of a good coach?

A good coach is one who is able to spot technical errors in players and rectify them at once, preferably with logic or explanation. He should also be a good psychologist who has to be both a friend and father. He must know what talents in a player are to be nurtured and developed.

The *highlight of the second Test was the world record score of 214 by Mithali Raj who shared in a record seventh wicket stand of* 157 *with Jhulan Goswami. Tell us something about Mithali's innings.*

19-year-old Mithali is an exceptionally talented player.She was first spotted by Diana Eduljee who got her recruited by the Railways. Her footwork is sure and her judgement is almost perfect. She has not only a sound defence but also a wide range of strokes. She initially had problems against the English leg spinner but she manage to play the leg spinner confidently after a while. After that Mithali played beautifully for almost 10 hours. She faced 407 balls and hit 19 boundaries. It turned out to be the highest individual score in women's Test cricket. Jhulan Goswami who shared the record stand with Mithali is also a great prospect. She is not only a useful batsman but also a lively medium fast bowler who moves the well.

What were the conditions in England during India's tour?

It rained a lot and after the rains it would become very cold. The wickets were generally soft. The bowlers used to get movement both in the air and off the wicket.

Of late, Indian women cricketers seem to be playing a lot of cricket both at home and abroad. How has this happened?

Credit for all this must go to the Secretary of the Women's Cricket Association of India, Anuradha Dutt. She has gone out of her way to ensure that Indian women cricketers get as much exposure as possible at the international level. Even the domestic cricket is now better organized.

In India, a lot of cricketers do very well at the junior level but seldom make it big. Why is it so?

There is one main reason for this. Many players give incorrect ages and play in smaller age-groups. As a result, when they are expected to peak, they are not able to as they have already passed their prime.

Finally, do you feel that T.V. must highlight decisions of umpires to the extent it does ?

Again, this is a good question. Without the human element cricket will never be the game of glorious uncertainties it is known to be. I personally feel T.V. replays should be used for showing batting and bowling techniques. It should also be used to show whether a catch has been taken properly or whether a shot is a six or a four. Again T.V. is a must for publicity and also to provide an opportunity to the general public to see places--they would normally have never got to see. However, I feel that it is not proper to highlight the umpires' decisions by showing them in slow motion replays when in reality they get only seconds to make them.

MITHALI RAJ – A STAR IN THE MAKING

WOMAN'S ERA-JANUARY (SECOND) 2003

Nineteen-year-old Mithali Raj is a youngster who possesses great talent. It is a matter of pride for Indian women's cricket, that this modest, friendly and charming player had the distinction of scoring 214 in the second cricket Test against England earlier this year. Her 214 is the highest individual score in women's Test cricket. I met Mithali recently in Delhi, when she was representing Indian Railways in the Rani Jhansi Cricket Tournament, and talked to her on cricket and her career to date.

When and how did you take to playing cricket?

I took to playing cricket at the age of nine. My brother Nitin used to play school-level cricket and he was the one who encouraged me initially. At home, I was the only one to get up late. So, to make me get up early my parents made me go with my elder brother for the morning cricket practice.

Who coached you in your early years?

Jyoti Prasad, the former Hyderabad Ranji Trophy player, was the first person to spot my cricketing talent. He used to conduct coaching camps for young boys. So, I went to the late Sampath Kumar Naidu, an NIS coach. Sampath Kumar was coach in our school - Keyes High School. He also conducted camps for girls. He honed my skills.

When did you make your debut for Andhra Pradesh and how did you come into the national team's reckoning?

I made my debut for Andhra Pradesh against Madhya Pradesh in the 1995 Nationals at Hyderabad. I was just about 13 then and there were many senior players in the team. It took me a couple of years to settle down in the senior side. In the 1997 Nationals at Kolkata, I scored an impressive 65 against Maharashtra. This knock of mine caught the eyes of the selectors and I was included in the list of probables for the 1997 World Cup. This was how I came into the national reckoning.

Please tell readers about women's cricket in Andhra Pradesh.

We are very fortunate that in Andhra Pradesh not only are there a lot of coaching camps for aspiring women cricketers, but we also have a proper set of 50-odd matches for our women players. Apart from a league, a number of other tournaments take place for our state women cricketers.

When did you make your international debut?

I made my international debut in the second match at Muzaffarnagar which was one of the five-match one-day series which Sri Lanka played in India in 1998. In the fifth and last one-dayer at Lucknow, I scored 101 not out.

Your first trip abroad with the Indian side was to England** in **1999. How did you perform on that tour?

Our team played three one-dayers and one Test on that tour. I was not very successful on that tour and managed to play in two of the one-dayers at Old Trafford and Trent Bridge. I opened for India in these matches. In a practice match against Ireland, I scored 123 not out. The wickets were soft in England with the ball moving a lot both in the air and off the wicket, and due to inexperience, I had a tough time

How did you perform in the World Cup in New Zealand the following year?

Our team performed quite well in the World Cup finishing third. I managed to play only three games before I got typhoid. In these three games, I scored 51 against the Netherlands, 65 against South Africa and 35 against England.

This year, India has played a lot of international cricket. How have you performed so far?

We started the year with a home series against England which included five one-dayers and one Test at Lucknow. In my debut Test in Lucknow I got a duck. However, useful unbeaten scores and vital wickets helped me to become the 'Woman of the Series' in the one-dayers. Our team did well. We drew the Test and won the one-day series 5-0.

Our team then went to South Africa. In South Africa, we lost the one-day series 1-2 as our players were not familiar with the Duckworth-Lewis system which is used when matches are weather-interrupted. However, we won the Test match at Cape Town by 10 wickets. It was a great feeling winning a Test match abroad. On this tour, I scored 65 in the second one-dayer and had scores of 55 and 9 not out in the Test.

What were the playing conditions like in South Africa?

The grounds were lovely and diving to stop the ball was not a problem. However, the wickets were very bouncy.

How was the England tour which followed the tour to South Africa?

We started our England tour with a triangular one-day series which had New Zealand as the third side. We did not perform well as we played this series without sufficient practice matches. Due to lack of practice matches, we found the conditions very difficult to play in. For example, before leaving for England we attended a camp in Delhi where the temperature was around 40°C and when we landed in England it was not even 20°C. The wickets too were soft and the ball moved a lot both in the air and off the wicket. In the Test series, the first Test was washed out, while the second one ended in a respectable draw.

The second Test at Taunton was the one in which you made history. Please, tell us about your knock in particular and the game in general.

Before the Test started, I was in tears because I felt that, as a specialist batsman, I had not contributed at all to the team's cause by way of runs. I sat down with my teammates and close friend Nooshin who was to be the scorer for that historic Test to find out what I ought to do. She told me that I had the talent and all I had to do was to be more watchful, patient and determined. All the players in the team including myself realized that our team's reputation was at stake in this match and we had to redeem ourselves.

For this Test, we included an extra bowler in place of a specialist batsman. England, after being put to bat, scored 333 runs. When I went to bat on the second day, our score was 45 for 2. My partner at that stage was my captain Anjum Chopra. The two of us retrieved the situation by putting on a decent partnership. Hemlata Kala, the last specialist batsman in the team, joined me next. She got a half century and the two of us added 80-odd runs for the fourth wicket. At draw of stumps on the second day, I was 45 not out. On the third day, after my partnership with Hemlata, I received great support from Jhulan Goswami who is basically a medium pacer. Jhulan and I added 157 for the seventh wicket which is also a world record. At the close of play on the third day, Jhulan and I were together with myself on 210 - the highest Test score by a player. On the last day I got out for 214 with Jhulan following soon after, scoring 62. We had at least redeemed ourselves. For the record I wish to state that I batted for almost 10 hours, faced 407 balls and struck 19 boundaries. It was an innings that really made all of us believe in ourselves.

Finally, what do you feel about women's cricket in India?

We need to have a better planned schedule so that we get time for rest and to be with our families. The cricket matches should be properly spaced out. Our fields need to improve. But things are really looking up and I am confident things will be better in the years to come.

AAKASH CHOPRA – ONE OF INDIA'S UNSUNG HEROES IN AUSTRALIA

ALIVE – MARCH 2004

Indian Test opener Aakash Chopra could not make a half -century in the recently-concluded Test series against Australia. However, he managed to do what most of the Test openers all over the world have failed to do against the Australian pace attack on Australian pitches i.e.not lose his wicket. In fact, former Australian fast bowler and India's new bowling coach, Bruce Reid, felt that Aakash Chopra was one of the unsung heroes for India as he almost always played out the new ball in the Test series, thus shielding the middle-order batsmen. I met 26-year-old Aakash Chopra at his Delhi residence soon after his return from Australia and spoke to him about his career to date.

When and how did you take to cricket?

I loved cricket since my childhood. In fact, I went to the famous coach, Mr. Tarak Sinha, at the age of seven to get lessons from him. I was not accepted then.

Who has coached you?

Mr. Tarak Sinha agreed to coach me two years later. Since then, he has been my only coach and I still go to him if I have a technical problem.

What is so special about Tarak Sinha?

Ustaadji is a very dedicated person. He possesses the eye and sixth sense to spot a potentially outstanding player early. He knows precisely how to mould a player. He plays on the strengths of a cricketer, making the best use of his talent. Moreover, he is quick to spot faults and can rectify them. He is an exceptional coach.

You have been a heavy scorer in domestic cricket. Please tell readers about some of your outstanding performances in domestic cricket.

I made my Ranji Trophy debut against the Services in Delhi during the 1997-98 season. I scored 150 on debut. My highest score in the Ranji Trophy is 222 against Himachal Pradesh at Delhi in 2002. I have seven centuries in Ranji Trophy. In Duleep Trophy matches, I have scored four centuries, the highest being 143 against Central Zone at Indore in 2002. I made my Deodhar Trophy debut last year and became the highest run-getter. My best performance was 210 not out against Central Zonea t Goa. In the Irani Trophy match against the Railways in Delhi in the 2002 season, I scored 93 and 69.

You played for India 'A' in 2002 and 2003 against Sri Lanka and the West Indies. Please tell us about your performances on those two tours.

In Sri Lanka, I was the highest run -getter, getting a hundred each in the one day and Test matches. In the West Indies, I was the second highest run-getter. My best score was 175 against Guyana at the Bourda Oval. I have fourteen first class hundreds to date.

A knee injury kept you out of the India 'A' Test tour of England. How did it come about?

It happened during the semi-final game against Tamil Nadu. We were playing football to keep fit for the upcoming match when a ligament tore. The injury took a serious turn.

You made your Test debut against New Zealand last year. Tell us about the series.

I was fortunate that after recovering from the knee injury, 1 got two chances against New Zealand before the first Test at Ahmedabad. In those two warm-up games I did well. In the first Test at Ahmedabad, I scored 42 and 31 and took 3 catches at short leg. In the second Test at Mohali, I scored 60 and 52, putting on a partnership ·of 164 with Sehwag in the first innings of the Test. I wish to mention here that I batted with a broken finger in the Mohali Test. This injury I suffered during practice.

How did you prepare for the Australian tour?

Honestly speaking, I could not prepare myself for the tour because of a broken finger. Of course, my talking to players like Sunil Gavaskar, Mohinder Amarnath and Chetan Chauhan before leaving for the tour was a big help.

How did you find the wickets in Australia?

The Brisbane wicket was a lot bouncier and offered movement. Adelaide was like any Indian wicket. The wicket on the first day at Melbourne was a bit damp. The bounce was inconsistent. Sydney was basically a good batting track.

What was it like touring with the Indian side?

It was an honour to be in the company of stars like Dravid, Tendulkar, Laxman and Ganguly. By watching them and talking to them one could learn a lot. ·

What approach must a batsman have to be successful in Australia?

To be successful in Australia as a batsman, you have to be decisive. You must know what deliveries to play and what to leave. You must be very careful about your shot selection.

How were the crowds in Australia?

The crowds in Australia were intelligent and unbiased. They loved and applauded our side as we provided good cricket.

You took some brilliant catches close-in on this tour. Did you make any preparation?

Being a newcomer, I was expecting that I would have to field close-in. I was mentally prepared for the role and so did reasonably well.

How did you find the Australian pacemen?

Gillespie was the best of the lot. He is a thorough professional as he knows precisely where to bowl to which batsman. Lee was the quickest I have faced to date. He has both pace and movement. Bracken moved the ball a lot while Williams, despite his wickets, is not exceptional.

What is your opinion about the batsmen you played with?

Sehwag is exceptional. He takes the pressure off his partner. I was lucky that we have known each other right from schooldays. Speaking the same language and being friends helped a lot. Watching Dravid bat is an education. He is a master technician. Playing with Dravid is a learning experience as you not only learn how to leave deliveries but also how to build an innings. Tendulkar is a genius. But what strikes you most about him is that he has no airs and is most helpful. He would go to a youngster and help him till the youngster felt comfortable. Ganguly is a great motivator. He does not act as captains generally do. He is friendly and helpful.

SHIKHAR DHAWAN – A STAR IN THE MAKING

ALIVE – APRIL 2004

India's left-handed opening batsman from Delhi, Shikhar Dhawan, was named the man of the tournament in the recently concluded ICC under-19 World Cup cricket tournament, held in Dhaka. Shikhar was the highest run-getter, scoring in all 505 runs in seven matches, at an average of 84.16. This included three centuries and a half-century. Shikhar has now been selected for the Border-Gavaskar cricket scholarship and will spend seven weeks in Australia from August this year. I met Shikhar at his residence soon after he returned from Bangladesh.

When and how did you take to playing cricket?

When I was 12 years old, I was taken by my cousin, who played for Sonnet Cricket Club, to the great coach of the club, Tarak Sinha. I was most fortunate that he accepted me as his trainee.

You have been around in the junior circuit for some time now. When did you first play for India at the age-group level?

I first represented India in the Asia Cup under-17 tournament at Dhaka in 2000-2001. The Indian side won the tournament. I played only three matches in the tournament. In my first match in the tournament, I scored 64 not out against Malaysia and won the man of the match award.

How did the present India under-19 team prepare for the Bangladesh tournament?

Before leaving for Bangladesh, we had a camp which was supervised by our coach Robin Singh. In the camp, a lot of stress was laid on fielding and catching.

What were the playing conditions like in Dhaka? How was your performance?

The weather was very humid. The pitches would be a bit damp to start with but would turn out to be good batting tracks. I got three centuries – 155 not out against Scotland, 120 against Bangladesh and 146 against Sri Lanka. I also scored 66 against South Africa. Unfortunately, we lost this game narrowly as we had no real partnership and to be frank, wickets were just thrown away. In the other three games, I played shots before settling down. As such, my scores were eight against the West Indies, four against New Zealand and six against Pakistan in the semi-final.

How was the semi-final encounter with Pakistan?

In the semi-final, we were without our skipper Ambati T. Rayudu, who was suspended by the match referee for time-wasting in the game against Sri Lanka. All said and done, Pakistan was a very competent side, possessing a good bowling attack, which could consistently bowl an excellent line and length. Their spinners, too, possessed a lot of talent. They were better than us on that day.

How was it like going back to Dhaka again with an Indian side?

Our schedule in Dhaka, this time, used to be practice, team meetings, playing matches and remaining in our hotel.

Who are your cricketing heroes?

I admire Andy Flower the most for his patience, running between the wickets and the wonderful way he rotates the strike. I also like the flair of Brian Lara and the natural aggression of Adam Gilchrist and Mathew Hayden.

Finally, what are your other interests?

I like playing volleyball and listening to music but cricket is my life. Honestly, I only like training in the gymnasium, practising in the nets and playing matches. I also like discussing my game with my coach and senior players of my club, like Aakash Chopra.

EKNATH SOLKAR – ONE OF THE WORLD'S GREATEST CLOSE–IN FIELDERS

ALIVE – JULY 2004

Eknath Solkar is probably the greatest close-in fielder Indian cricket or even world cricket has ever seen. In the late 60s and early 70s, Mumbai's Solkar stood at forward short leg for our all-time great spinners and brought off some of the greatest and bravest catches taken in the history of the game. Those were the days when close-in fielders had no protection at all.

I met and spoke to this 56 year old all-time great Indian fielder, batsman for a crisis and useful bowler at Bangalore where he was sharing his fielding expertise with the trainees at the National Cricket Academy.

When and how did you take to the game?

My father was the head of the ground staff at the Hindu Gymkhana ground in Mumbai. I was born and brought up there. I grew up watching matches while helping the authorities by maintaining the score board during the matches. I also practised at the ground, but I learnt the game mainly by observing others.

Were you coached by anyone?

The late great Vinoo Mankad and Laxman Kenny- the elder brother of Test player Ramnath Kenny - conducted nets at the Hindu Gymkhana ground which I was fortunate enough to attend.

Could you tell readers about your days as an Indian schoolboys cricketer?

In those days, cricketers in India got international exposure at the schoolboys level. I toured Sri Lanka in 1964 with the Indian schoolboys side. In 1965-66, I captained the Indian schoolboys side against the visiting English side.

When did you make your Ranji Trophy debut for Mumbai and how long did you represent your state?

I made my Ranji Trophy debut for Mumbai in 1966 against Saurashtra at Jamnagar. On my debut, I took 6 for 36 with my left arm spin and scored 41 not out. My 6 for 36 remained my best figures in Ranji Trophy. As a batsman, my highest score in Ranji Trophy was 145 against Maharashtra at Nasik in 1974. I continued to play for Mumbai till 1981. That year I was captain of the side which won the Ranji Trophy. I retired after that. I wish to add that Mumbai won the Ranji Trophy every year from 1966 till 1981.

Which Ranji Trophy wins do you remember the most?

Of course, I cherish the 1981 win as I was the captain. But the win I have very fond memories of was in 1967-68 when despite being a relative newcomer and youngster, I was fortunate to play a key role in our state winning the title that year. That year we were without a number of senior, key players who were on National duty in Australia and New Zealand.

Which was your most memorable innings in Test cricket?

Two innings of mine in Test cricket come to mind immediately. The first one was my only Test century-102 against the West Indies in the sixth Test at the Wankhade stadium in 1974-75. In fact, this match was the first ever Test played at this venue. The second one was my 65 against the West Indies in the first Test at Sabina Park in Kingston, Jamaica in 1971. This innings was a crucial one as my big partnership of 186 with Dilip Sardesai not only helped India recover from a terrible 75-5, but also gave our team the confidence that we can put pressure on the West Indies and even defeat them. In that Test, we took the first innings lead for the first time in a Test against the West Indies and even made them follow on.

Please tell the readers about those historic wins over the West Indies and England in 1971.

In the West Indies, the first Test at Jamaica turned out to be a great confidence booster. In the Tests, Gavaskar batted exceptionally well, being well supported by Dilip Sardesai in particular. Others like Prasanna and myself chipped in with useful contributions. The spinners Venkat and Salim Durrani in particular bowled really well. Bedi and Prasanna also played their parts too. The catching was also very good.

On the English tour that followed, the success in the West Indies gave us a lot of confidence. We were happy to have the experienced Farookh Engineer in our Test team. Engineer had a lot of experience playing for Lancashire in English county cricket. Of course, the magical spell by Chandrasekhar in the third and final Test at the Oval helped us to win that Test and the series.

In the international scene, you were used both as a new ball bowler and as a spinner. What were your experiences at the international level as a left-arm bowler?

My happiest memory as a Test bowler was when I used the new ball during the 1971 Test series in England. I gave the great Geoffrey Boycott a lot of trouble getting him caught in the slips frequently. As a spinner, I have dismissed great batsmen like the West Indians Sobers and Kanhai and Ian Redpath of Australia.

Who is the best batsman you have bowled to in Test cricket?

Without doubt, the best batsman I have bowled to in Tests was Sir Garfield Sobers. Sobers was a master batsman.

Whom would you rate as the best fast bowler you have faced in Test cricket?

Andy Roberts of the West Indies was the best fast bowler I have ever faced. Roberts was quick and accurate. He bowled very fast and deceptive bouncers. He also had the knack of studying the weakness of a batsman very quickly.

You have played alongside Sunil Gavaskar and Gundappa Vishwanath –two of the finest batsmen the world has ever seen. Please tell us about them.

Gavaskar was technically perfect. He also possessed great powers of concentration and was both dedicated and determined. Vishwanath was a genius. He was sheer class. He was a touch artist who could make the best of bowling attacks look as if it were ordinary. The worst of wickets would not affect him:

You had a great hand in the successes of our great spin quartet-off spinners Prasanna and Venkataraghavan, left arm spinner Bedi and leg spinner Chandrasekhar. Please tell the readers about them.

Prasanna and Bedi were masters of flight. They could, with their sharp turn, flight and variations, make the best of batsmen look like novices. Chandra was special. He was quick and when he got his length and line right, he was unplayable on any wicket. Venkat was steady and accurate. On a bad and helpful wicket, he could be devastating.

What do you think are the qualities required to be a top-class fielder?

Fielding came naturally to me and I enjoyed fielding anywhere. To be an outstanding fielder particularly close-in, one must have sharp reflexes, good anticipation, keen eyesight and plenty of courage. Most important of all, one must enjoy fielding.

You took a number of brilliant catches in your Test career. Could you name five of your best catches?

Of the five catches, I will be mentioning, four of them were taken close to the wicket while the fifth one was taken in the out-field. The close-in catches were taken in the area between short square leg and forward short leg. They were all equally good. I will mention them chronologically. So here it goes. In the fifth and final Test against Australia at Chennai in 1960-70, I took a really good catch of Keith Stackpole off Venkat. The next one was of Alan Knott in the third and final Test against England at the Oval in 1971. I dived full length forward to catch Knott. This catch was one of the turning points of the Test. In the home series against England in 1972-73, 1 held the next two outstanding catches. Tony Lewis was snapped up by me at short square off Bedi while sweeping in the second Test at Calcutta. Again, Mike Denness was taken by me off Prasanna. This catch was quite remarkable as the ball came of the outside edge to me. I was almost totally unsighted. The last one was held by me at long-off. I dived forward and held Clive Lloyd in the first Test at Bangalore in 1974-75.

Finally, what are the qualities that help one to become a successful Test cricketer?

The qualities that help one to become a successful Test cricketer are talent, technique, temperament, courage, dedication, determination and a sense of purpose. Luck and the ability to take success and failure in one's stride also helps.

BALBIR SINGH (SR.) – A GREAT OF INDIAN HOCKEY

ALIVE – MARCH 2005

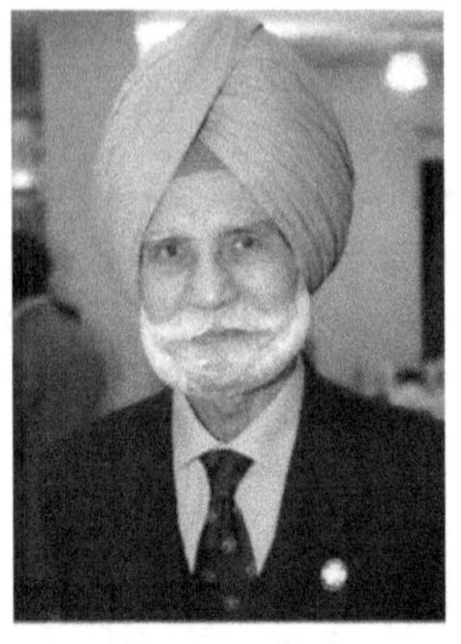

I was going down the stairs of the V. I. P. pavilion of the Chandigarh Hockey Stadium after doing the television commentary of the India-Spain hockey test, when I passed an elderly Sikh gentleman who was sporting the Indian blazer which had 1948, 1952 and 1956 Olympic badges on it. I stopped, looked hard and immediately realised that I was face to face with 81-year-old Balbir Singh, one of the two Indian hockey players to have not only won three Olympic Hockey gold medals but also led India in one of those triumphs. The other player to have achieved this feat is the legendary Dhyan Chand, who is no more. A couple of hours later, I was at Padma Shri Balbir Singh's residence. Our hockey legend kept me spell-bound with his amazing memory and honest and thoughtful observations on the game and the people who ran and played it.

Who had the greatest influence on your development?

My father, Dalip Singh, was a great person. A strict disciplinarian, he instilled in me values which helped me to achieve whatever I did in life.

Who was the best coach you have had?

Without doubt, it was the late Harbail Singh. To this day, I am indebted to him for nearly all that I achieved in hockey. Harbail was my coach, mentor, guru, philosopher and guide. He was the one who moulded my game on the right lines.

You were closely associated with Ashwini Kumar - one of India's greatest administrators in hockey. Tell us something about him.

Ashwini Kumar is and was a genius - a brilliant police officer, an outstanding musician, a great writer and, most important of all, a great and lovely human being. He always had in mind what was best for others. He went out of his way to help sportsmen. If Punjab became a power to reckon with in the field of sports after partition, it was mainly due to Ashwini Kumar. He played a major role in my grooming, making me a coach at the age of 24. He is and was greatly respected by the players too.

What helped you to attain your level of brilliance as a player?

I acquired a great deal of my mobility, agility, wrist work and, above all, quickness of eye by practising with a tennis ball against a wall, when very young.

Your performances in the three Olympics you participated in were remarkable. Please enlighten us.

In the 1948 Olympics at London, I played two matches and scored 8 of the 13 goals, including 2 of the 4 in the final. Four years later, in the Helsinki Olympics, I scored 9 of the 13 goals our team scored in three matches -3 of my goals were in the semi-final. In the final, I scored 5 out of the 6 goals — a record to date. In the 1956 Melbourne Olympics, where I was fortunate to lead the side, we completed a hat-trick of Olympic gold medals. I played only three games. In the first half of the opening match against Afghanistan, I fractured a finger in my right hand after having scored 5 goals. After that game, I played only in the semi-final and final with a fractured hand.

How did you manage to play such important games with a fractured hand?

For the 1956 Olympics, the Indian side depended a lot on me. So, after my injury in the first match, it was decided that I would play only in the semi-final and final. Each member of the team was told to keep my injury and the doctor's report a closely-guarded secret. Opponents considered me the most dangerous centre-forward of post-war years. The idea of playing me with an injury was to keep defenders on me constantly. In the semi-final, against Germany, the tactic paid off and we won 1-0. Even in the final, Pakistan had two of their defenders on me. This eased the pressure on the inside players. The full back converted a penalty corner, then called short corner, and we won 1-0.

You have also been a coach and manager of the Indian side. Could you tell us about the great 1975 World Cup win?

The tournament that comes to mind first was our gold medal in the 1975 World Cup at Kuala Lumpur. We were a well-knit unit and the players were greatly helped by Rajinder Kalra, both physically and psychologically.

What went wrong in the 1982 Delhi Asiad?

The Indian team for the 1982 Asiad was not a bad one. The mauling we suffered at the hands of Pakistan in the final was due to psychological reasons. The team just collapsed that day. Come to think of it that in 1982, India got the bronze medal in the Champions Trophy at Amsterdam and the silver medal in the Esanda Cup at Melbourne. In both the tournaments we beat Pakistan. I was with the team both in Amsterdam and Melbourne.

Who was the best goal-keeper you have played with or against?

Without doubt, it was my Indian teammate, Francis. Everything was perfect about Francis. He was very safe, very cool and possessed excellent reflexes and wonderful anticipation. Francis would not aimlessly kick a ball; instead, he would initiate a counter-attack for his side.

Who was the best back you have played against?

There is no greater challenge for a forward than to beat a cool and tough defender. R. S. Gentle, during my best playing days, was the one who towered above the rest with his hard yet clear tackling. I loved playing against him. In fact, the goals that have given me the most satisfaction have been the ones I have scored with Gentle in the opposite ranks.

You succeeded Dhyan Chand as India's centre-forward. What was so special about him?

The great Dhyan Chand was much senior to me. However, I have seen him in action. He was a great goal scorer. Apart from his scoring skill, he had masterly control, which enabled him to pass accurately and dribble well.

Finally, what are your views on having foreign coaches?

I do not think we need to look for foreign coaches. Our coaches are good. I am confident that the best we have should be given more exposure and time with the teams, so that the improvement which takes place lasts for a long period. The coaches picked should be quick learners, very observant and innovative and practical in their approach. Foreign coaches have problems relating to our language, habits and culture. Moreover, they are less patient with other players. Throwing out talented players on the pretext of being supposedly indisciplined is not done. Talented players should be brought around and their strengths should be utilised to the full.

HARBINDER SINGH – A FINE HOCKEY CENTRE – FORWARD

ALIVE – MAY 2005

Harbinder Singh, an Arjuna Award winner and former Hockey Olympian, was one of the finest centre-forwards our country has ever produced. Despite his outstanding achievements, Harbinder is most unassuming and modest. I met the 61-year-old hero of yesteryear, recently and spoke to him at his residence in New Delhi about his career in particular and Indian hockey in general.

When and how did you take to hockey?

My father, Sardar Balbir Singh, was in the Indian Army. He was an excellent hockey player, who toured Sri Lanka with the legendary Dhyan Chand. So, from childhood we saw a lot of hockey. I picked up the game by watching the army players in action. In school, I played hockey and football with great fervour. Former East Bengal soccer star striker, Gurkripal Singh, played football with me in Jalandhar.

Did the stay in Jalandhar, during your school and college years, help you to become a better hockey player?

Punjab had a very rich hockey culture at that time. Every village would have a number of teams. There would be regular competitions at almost all levels. We became much better players because of the opportunities we got of playing with and observing great players at close range.

At that time, the standard of hockey in the university was also very high. When did you make it to the Punjab University team?

I represented Punjab University from 1959 to 1961. In 1959, I also won a gold medal for the Punjab University Athletics team. In 1961, I was a member of the team which won the inter-university title.

Could you briefly describe your progress in hockey immediately after this?

In 1961, I made my debut for Punjab in the National Hockey Championships. We lost in the final that year but won the title the following year. In the same year, while in my first year in college, I was selected as a member of the Indian Senior Hockey side, which toured New Zealand and Australia.

Please tell readers about your achievements at the national level.

In addition to my being a member of the Punjab side, which won the national title in 1962, I was also a member of the Indian Railways team which won the national title 7 times (5 times in succession from 1963 to 1968). Incidentally, I also won a gold medal while representing the Railways in the 4x100 m relay race in the 1967 National Championship. .

What about your achievements at the international level?

I was privileged to represent India thrice in the Olympics and in two Asian Games. We won a gold medal in 1964 at the Tokyo Olympics and bronze medals in the 1968 Mexico and 1972 Munich Olympics. In the Asian Games, we won a gold medal in 1966 and a silver medal in 1970 where I captained the side. Both the 1966 and 1970 Asian Games were held in Bangkok.

How did your being a good athlete help your performance in hockey?

Being a good athlete helped me in overtaking or outpacing opposition defenders. On rare occasions, whenever required, I could easily rush back to help my defence.

Which was the most memorable game of your career?

I would rate the 1964 Tokyo Olympics final against Pakistan, which we won, as the most memorable game of my career. It was a crucial game, as we had lost the gold medal to Pakistan in the 1960 Rome Olympics. We just had to win that game. The first 8 to

10 minutes of that game were very rough and played in poor spirit. At that stage, the umpires called both the teams and said that, if the rough play and foul language did not stop, then they would be forced to use red cards. Realising the implication of the warning, both sides then played fast,

attacking, brilliant and clean hockey for the rest of the game. We finally managed to win the gold medal. Mohinder Lal, who scored the gold-winning penalty stroke that day, was my room-mate during the Olympics. Earlier, after breakfast, Mohinder Lal had told me that he had dreamt that India would be awarded a penalty stroke in the final. He also told me that the Pakistan goal-keeper was short. So, if a penalty stroke was awarded, he would place the ball over the goalkeeper's head. As fate would have it, Mohinder Lal's dream came true! He got the chance to do as he had planned in the morning, and India won the gold medal.

Which was your most memorable tournament?

The 1968 Olympics at Mexico was my most memorable tournament. I scored six goals and was the second top scorer. I was also selected in the World Hockey Eleven at the conclusion of the tournament.

Who was the best goalkeeper you have played against?

The Japanese goalkeeper I played against in the 1964 Tokyo Olympics was, without doubt, the best goal-keeper I have played against. Of course, our own Shankar Laxman was also superb. Talking about Laxman, I cannot forget the three successive saves he brought off in the last two minutes of the 1964 Tokyo Olympics final against Pakistan. Laxman first saved a direct hit, then a rebound and then another rebound which followed immediately after.

Who was the best defender you have played against?

Without doubt, it was our own Prithipal Singh. He was the best player of the 1960 Rome Olympics. He was a good full-back, with a very commanding personality. His penalty corner conversions were superb. Such was his presence, that the forwards in the opposition would shy away from him.

What ails Indian hockey today?

I feel that the main problem Indian hockey faces is the inability of the Hockey Federation or the Government to provide more astro- turf pitches in the country so that children pick up the game on that turf from an early age. In our time, matches were played on the same turf which we were used to from childhood. So, we were much better placed in international competitions. Another problem is that the competition for places in the team is much less. For example, India's right-winger during my time — Joginder Singh found it difficult to make it to the Railways side. Nowadays, people are becoming automatic choices.

Do we need a foreign coach?

If a foreign coach is to be appointed, he has to be a top class one. I wish to add here that the person selected must be given the job for at least four years.

What is your opinion of the National Hockey League?

I think it is a very good step. It has made hockey more professional. The players have also started earning more. Most importantly, even our hockey players are becoming idols of school-children as the League matches are gaining popularity.

ANJU JAIN – FIRST INDIAN WOMAN CRICKETER TO PLAY FOUR WORLD CUPS

WOMAN'S ERA – JUNE (SECOND) 2005

This year's World Cup cricket tournament for women saw Anju Jain, India's wicket-keeper and opener, achieve a rare feat. Anju, a former Indian captain, became the first Indian woman cricketer to represent India in four World Cups – 1993,1997,2000 and 2005. In fact, in the 2000 World Cup, she captained the team which finished third- the best ever performance by an Indian team till 2005.

How did you take to cricket?

My father,Amrit Lal Jain, was a cricketer. In fact, he was a wicket-keeper. He was in the Delhi Ranji Trophy squad in the early 1970s. So, cricket is in my blood.

Have you been coached?

I was first coached by Sunita Sharma at the National Stadium when I was 14 years of age. Even now when I have some problems, I go to her.

You have been on the international scene for about a decade now.What changes do you find in international cricket?

In the nineties, a total of 150 was considered a good score. Nowadays, even 250 is gettable. The standard of the game has improved greatly. The facilities are better and sponsorship and publicity are more.

Do any problems still exist in women's cricket in India?

I feel there should be more job opportunities for women cricketers. Nowadays, only the Railways and Air India provide jobs. It would be better if more companies provide greater job opportunities for talented players.

What achievement at the national level do you recall with pride?

I have a number of achievements at the national level. However, my record of scoring three successive centuries in the quarter-final, semi-final and final of the All India Inter-Varsity tournament in 1995-96 is what gives me great satisfaction. That record of mine is still to be bettered.

Any disappointment in your career?

I was hurt and am still hurt at having been left out from the Indian side for 18 months from mid-2002 till 2004. Despite scoring well in the domestic circuit, I was left out without any reason being given.

Which period of your career do you remember fondly?

I can never forget the comeback chance I got against New Zealand last year after being banished for 18 months. It was a crucial series for me. Against New Zealand, I got 54 in the only Test and two half-centuries in the five one-dayers. At Aurangabad,my 59 got me the player of the match award.

Who is the best bowler you faced in South Africa recently?

Cathryn Fitzpatrick of Australia was by far the best bowler I faced. She was quick and possessed excellent control and a lot of variation.

Who is the best batter you played against in South Africa?

Karen Rolton of Australia was undoubtedly the best. She is technically sound and has all the strokes. She is an excellent judge of the game and knows how to pace her innings.to suit the side.

Finally, what was so special about the Australian side?

They are a very professional side. Their players possess a high level of skills and are very positive with a never-say-die spirit.

Note: - In 2018, Anju Jain coached the Bangladesh women's cricket team which defeated India to win the Asia Cup.

GAUTAM GAMBHIR – THE IDEAL OPENING PARTNER FOR SEHWAG

ALIVE – JULY 2005

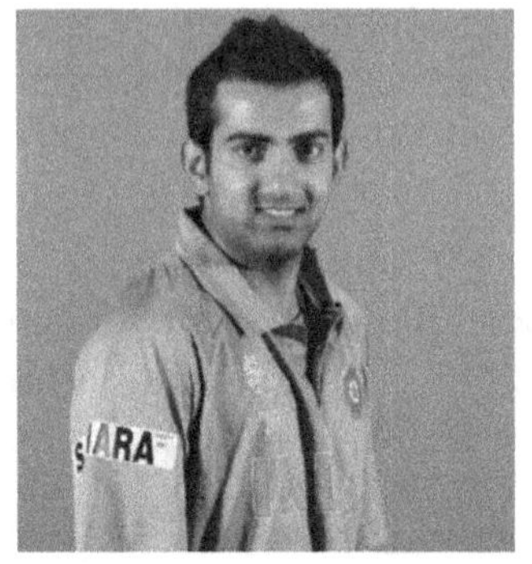

The latest opening partner in Test matches, for the brilliant Virender Sehwag, is his Delhi team-mate, Gautam Gambhir. The 23-year-old Gautam, who bats left-handed, possesses the wonderful knack of converting a good start into a long innings and a three-figure score.

Gautam is blessed with a fine and balanced cricketing brain and should serve India well for quite some time to come. For the record, in eight Tests so far, Gautam has scored 486 runs, at an average of 40.5. He has one century (139 vs. Bangladesh) and two half-centuries to his credit. I spoke to Gautam Gambhir at his residence, recently.

How did you take to cricket?

When I was in class 3 or 4, I attended a cricket coaching camp. In the camp, not only did I take an instant liking for the game but the people incharge of the camp also found that I had talent that ought to be nurtured.

Who has been your coach?

My only coach to date has been Mr. Sanjay Bharadwaj.

Any notable achievements at the under-19 level, where you played quite a bit?

I played three years for the Delhi under-19 side. I also captained the team. I scored 218 not out against Punjab. During the under-19 match against England, I scored 216 at Chepauk in Chennai. Unfortunately, I was not picked for the Indian under-19 side that played in the World Cup at Sri Lanka.

When did you make your Ranji Trophy debut?

I made my Ranji debut while in school, against Rajasthan in Delhi. I scored 35.

What has been your best effort in Ranji Trophy to date?

I have scored two double centuries in Ranji Trophy so far. Both of them have been against the Railways —216 at the Karnail Singh Stadium, Delhi and — my best so far — 233 not out, was at the Feroze Shah Kotla ground, Delhi.

Have you scored any other double century in high level first-class cricket?

When Heath Streak led the Zimbabwe side to India in 2001-02, I scored 218 in a single day, for the Board President's XI against the visitors at Vijayawada.

How many Duleep trophy matches have you been able to play and what have been your performances in that tournament?

I have played five Duleep trophy games to date. In these matches, I scored three half-centuries. I also scored a century against the West Zone in 2003.

You have toured with India 'A' sides. Which countries did you tour?

Over the last three years, I have been a member of the India 'A' sides which have toured Sri Lanka, the West Indies, England in 2003 and Zimbabwe and Kenya last year.

What has been your performance on those tours?

In Sri Lanka, I scored two centuries and two half-centuries, while in the West Indies, I was the highest run-getter, scoring 650 runs in seven games. On the tour of England, I scored two centuries and two half-centuries. One of those half-centuries was an innings of 80 against the full South African side, which was touring England then. I got a hundred each in Zimbabwe and Kenya.

Tell us about the three-nation limited-over tournament which was held in Kenya.

In the tri-nation tournament, Pakistan also participated. The Pakistan team was a really good one and included players like Naved Latif, Taufiq Omar, Salman Butt, Rao Iftikar and Bazid Khan. India won all the games and I scored 122 against Pakistan.

What qualities must a player possess to be a successful Test cricketer?

In Test cricket, a batsman needs to have not only a sound technique but also an unflappable temperament. It is this temperament which gives a player the mental strength to fight it out in tough situations and collect runs judiciously.

Which areas of your game do you feel need to be worked on still?

I need to tighten my game outside the off-stump. I need to move across more to the pitch of the ball. Again, I am doing my best not to play across the line.

The Indian side has some superstars as its senior players. How have they been with you — a relative newcomer?

All the senior players have been both helpful and encouraging. The great thing is that they are always available. My captains, too, have been most supportive.

Who is the best bowler you have faced in your career to date?

Without a doubt, it is Shaun Pollock of South Africa. Apart from being very steady, accurate and straight, he always makes the batsman think and play. Rotation of the strike is not easy when Shaun Pollock is the bowler.

Finally, apart from establishing yourself as India's opener, particularly at the Test level, do you have any other ambition?

Yes, it is my dream to be a member of the Delhi team which wins the Ranji Trophy as I have heard so much from the senior players about how thrilled they used to be on such occasions. So, I too, am really looking forward to this experience.

ANSHUMAN GAEKWAD – A GRITTY OPENER AND A THINKING CRICKETER

ALIVE – FEBRUARY 2006

52-year-old Anshuman Gaekwad, a former Indian cricketer, was in his time a sound batsman. His main quality was exemplary courage and he was an inspiration to his teammates. Anshuman also possesses one of the best cricketing brains in Indian cricket and has served as coach of the Indian team and National selector. I spoke to Anshuman Gaekwad recently in Delhi about his cricketing experiences.

From whom did you get your early cricketing lessons?

My father D.K. Gaekwad was a former captain of the Indian team and helped me a lot in my early years. Apart from that, I was fortunate to learn the nuances of the game from renowned former cricketers like Vijay Hazare and J.M. Ghorpade. Vijay Hazare was one of the greatest batsmen Indian cricket has ever produced. He scored a century in each innings against the Australian side led by the great Don Bradman in the 1947-48 Indian tour of Australia.

Could you tell readers about your Test debut?

It was in Kolkata, against the West Indies, in 1974-75. I played that Test as a middle order batsman. In fact, I came into bat soon after our captain Mansur Ali Khan Pataudi retired hurt, after being hit on the chin by a bouncer from Andy Roberts. Even in those days, the Eden Gardens was a big stadium, with a capacity crowd of 40,000 to 50,000. I had to face a fiery Roberts, who was bowling at his fastest. I saw through that over and compiled a most satisfactory 36. The knock gave me a lot of confidence too.

You were a member of the Indian side that participated in the 1975 and 1979 World Cups. Tell us something about these two tournaments.

In the 1975 World Cup, the Indian side had little or no idea as to what one-day cricket was. That is why we performed miserably except for a few noteworthy individual performances. In the 1979 World Cup, we just seemed incapable of winning as, even then, we did not have much experience in one-day cricket.

During the 1976 tour of the West Indies, India chased 403 to win the third Test at Port of Spain. Can you recall that historic win?

India had a strong batting line-up and the West Indies bowling was not really of outstanding quality. Initially, we played normal cricket, session by session. Then, when we found that we had wickets in hand and the target was reachable, we went for it. It was a team effort, with G.R. Vishwanath playing the leading role with his class batting. We won the game scoring a record 406 for 4.

The last Test at Sabina Park, Jamaica, is remembered for the 'bloodbath' started by captain Clive Lloyd and paceman Michael Holding. Tell us about that match.

This Test will always be remembered for the most intimidatory bowling of the West Indies paceman, Michael Holding. India had reached 205 for 1 and West Indies skipper Clive Lloyd felt that the Test and the series might be lost. It was then that Holding switched to round-the-wicket and attacked our bodies with fearsome pace on a track that had uneven bounce. I got 80 but was hit on the back of the head. Vishwanath was also badly hit on the finger, while Brijesh Patel was hit by a ball which flew off the bat. Bedi, our skipper, declared our innings closed at 306-6. In our second innings, we could get only 97 as five of our players — myself, Vishwanath, Patel, Bedi and Chandrasekhar were injured (the last two while fielding). It was cricket at its worst.

Why is it we could not defeat a depleted Australian side on the 1977-78 tour?

Yes, considering how strong our team was and how depleted the Australian team was, we should have won that closely-fought series. In the decisive final Test, Prasanna was injuredand I was forced to bowl a lot of off-spin. The Aussies are fighters and, maybe, it was that trait that enabled them to win that series.

Tell us about your Pakistan tours.

The 1978 tour of Pakistan was supposed to be a diplomatic; or rather, a friendship tour. The Pakistanis outplayed us. Zaheer Abbas, in particular, was in superb form, tormenting our master spin bowlers. He was uncontrollable. The 1982-83 tour was dominated by Imran Khan. The wickets helped seam movement and Imran bowled with fire and variation and was unplayable on most occasions.

What is required of an opener to be successful in Test cricket?

To be a successful opener in Tests, a player must possess temperament, technique, courage and common sense, which teaches him to exploit his strengths and play within his limitations.

You have played alongside some of the best batsmen India has produced. Please share your thoughts about them with us.

Gavaskar was a perfectionist, supremely confident and intelligent. On a good track, bowling to him was a hard task. Viswanath was an artist. Even the best bowlers had a problem bowling to him on both bad and helpful tracks. Mohinder Amarnath was a gutsy and cool customer, while Dilip Vengsarkar was calculative, technically and temperamentally very sound.

Your opinion on some of India's greatest spinners?

Off-spinner Prasanna was a master of flight and variation, while Venkataraghavan, the other off-spinner, was a very dangerous bowler on a helpful wicket. In fact, on helpful wickets, he was more dangerous than Prasanna. Left-arm spinner Bedi was very accurate and a master of flight, possessing great control over length and line. Leg-spinner Chandrasekhar was an unpredictable bowler and a match-winner on his day.

As an opener, you have played against some of the greatest fast bowlers in the world. Please share your views about them?

Andy Roberts was deceptively quick. Joel Garner was 6'7" tall and was difficult to face because of the height from which he bowled. Colin Croft was very quick and thus dangerous. Malcolm Marshall was skiddy, while Michael Holding bowled quick with a beautiful action. So much about the West Indians. New Zealander Richard Hadlee possessed great control over length, line and movement. He was also deceptively quick off the wicket. Pakistan had two fine bowlers in Imran and Sarfraz. Imran was quick and bowled with an open chest action. He bowled an in-cutter but what made him more dangerous was the outswinger he bowled with the open-chested action. Sarfraz was an intelligent bowler and an excellent mover of the ball.

Please tell readers about your experience as India's coach.

I enjoyed coaching the Indian side. Being the coach of the National team is very testing and challenging. It involves a lot of work — both present and future planning. There is so much work that you feel 24 hours are insufficient.

Finally, as a former selector, do you feel, India should have only three National selectors?

If you ask me, for a country like India, even five selectors are not enough.

JHULAN GOSWAMI – KAPIL DEV OF INDIAN WOMEN'S CRICKET

WOMAN'S ERA – SEPTEMBER (SECOND) 2006

23-year old Jhulan Goswami of Bengal, a lively medium-fast bowler and an attacking bat became the first Indian bowler to take 10 wickets in a Test in the first week of September this year. She achieved this distinction in the second and final Test against England at Taunton taking 5 for 33 in the first and 5 for 45 in the second innings. Her performance was greatly instrumental in India winning the Test and the series. Jhulan who took 15 wickets in the two Tests bagged both the woman of the match and series awards. I met Jhulan before she left for England and spoke to her about her cricket career.

Where do you hail from?

I come from Nadia district in West Bengal.

When did you take to cricket?

I started playing cricket at the age of 15 while studying at Babuji Balika Vidyamandir at Chakdaha.

Did you take coaching at that stage?

Yes, I was fortunate to meet Mr Swapan Sadhu, a cricket coach. Mr Sadhu has taught me everything, I know about the game. He has cared for me both on and off the field. He inculcated in me discipline. Even now if I have a problem, I go to him for advice.

When did you make your debut for Bengal in the Senior Nationals?

I made my debut for Bengal in February 2000 in the Nationals at Jorhat.

When did you make your debut for India?

I made both-my one day and Test debut-for India in January 2002 against England at home. My one day International debut was at Chennai on 6 January while my Test debut was at Lucknow on 14 January.

Which has been your best bowling performance in International cricket?

In one day internationals, my best performance was against England last year when I took 5 for 16 off 10 overs in the fourth one dayer at Silchar.. My spell helped in bowling England out for 50. Earlier in the World Cup in South Africa, I had taken 4 for 16 against the West Indies at Pretoria. In Test cricket, I again achieved my best figures in last year's Test against England at New Delhi. I finished with figures of 5 for 25 off 20 overs in England's first innings.

You did play a bright innings in a Test against England last year. However, your most impressive batting performance in international cricket was your 62 against England in the Test at Taunton in 2002. Please tell the readers about that knock.

That innings is something which I shall never forget for the rest of my life. This is because I shared in a world record 157 run partnership for the seventh wicket with Mithali Raj who scored 214. For me, the knock gave me a lot of confidence as my technique and temperament passed the acid test of Test cricket and that too abroad.

What were your performances like in the one day series against England at home last year where you were the joint player of the series?

It was my performance as a bowler that helped me to share the award. In five matches, I picked up 10 wickets. at an average of 11.50. My best performance was 5 for 16 in the fourth one day at Silchar.

Among the batters you have bowled to in international cricket, whom do you consider the most difficult to bowl to?

In my opinion, it is Rebecca Rolles of New Zealand. She is a very sound player who can improvise when required. Among the Indian players, Mithali Raj is outstanding. Former Indian skipper, Purnima Rao was very difficult to bowl to because of her unorthodox style.

Finally, who is your cricketing idol?

Without doubt it is Glen McGrath of Australia. What I admire most about him is his consistency and the superb length and line he always maintains. I only wish that as a bowler, I perform like him for India. Her wish has come true as like McGrath she, too, has proved to be a menace to the English cricketers.

2012-August 2018

E.A.S. Prasanna, Aditi Ashok, Anjali Bhagwat, Col.R.S. Rathore, Vijay Kumar, Manika Batra, K. Sasikiran, Raj Kr. Sharma, P.R. Man Singh, Unmukt Chand, Randhir Singh, B.S. Bedi, Sudha Chaudhry, Sushil Kumar, Rani Rampal, Ritu Rani, Deepali Deshpande, Parimarjan Negi, S. Rangaswamy, Jitu Rai, Anirban Lahiri, S.S. P. Chawrasia, Kapil Dev, Sakshi Malik, Deepa Malik, Rishabh Pant, Dipa Karmakar, G. S. Randhawa, Harendra Singh, G.R. Vishwanath, Abhinav Bindra and Sudha Shah

ERAPALLI PRASANNA – A TOP-CLASS OFF SPIN BOWLER

ALIVE – NOVEMBER 2012

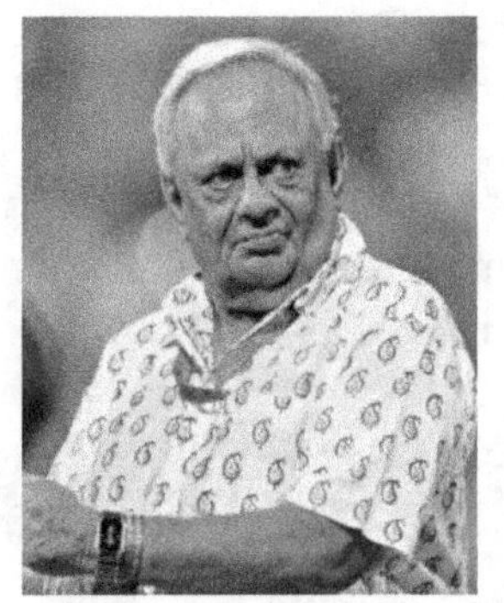

One of the world's finest off spin bowlers ever and probably India's greatest ever, Erapalli Prasana dominated the international scene from 1967 till 1970 in particular (in those days we had a maximum of eight Tests in a year). Of course, he continued to bowl well at Test level till 1978.

Padma Shri Erapalli Prasanna of Karnataka was a spectator's delight but a batsman's nightmare with his sharp turn, drifters and superb variation of flight. I met Erapalli Prasanna in Bangalore and spoke to him about his career in particular and cricket in general.

When did you come on to the National scene for the first time?

It was in the early sixties when I was studying for engineering that I performed well enough to make it to the national side. To be precise, it was 1961. England or M.C.C. under the captaincy of Ted Dexter was touring India then. I performed impressively for the Combined Universities against the tourists, took the wicket of the great Ken Barrington while playing for the Board President's XI and also captured 6 wickets for South Zone against the visitors. My performance impressed the selectors and I made my Test debut against England in the fifth Test at Madras.

You were then selected to tour the West Indies with the Indian team in 1962. What was your experience on that tour?

It was a great learning experience for me as there were many senior Indian players like Vijay Manjrekar and Polly Umrigar with whom I was touring abroad for the first time. I also got the opportunity to bowl to great West Indian batsmen like Sobers, Kanhai, Worrell and Hunte. I played only the second Test at Jamaica and took 3 for 122 off 50 overs. The tour taught me how to bowl to top class batsmen on goodish wickets.

Could you tell readers about some of the great West Indian players you bowled to and faced on that tour?

Let me start with the all-rounder Gary Sobers first. As a batsman, Sobers was out of the world. He was technically sound and possessed all the strokes.

Sobers was also a more than useful left-arm medium fast and spin bowler too. As a fielder particularly close in he was brilliant.

Rohan Kanhai was a technically sound player who could innovate. His falling sweep was quite unique.

Among the bowlers, Wesley Hall and Lance Gibbs were top quality. Hall was a fearsome fast bowler who was really quick, while Lance Gibbs was a tall off-spinner who possessed great control over flight and turn. It was not easy for batsmen to easily come down the wicket to him.

Despite becoming a Test cricketer even before your 22nd birthday, you took a break from top-level cricket for about four years (1962-1966). Why?

Yes, I took a break from serious competitive cricket from 1962-1966 for various reasons. My father died during this period and I also felt that I had to complete my engineering degree. By mid-1966, I completed my engineering.

How did you make a comeback to the Indian team?

The West Indies who were touring India in 1966 played the South Zone at Bangalore. In that game, I took eight wickets for South Zone and was selected for the third and final Test at Madras. I had a reasonably good Test taking five wickets in the match.

You toured England in 1967. The team except for a few players performed poorly. What happened?

To be honest, our team lacked the experience of English conditions – weather and wickets. In batting, Wadekar was the most consistent of the lot while there were some good performances by skipper Pataudi, Engineer and Hanumant Singh. Pataudi's 64 and 148 in the first Test at Leeds was an outstanding performance. In bowling, Chandrasekhar was the star taking 16 wickets. Only in the third Test at Edgbaston did our spinners make an impact. We played four spinners in that Test with Chandrasekhar and myself finishing with six and seven wickets respectively.

England had an all-time great batsman in Tom Graveney. Despite touring in the first half of the English summer we did reasonably well. We did learn a lot on the tour and this helped us to win in 1971.

The next four series - 1967 – 68 in Australia, 1968 in New Zealand and the visits of New Zealand and Australia to India in 1969 saw you at your peak. Please tell us about that outstanding phase of your career.

I did have some fine performances for India from 1971 – 1978 but the 1967 – 1969 period was probably the best period of my international career. My skipper Pataudi understood me well and trusted me wholly. It was this that brought the best of me. In just 16 Tests, I captured 95 wickets - 51 vs. Australia in nine Tests and 44 vs. New Zealand in seven Tests. We had excellent close in fielders like Solkar, Venkat, Wadekar and Abid Ali. Solkar became a big threat for opposition batsmen in 1971 and 1972-73 in particular.

The big regret is that against Australia in both the 1967 and 1969 series we lost matches we should have won. This used to happen to us against teams like England and West Indies too.

The turnaround for Indian Cricket came in 1971 when we defeated the West Indies and England for the first time abroad. How did this happen and what was your role?

1971 was a great year for Indian cricket with everything going right for us. In 1969, a lot of good talent was discovered in the form of Vishwanath, Solkar and Mohinder Amarnath. The spinners were maturing, and the close catching was of high quality. The 1971 side to the West Indies was a mixture of youth and experience selected on the basis of current form and keeping in mind the conditions in the West Indies.

Apart from the top class spin attack we possessed, the experience of Sardesai, Durani and Jaisimha was added. New cap Gavaskar was a great choice. Sardesai played crucial knocks. Durani bowled the match-winning spell in the second Test at Port of Spain while Jaisimha gave excellent inputs.

I got 11 wickets in the three Tests I played. However, it was with the bat, I made a large contribution putting on 122 for the ninth wicket with Dilip Sardesai in the first Test at Jamaica. Sardesai scored 212 while I got 25 in that innings.

You also had a number of other outstanding performances till that miserable tour of Pakistan in 1978. Could you tell us about them?

On the individual front, there were quite a few good performances. The best one would be in the first Test at Auckland in 1976 vs. New Zealand where I took 3 for 64 and 8 for 76 (11-140) helping India to win the Test.

Again, in 1974-75, I took 5 for 70 and 4 for 41 against the West Indies in the fourth Test at Madras and helped India win.

Another performance I remember was my 4 for 16 in England's second innings in the third Test at Madras in 1972-73 where we won a close game.

Finally, my 1 for 14 and 4 for 51 in the fourth Test against Australia at Sydney in 1977-78 which helped us to win the Test convincingly.

Please tell us about the best batsmen you have bowled to or seen.

Tom Graveney of England was the best player I have bowled to. Sobers, Kanhai and Ian Chappell also played spin really well.

Among the Indian batsmen, Vijay Manjrekar, Sunil Gavaskar and Vishwanath were outstanding. Of the Indian left-handers I have bowled to Wadekar, Ambar Roy and Milkha Singh were really good. Wadekar's fine temperament and ruthlessness as a batsman helped him reach the levels he reached.

ADITI ASHOK – A WOMAN GOLFER OF GREAT PROMISE.

WOMAN'S ERA – JANUARY (SECOND) 2013

Aditi Ashok of Karnataka is a woman golfer of great potential. Aditi, at present, is the best junior women's golfer in the country. She is also the second leading women's golfer in India. Her love for golf can be seen from the fact that she is also a class B qualified referee making her eligible to officiate national junior events. All this at 14. I met Aditi recently and found her to be an intelligent and a focussed player with one big aim in mind – to make it to the LPGA Hall of Fame. Aditi spoke to me about how she took to the game, her career to date and her ultimate aim.

How did you take to golf at such as early age- almost 5 ½ years?

My parents were having breakfast at the Karnataka Golf Association course. I went out of curiosity to the tee nearby. The coach gave me a small club for fun and believe it or not I took a liking for the sport. I played my first round of 18 holes at six years two months at my home club – the Bangalore Golf Club. For me Golf has been everything and my parents have most of the time been with me so that I grow up to become a golfing great.

Who have been your coaches to date?

My first coach was Col. Nagaraj who taught me the basics at the KGA course. After attending some group coaching, I started being coached by Mr. Tarun Sardesai in 2005. Mr. Sardesai is a category A coach. From last year, my coach has been Mr. Steven Giuliano, a PGA coach based in Malaysia.

Apart from my coaches, I wish to express my gratitude to my home club – the Bangalore Golf Club. For me it is really a home club as I can play and practise there anywhere and at any time with no restrictions. My school Frank Anthony Public School, Bangalore has always cooperated with me.

You have won a number of titles and been the youngest to achieve that distinction. Please tell readers what those titles were.

First of all, the age of 9, I became the youngest amateur in India to win the Bronze title at the All India Ladies Amateur Golf Open Championship in 2008. In January 2011, at the age of 12, I became the youngest amateur in India to win an amateur open title – the All India Ladies Amateur Golf Open Championship for the Billoo Sethi Trophy. The same year, I became the youngest and first Indian amateur to have participated at the Asia-Pacific Invitational for the Queen Sirikit Cup in Thailand. Finally, in September 2011, I became the youngest player in the world at 13 years and five months to win the WGAI's Clover Greens, Women's Professional tournament as an amateur.

What have been your other big achievements at the national level to date?

Last season, I won the All India Women's match-play championship. This season, I finished as the leading junior women's golfer in India winning the final tournament of the National junior tour in Kolkata. Unfortunately, I lost in the semi-final of the All India Women's match-play competition this year. My best moment came when I had an eighth-place finish at the Hero Honda Women's Open.

You have represented the country in international tournaments abroad. Could you tell readers about them?

I have been representing the country since 2010 in different competitions. At the junior level, I participated in the Junior Open, U.K in 2012, Evian Masters Junior Cup, France in 2010, 2011 and 2012; 100 Plus Malaysian Juniors, in 2011, the Asia Pacific Junior Golf Championship in Thailand and Myanmar in 2011 and 2012 respectively and the Faldo Series Asia grand final in China in 2012.

At the ladies level, I have represented India in the Asia – Pacific Invitational Ladies Amateur Team Championship for the Queen Sirikit Cup in India and Singapore in 2011 and 2012 respectively. I was also a part of the Indian side that participated in the World Amateur team championship for the Espirito Santo Trophy in September 2012 in Antalya, Turkey. This was the first time India participated in the prestigious world amateur team championship.

What awards have you won for far?

Last year, I won the Rolex Award of Excellence as the number one junior golfer. I was also the Toyota IGU player of the year last year. The Sports Authority of India gave me a cash award of Rupees 5 lakhs last year for my training abroad. I went to Malaysia to be trained by a PGA coach Mr. Steven Giuliano. This year I have also won the Toyota player of the year award.

Could you tell readers about the training you underwent in Kuala Lumpur?

The training was for ten days- six to eight hours per day, on a one to one basis. Every aspect of the game was touched on and I am still in touch with my coach Mr. Steven Giuliano.

How does playing golf help a youngster?

Playing golf helps a youngster as he or she develops qualities like honesty, integrity, responsibility, patience and perseverance – all essential for a person to become successful.

ANJALI BHAGWAT – AN INSPIRATION TO YOUNG WOMEN SHOOTERS

WOMAN'S ERA-FEBRUARY (SECOND) 2013

43-year-old Anjali Bhagwat has been an inspiration to the new generation of Indian women shooters. For Anjali, shooting is her life and her dedication, love and involvement in the sport is something that impresses anyone immediately. I met Anjali in Delhi recently and spoke to her about her shooting career and Indian shooting.

How did you get interested in shooting?

My first brush with shooting occurred during my stint as a cadet in the NCC. In fact, I joined Kirti College in Mumbai because of its affinity to NCC. As part of the curriculum, I went to the Maharashtra Rifle Association. I started actively shooting at the age of 19 and within seven days of holding a gun, I took part in the National Championships in 1988 and won a silver medal.

Who have been your coaches?

My first coach was Sanjay Chakravarty. He taught me the basics. In 1999, Hungarian Lazlo Szucsak was my coach. Unfortunately, he was with us for a year initially. Fortunately, he came back to coach in India from 2005 till 2008. Lazlo Szucsak was one of the best coaches in the world. He really polished my skills and fine-tuned my game. He taught me how to use the accessories and intelligently adapt to new conditions and situations. From 2009 till 2012, I have been coached by Stanislav Lapidus who is also a very good coach.

Please tell readers about the main competitions you have participated in.

I have had the honour of representing India in all the international competitions. The main ones were the Olympics, World Cup finals,

World Championships, Asian Games, Asian Championships, Afro-Asian Games and Commonwealth Games.

You have a number of big achievements in shooting particularly at the international level. Could you let readers know about your main ones?

Apart from winning a number of medals including gold in major competitions, I also have had a number of firsts to my name. First of all, when I qualified for the finals of the 2000 Olympics, I became the first Indian woman shooter to achieve this feat. Winning the prestigious ISSF Champion of Champions award in Munich in 2002 was another first. The same year, I became the first Indian to be ranked world no.1 among women in the 10 m Air Rifle event. In 2003, I became the first Indian shooter to win golds in the World Cup in Atlanta (USA) and the World Cup finals in Milan with identical scores of 399/400.

Please tell us in detail about the win in Munich in 2002.

My greatest moment was winning the ISSF (International Shooting Sports Federation) Champion of Champions award in Munich in 2002. Apart from being the only Indian to have won the ISSF Champions Trophy, I must make it clear that the competition was very tough. For this competition, the top ten World Cup medal winners (5 men and five women) are invited. Men and women have to play against each other. Following the procedure of elimination, the top two shooters fight it out to finish a winner. I was successful.

You have contributed greatly towards shooting as a sport for women in India – in fact, an inspiration to the younger generation. What honours has the Indian Government conferred on you?

The Government of India has conferred on me two huge honours – the Arjuna Award in 2000 and the Rajiv Gandhi Khel Ratna Award in 2002. I am of course grateful to the Government for recognizing my efforts. A lot of credit should go to my family members and my coaches.

How and why has shooting become an Olympic medal-winning sport in India?

Some of our men shooters like Rajyavardhan Rathore and Abhinav Bindra in particular worked very hard to achieve what they did. Rajyavardhan Rathore inspired all of us with his silver medal in the 2004 Athens Olympics. The Government, too, has been doing all it can for the shooters – best infrastructure, excellent coaches, training abroad and better allowances. Even the Indian Army, in particular, has been helping its shooters. Because of the Olympic successes, shooting has become popular at the school level too. In Mumbai and Pune, many schools have facilities for shooting in their campuses. People now feel that they can win medals in the Olympics too and so the sport has become popular. Finally, even corporates are helping out.

I understand that you are into coaching too. Please tell readers about the coaching aspect of your shooting career.

I am involved in a coaching scheme run by the Maharashtra State Government. Children are selected on the basis of their talent from remote areas and are made to stay in a place. All basic needs like shelter, food and education are taken care of by the Government. I coach shooting. Of course, I keep on guiding players who seek my assistance.

Finally, how does Shooting help youngsters who take to the sport?

Shooting helps a youngster to develop mainly concentration, accuracy and patience. It is a wonderful sport to keep one properly busy.

RAJYAVARDHAN SINGH RATHORE – FIRST INDIAN INDIVIDUAL OLYMPIC MEDAL WINNER IN THIS CENTURY

ALIVE – MARCH 2013

43-year-old Rajyavardhan Rathore won the silver medal in the shooting event of the 2004 Athens Olympics and became the first Indian individual Olympic medal winner in this century. I met Col. Rathore recently in Delhi and what strikes anyone about him is his self-confidence, politeness, unassuming nature, excellent manners, memory power and punctuality. After asking him about his career in shooting I got to know about what he felt about the sport in India.

Please tell readers about your early background and the sporting interests of your younger days.

I hail from an army family. My father was a Colonel in the army while my mother has been a teacher. The two sports to which I was greatly attached when young were shooting and cricket.

What made you take up shooting ahead of cricket?

You will be surprised to know that I was about to make it to the Madhya Pradesh Ranji Trophy team when I was only in class 10. My mother told me not to go for the trials as she was keen that I complete my basic education. I then joined the NDA (National Defence Academy) where slowly but surely my interest and progress in shooting grew.

When did you take to shooting seriously?

My studies at the Indian Military Academy where I won the 'Sword of Honour' and then my stint in Kargil and other duties made me take up shooting seriously as a sport as late as 1998. But since 1998, it has only been hard scientific training and rigorous practice.

How did you qualify for the 2004 Athens Olympics?

I had achieved a lot of success in different competitions all over the world. However, my bronze medal at the World Championship in Cyprus helped me to qualify for the 2004 Olympics.

Now I wish to take you back to 18 August 2004 in Athens when with one round to go and just one point ahead, you needed to get both your shots right to win the Olympic men's double trap shooting event. What were your thoughts then?

To be honest, I had put all pressure aside and was totally focussed on the target. I saw nothing else but the target. I must add here that despite my best efforts it was indeed Sheikh Ahmed al-Maktoum of UAE's day. He was that day absolutely unbeatable .

How did you feel standing on the podium to receive your medal?

It felt absolutely great. It really felt good to win a medal for the country but it felt better as millions of my countrymen were really proud of me.

At the presentation there was a sight which all Indians still remember - your draping the country's flag around you. What were your thoughts then?

I wanted something close to a symbol which represented my country and I felt that our national flag was the best possible thing. So I wrapped the National flag all around me. I cannot say how inspired and thrilled I felt that time.

Which other performance after the Olympics do you remember with great fondness?

Though I have had notable successes before and after my 2004 Olympic feat, I remember fondly the first Asian Shot Gun Shooting Championship at Kuala Lumpur in 2011. In that competition. I equalled Russian Vitaly Fokeer's mark set at the World Cup held in Concepcion, Chile in March 2011 and won the gold medal in the double trap event. In the team event of which I was a member, we won the bronze. The individual performance of mine is an event I will always remember as my ability and temperament were really tested.

What honours have been conferred on you because of your achievements in the sport 'Shooting'?

The Indian Army with whom I am serving has given also possible recognition. They have also provided me with all possible assistance in my training, practice and facilities. The Government of India conferred on me the Arjuna Award in 2003 and the Rajiv Gandhi Khel Ratna Award in 2004.

You were India's first individual Olympic medalist in this century and silver medalist after many years. What special qualities are required to achieve such a big feat?

First of all, an individual must have a personal hunger to achieve. He or she needs to be perfect technique-wise and most important of all unruffled in tight and tense situations. Here I wish to mention that our culture and religious books provide a lot of wisdom which if appropriately applied brings success. The goal must be clearly defined and we must work unrelentingly towards it, with total focus. Finally, if we have the blessings of elders and God is with us, success is assured.

Finally, you passed through a tough period in 2009 and 2010 when you were about to quit the sport due to a number of reasons. Who stood by you then?

For helping me to continue in the game first and foremost, I must thank my family. My wife was and is a great pillar of strength. In fact, she has been a friend and philosopher. Honestly, it feels good that even if you do not have faith in yourself, there are others who have faith in you.

VIJAY KUMAR – LONDON OLYMPICS SHOOTING SILVER MEDALIST

ALIVE – APRIL 2013

In the 2012 London Olympics, India won two silver medals – Sushil Kumar, who had won a bronze medal in wrestling in the 2008 Beijing Olympics, was one of them. The other was 27-year-old Vijay Kumar who hails from Harsaur village in Himachal Pradesh. Vijay Kumar who serves in the Indian Army got the second position in the 25m rapid fire pistol event. What struck one most about Vijay Kumar was his unassuming nature despite all his success. I met Vijay Kumar recently in Delhi and spoke to him about his life and career.

Could you tell us about your life until you joined the Army?

My father served in the Indian Army. Though we were not very well off, my father inculcated a deep sense of values in us. After completing my formal education, I joined the Indian Army at the age of 18 in order to fulfill my dream of serving the army and also support my family.

What role has the army played in your development as a shooter?

Whatever I am today is largely due to the Indian Army. Initially, it was after joining the Army that I was able to sharpen my shooting skills. In a few years, I became the best pistol shooter in the Army and started winning competitions both at Army and National Levels. The Army has provided all of us with a top-class foreign coach- Pavel Smirnov. I am particularly happy that he will be around for another four years. The Army ensures that we get the best equipment with ammunition and training facilities including foreign exposure.

Which coach of yours has had the greatest impact on you and your development?

Without a doubt, it has been Pavel Smirnov. He plans out everything for me from general training to improvement in technique. Before the London Olympics for example, he had worked out everything so well that I peaked at the right time – the shooting event at the London Olympics. In my best interest, he was very strict about my activities. For instance, four months prior to the London Olympics, when we were rigorously training in Europe picking up vital tips on competition and acclimatization, I was not allowed to make or take more than one call a day. Shooting was not to be discussed in those calls. The isolation was complete when a fortnight before the Olympics the face book and twitter accounts were de-activated.

What is your normal training schedule?

I usually train for six to seven hours a day. I also do physical training for about two hours daily. Apart from this, when I feel free I also enjoy playing badminton, table tennis and billiards. I also like cycling.

You got a silver medal on your debut Olympics in London. What more do you need to do to get a gold medal in the next Olympics?

My coach has told me not to worry about results. He only stresses on the fact that I must practise, follow the schedules given, work on and master my technique and also focus on the competitions in between. He is confident that the best result will surely come.

What have been the main competitions you have represented India in and what have been your major achievements?

I won a silver medal in the 2012 London Olympics. It was my debut Olympics. I have also won Gold, Silver and Bronze medals in the Commonwealth Games (2006 and 2010), Asian Games (2006 and 2010) and the World Shooting Championships.

How have your performances been recognized?

In 2006, I won the Arjuna Award. Last year, I won the Rajiv Gandhi Khel Ratna award and this year when the Republic Day honours were announced. I learnt I had been nominated for a Padma Shri. The Army also gave me the highest promotion possible. In addition, I have earned the love of the people of India which means a lot to me.

What are the reasons for our successes in Olympic shooting in the last decade?

Actually,the mental block about winning Olympic medals in shooting was broken by Rajyavardhan Rathore in the 2004 Athens Olympics. Now more people are taking to shooting seriously and we have some top class shooting ranges in the country too. Good shooters are also getting a lot of support from the government.

How does Shooting help develop a person?

Shooting helps a person develop qualities like self-control, discipline, patience, concentration and the ability to fight with and overcome odds.

Finally, what is your message for youngsters?

I feel youngsters must be disciplined, use their heads, have a goal and remain focussed on it. Having a good guru is a must. They must never bother about setbacks. Then they will surely succeed

MANIKA BATRA – ONE OF INDIA'S MOST PROMISING T.T. PLAYERS

WOMAN'S ERA – JUNE (FIRST) 2013

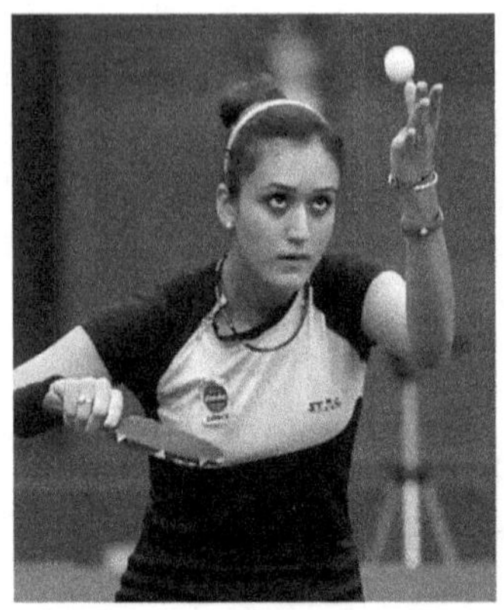

The star of the last National Table Tennis championships for Women at Raipur earlier this year was Manika Batra, a 17-year-old school student from Delhi, who with two brilliant wins steered Delhi to a historic triumph over the reputed Petroleum Board and become Women's National Team Champions after a decade. Manika represented India in the recently concluded Commonwealth Table Tennis Championships in New Delhi and won a bronze medal. I met Manika and spoke to her about her career and her experiences in the game both in India and abroad.

When and how did you take to the game?

I took to the game quite early at the age of five as my elder brother and my elder sister were already playing the game.

Who has been your coach?

From the age of five, I have had one coach- Mr. Sandeep Gupta. Mr. Gupta coached me in the school and also coaches me at the Hansraj Stag Academy. He has made me the player I am.

What kind of schedule does your coach make you follow?

My training schedule is quite hectic. Apart from doing physical training, I practise six to seven hours a day. He also helps me psychologically, so that my temperament improves.

Could you tell us about your performances in the final at the Nationals in Raipur earlier this year?

It was really a great period of my life. In the team event, I won two of Delhi's three matches including one against a player of the calibre of Ankita Das. I also partnered Utkarsh Gupta in the mixed doubles event to win the title.

I owe a lot to my coach for having developed in me the ability to stay cool in tight situations. Talking about keeping cool, I wish to mention here my win over Poulami Ghatak, then Indian number one, in the 2011 Inter-Institutional Competition which earned me a scholarship with IOC at the age of 15. I can join the Indian Oil Corporation officially once I become 18 years of age.

Could you tell readers about some of your best performances both in India and abroad?

At the Junior level in International events, I have performed quite well. In 2010, in the Global Cadet Challenge championship in Hyderabad, I finished third. Again in 2012, I secured the seventh position in the Junior Girls team event of the Asian Junior Championships in China. While in the Volkswagen World Junior Championship the same year in Hyderabad I reached the pre-quarter-final stage where I lost to the World No. 4.

At the National level, I started performing well at the senior level from last year. In the PSPB inter-unit tournament in New Delhi last year, I secured the first position in the women's singles event. The same year, I received the first position in the mixed doubles event in the Senior Nationals in Lucknow. Again, in the All India Public Sector tournament in Kolkata, I secured the first position in the team event.

However, my greatest moment to date, was in the Nationals at Raipur earlier this year, where I got the first positions in the team's event and the mixed doubles event too. I wish to also add that my bronze medal in the singles event of the Commonwealth Table Tennis Championships gave me a lot of satisfaction and self-confidence as I was playing against much senior players at the International level.

What must our women players need to do to reach the same level as badminton stars Saina Nehwal or even P.V. Sindhu who have made it big internationally?

I think we need to become much fitter, work harder, plan better and be really self-motivated. We need to feel that we can reach the next level and beat anyone.

Finally, how does the game Table Tennis help a school student?

By playing table tennis, we develop our focus, concentration and agility. We develop quick reflexes and learn how to be patient and aggressive when required.

KRISHNAN SASIKIRAN – AN OUTSTANDING CHESS PLAYER

ALIVE – JUNE 2013

32-year-old Krishnan Sasikiran is one of India's leading chess players at present. Sasikaran who hails from Chennai is an Indian Grandmaster who earned the title at the 2000 Commonwealth Championship. I met Sasikiran in Delhi recently and spoke to him about his career and the game chess.

When did you take to Chess?

Like most youngsters in Chennai, I took to Chess early at the age of nine. I took part in the under-10 state competition in 1990.

When did you achieve your first major success?

My first major success came in 1995 when I won the under-18 National Championships in Bengaluru. I was 14 then and till that time I had not won a big title. My father used to smoke a lot. So I told my father that if I won the title, he must stop smoking. I did win the title and the victory saw my father get rid of his smoking habit. After this win, I started making proper progress in my chess career by first of all winning the National 'B' title in Kolkata in 1997 and following it up with a good performance in the National 'A' Championship in Muzzafarpur the following year. My performance at Muzzafarpur helped me to qualify for the Olympiad in 1998 at Elista (Russia).

Could you tell readers about some of your other outstanding achievements in the sport?

In 2006, I was a member of the Indian team that won the Gold medal in the Asian Games at Doha. In January 2007, I became the second player from India to reach a FIDE rating of 2700. Earlier in 2001, I won the prestigious Hastings International Chess tournament and in 2003 the 4th Asia Individual Championship. I have so far participated in eight Olympiads since 1998.

Why is the standard of Chess in Tamil Nadu so high?

Chess is compulsory in all Tamil Nadu schools right from class I. In fact, it is a subject. There are plenty of tournaments too. Also, we must not forget that Tamil Nadu has produced one of the greatest chess players the world has seen –Vishwanathan Anand. So, youngsters in Tamil Nadu have a role model to look upto. Of course, West Bengal and Maharashtra produce quality chess players too. Tamil Nadu also has a number of good coaches in addition to organising numerous chess competitions for different age-levels.

What are the qualities required by a person to become a successful chess player?

According to me, the two main qualities required for a person to become a good chess player are first of all an interest in the sport and secondly the ability to work hard and intelligently. I personally believe that everything can be learned if one wishes to learn and improve.

Can one make a career by playing chess?

In India, top ranking players get secure and well-paid jobs. I am working with the ONGC. In Chess to make money professionally one has to have a FIDE rating of 2600. Then one gets opportunities to participate in big money tournaments.

Finally, could you tell readers why Russians in particular are so good at Chess?

Russia is very scientific about the game Chess. First of all, the game has a great tradition. There are plenty of top-level coaches. Chess academies of the highest quality are available for aspiring youngsters. The level of competition at every stage is very high so players who make it to the top are of the highest quality. Other European countries also nurture chess and have produced great players.

RAJ KUMAR SHARMA – COACH OF VIRAT KOHLI

ALIVE – AUGUST 2014

Today, the cricketing world talks about Virat Kohli, the batting star of India and the world, but only a few know about the man (Raj Kumar Sharma) who has been Virat's coach, mentor and guide since 1998 when Virat was hardly ten years of age. I met 49-year-old Raj Kumar Sharma recently and spoke to him about his playing career, coaching experiences and Virat Kohli - the man and the player. Coach Raj Kumar Sharma was mainly an off-spinner who also battled usefully.

Please tell readers about some of your main achievements as a cricket player.

At the college level, I have played in the All India Rohinton Baria Trophy tournament and the Vizzy trophy. I represented the Delhi Ranji Trophy side from 1986 to 1992. I even played against the Pakistan touring team in 1986.

When did you take to coaching?

I played professional cricket in Bangladesh from 1993 to 1995. While playing for Easkaton Sabuj Sangha Club in Bangladesh, I coached youngsters there.

What are your qualifications as a cricket coach?

I am a level B coach from the National Cricket Academy, Bengaluru.

What have been your earlier coaching stints?

I have been coach of the different Delhi sides – under-19, under-22 and Ranji Trophy. I have also coached North Zone sides. The Board also appointed me as coach of its Zonal Cricket

Academy for the North Zone in 2006 and 2007 and the West Zone in 2009.

What other cricketing duties have you performed?

I have been a selector, cricket manager of the Delhi Ranji Trophy side and also served as a Match Referee for the BCCI for various Ranji and Deodhar Trophy matches.

When did you take to serious full-time cricket coaching?

After returning from Bangladesh, I joined Playmakers Academy and coached alongwith many senior Test stars like Chetan Chauhan. In 1998, I decided to start my own cricket coaching centre – West Delhi Cricket Academy at Paschim Vihar.

How did you manage to establish your Academy?

Initially, it was very difficult but God has been kind. I started coaching initially at Xavier Convent, Paschim Vihar. On the first day itself 300 children came for admission. The final number I started with was 150, Virat Kohli, then a boy of nearly ten years of age, was one of them.

Today, due to God's grace, the academy has four centres–St Sophia's School, Paschim Vihar, DDA Sports Complex, Hari Nagar, DDA Sports Complex, Dwarka and S.D. Public School, Kirti Nagar. Each centre has a large number of students but we ensure and take care that every trainee gets full value for his money. We have in all 20 coaches with each centre getting a minimum of three days and a maximum of four days' coaching.

What are the timings and what aspects are stressed on?

The trainees are between the ages of 8 to 18. Trials are held for boys who are 13 plus. The timings are after school hours usually 3.30 p.m. – 7.00 p.m. The training consists of physical training, nets and fielding. Stress is laid on match situations. Regular matches are held and videos recordings are done alongwith video analysis. Thanks to Virat Kohli's help, the centres have the best of facilities and equipment. We have bowling machines, mechanized rollers, international standard turf wickets and the best and latest training equipment. We also have a club side called Professional Management Club which is affiliated to the DDCA. The team has been champions in the DDCA Super Elite Group.

Are there any differences between training methods in India and abroad?

In India, we have the National Cricket Academy in Bengaluru which is modelled on the Australian Cricket Academy. Our training and facilities are at par with those abroad. We also have the MRF Pace Foundation in Chennai to train pacemen. Dennis Lillee was the head before Glen McGrath took over.

How has cricket become such a passion among our youngsters?

The BCCI is very well structured and organized. Players and umpires are paid very well at all levels. Career options are there in cricket. Again, playing in IPL has provided players with a lot of money. Hence, cricket has become a passion with our youngsters.

When did Virat Kohli come to you?

Virat Kohli came to me on the first day of our academy in 1998. He was very different from other nine-year-olds. He was strongly built. He could hit the ball hard and throw the ball with speed and power. He was too good for the others in his age group and so within a short while I shifted him to the under-15 group. Here also he played well and with confidence.

What was special about Virat?

Virat liked to take responsibility. He enjoyed challenges and still enjoys them. He is focussed, dedicated and hungry for success. The only shortcoming he has is his over-confidence – the feeling that he can do anything with any bowler. I keep reminding him about it.

What would you say were the three most important moments in Virat's career?

The first incident was in his debut Ranji season in 2006. During the Super League Ranji Trophy match vs. Karnataka at Delhi,

Delhi were in danger of following on with Virat batting on 40. The next morning his father passed away. Virat rang me up in Australia (I was with my Academy team) and asked me for advice. It was a difficult situation but I told him that for his state and himself he needed to play. Virat went to the ground and batted. He scored a chanceless 90 being given out to what he felt was an incorrect decision. After his dismissal, Virat attended his father's cremation. I remember he rang me up late that evening and cried – believe it or not it was because he missed a hundred.

In 2008, Virat captained the Indian under-19 side which won the under-19 World Cup at Kuala Lumpur. I was there. Virat got a contract from RCB for the IPL. He totally lost balance and focus and went through a terrible period. I really had to be very strict with him to bring him back on track. I think he has turned the corner.

Again, in the 2011 tour of Australia, Virat started to lose self-belief after the first two Tests. I spoke to him regularly and for long durations. I was so worried that I even suggested to him that I was prepared to go to Australia and be with him. Virat said that that was not required and his composure would come back. He said that if the skipper played him in the third Test, he would prove himself. The rest is history. Dhoni played him and Virat had scores of 44 (top scorer) and 75 (top scorer) in the third Test at Perth and 116 (top scorer) and 22 run out in the fourth Test at Adelaide.

How would you sum up Virat?

Brilliant cricketer, mature guy with a wise head on his shoulders, not a proud person but supremely confident and finally has a heart of gold – the youngsters in the academy will tell you.

Any other stars in the making from your Academies?

Rajesh Sharma – a right-hand middle-order batsman, Pradeep Malik – an attacking opener and wicketkeeper and Pulkit Narang-probably the best off-spinner in Delhi are outstanding prospects who can go far.

Finally, what qualities must a player possess to make it to the top?

God – gifted talent, total focus and commitment and of course, be hard working.

P.R. MAN SINGH – MANAGER OF 1983 INDIAN CRICKET WORLD CUP WINNING TEAM

ALIVE – OCTOBER 2014

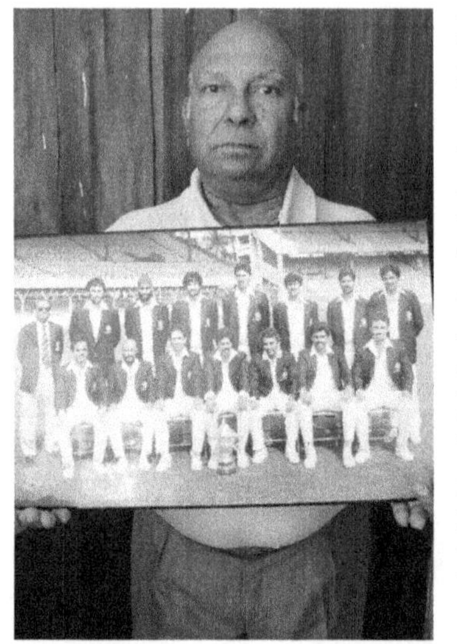

Every Indian cricket lover remembers India's great win in the 1983 World Cup defeating holders West Indies in the final at Lord's. But only a few remember 75-year-old PR Man Singh – the manager of the side and the only official with the side. I met Man Singh at his Hyderabad office and spoke to him about his career as a cricketer, administrator and of course as the manager of the successful 1983 Indian World Cup winning side.

You have a great reputation as a cricket administrator and one who has done a lot for the development of young cricketers. Till what level did you play the game?

I was good enough to represent Hyderabad in the Ranji Trophy during the years 1965 and 1966.

How did you enter cricket administration?

At that time I came in contact with a thorough gentleman in Ghulam Ahmed, a good off-spinner, who had represented and also captained the country's cricket team. Ghulam Ahmed spoke to me and convinced me that I could contribute more to cricket if I took up cricket administration. He felt that I possessed the necessary qualities to succeed. This meeting took place in 1967. Soon after, I started working with Ghulam Ahmed learning the nuances of cricket administration every day from him.

When did you take to serious cricket administration?

Working with Ghulam Ahmed was the best thing that happened to me. I learned so much from him that I became Secretary of the Hyderabad Cricket Association in 1976. I remained as Secretary till 1991. I am proud to say that during my tenure as Secretary there were many positive changes relating to the betterment of cricket in the state. Players started to play a greater role in the improvement of the game. We also had quite a few players from Hyderabad making it to the Indian side -Azharuddin to name one. Of course, Hyderabad has produced players of the calibre of Mansur Ali Khan Pataudi, M.L. Jaisimha, A.A. Baig and V.V.S. Laxman.

You were famous for the Hyderabad Blues tours you used to organize for promising youngsters from all over the country. Please throw light on those tours.

I got the idea of the Hyderabad Blues tours from two well-known journalists who also conducted similar tours. The two journalists were E.W. Swanton who organized 'The Arabs' and Ron Roberts who formed 'the Gay Cavaliers.' My idea was basically to give international exposure to young Indian players through the Hyderabad Blues tours. Till the end of the 1970s, almost every Indian Test cricketer had played for the Hyderabad Blues. The Moin-ud-dowla tournament which used to be conducted in Hyderabad was an important event in the Indian cricket calendar. All the leading Indian cricketers participated in it.

You were the manager of the Indian side that won the 1983 World Cup. How did the team manage to win without a coach or a physio?

The team was a very well balanced one. It had a number of all-rounders and could bat upto number eleven. There were a number of outstanding fielders and a very safe wicket keeper in the side too. The players were mature and committed being well aware of what was required of them to do well. You will be surprised to know that before the team left there was no conditioning camp, no media hype and even no farewell party. All this worked in our favour as it brought us closer to each other. We knew we had nothing to lose so everyone put in his best.

What was your role during the 1983 World Cup?

Being an officer of the Board of Control for Cricket in India, I made it very clear in the very first meeting that I was not a boss or an agent of the BCCI. I was like an elder brother to them. On the tour, I tried to ensure that the personal problems or inconveniences of the players were looked after so that they could give off their best in the matches. I was fortunate to have known nearly all the players at a personal level for quite a few years. The one- to - one relationship helped me to have an excellent rapport with all of them. This helped me to solve personality clashes which in turn helped maintain team unity. I also tried to ensure that the players had nothing to worry about off the field issues.

Could you tell readers about Kapil Dev's great innings of 175 not out vs Zimbabwe at Tunbridge Wells?

Kapil's innings of 175 not out was one of the greatest one-day innings played by an Indian batsman in a tight situation (India were 17 for 5). That day, Kapil simply blasted the Zimbabwe bowlers. His shots either scorched the turf to reach the boundary or went out of the ground. Kapil was well supported by Roger Binny, Madan Lal and Kirmani.

Finally, please tell us about that great final where India made history - probably your greatest day too.

To be honest, God was with us throughout the tournament, In the early part, we defeated the holders, West Indies, while Zimbabwe upset Australia. Things thus became easier for us. The selection of Kirti Azad in the first eleven turned out to be a masterstroke. In the tournament, the seniors in the side played a huge role on the field. The younger players also gave their best. In the final, Srikkanth played with courage and aggression to top score. MohinderAmarnath and the lower order batsmen also chipped in. When the West Indies batted, Greenidge was bowled by Sandhu without playing a shot, while Kapil Dev's catch of Richards was out of the world. The wicket of Richards turned the game India's way. Madan got the wicket because of his insistence in bowling and persistence in using the short ball. Dujon and

Marshall were putting on a stand when four of our seniors – Kapil, Sunil, Mohinder and Kirmani got together and decided that Mohinder should bowl. Mohinder struck crucial blows and put India on the road to victory. It was truly a memorable and most unforgettable day.

UNMUKT CHAND – CAPTAIN OF THE UNDER-19 CRICKET WORLD CUP CHAMPION TEAM

ALIVE – DECEMBER 2014

21-year-old Unmukt Chand is a quality right-hand opening batsman who has immense talent, a sharp cricketing mind and the big match temperament to be a huge success at the highest level the moment the break comes. I met Unmukt at his residence to talk to him on his cricketing experiences and the wonderful book he has written at so young an age.

Who are the people who motivated you to take to the game as early as you did?

My parents have sacrificed their all to ensure that I become a good cricketer. Special mention must also be made of my uncle Mr. Sundar Chand Thakur who has really helped and guided me not only in cricket but all aspects of life.

When did you start taking proper coaching and who have been your coaches?

I started playing cricket in my society when I was about six to seven years old. My father, Mr. Bharat Chand Thakur, presently a Vice Principal in a Government School, felt that I had the talent and keenness and so took me to the National Stadium at the age of eight to be coached by Mr. M.P. Singh. In 2008, I joined Lal Bahadur Shastri Club and was coached by Mr. Sanjay Bhardwaj. I am still with him. Both Mr. M.P. Singh and Mr. Bhardwaj have done a lot for me. My uncle also played a great role in my development.

Who else influenced you and your cricket in your early teens?

When I was 12, I was selected by the cricketing legend Bishan Singh Bedi Sir, to attend a month-long camp at Dharmashala.

It was the first time I travelled without my parents and family members. The camp helped me to develop both as a player and as a human being. Bedi Sir also took me to Sydney in Australia with his senior club team. I played a few matches and had my first taste of the bouncy wickets in Australia.

How useful were the under-16 camps which you attended at both the Zonal Cricket Academy and the National Cricket Academy?

I earned my place in the Zonal Cricket Academy (North Zone Camp) by scoring three consecutive half-centuries in the knock-out rounds for Delhi in the under-16 Vijay Merchant Trophy (2008-09). At the Zonal Camp, I learned a lot. Our basics were improved, we were made fitter and we also discussed the history of the game.

I was lucky, that very year, I represented North Zone in the All India Under-16 Hanumant Singh Trophy tournament. I scored 402 runs and was declared the Man of the tournament. I made it to the under-19 side and got to play at the National Cricket Academy for three consecutive years. Training at the NCA in Bengaluru has made me aware of myself and my batting. The best thing there is the video footage that is taken of players playing. The facilities at the NCA are really superb.

How did being captain of the victorious Indian team in the under-19 World Cup in Australia in 2012 help you to grow as a skipper and as a player?

As a captain, I learned how to manage a team. I also learned to take suggestions from others including teammates which benefitted the team. I also learned to say enough was enough when suggestions were unnecessary and uncalled for. I learned how to take decisions with thought and face the consequences. Finally, I was able to instill positivity in my team and develop a winning attitude.

As a player, I learned to unearth my potential and rise to the occasion. The responsibility in me came through in the final during my match-winning century vs. Australia.

Why do many players fade away even after doing well at the under-19 level?

The transition from the under-19 to the next level is not easy. It requires talent, character, family support, a lot of hard work and consistency. After the under-19 level, one enters the man's world and one is all by oneself. One has to have one's priorities right to succeed.

What has troubled you over the last season or two?

The last year or so has been a transitional phase for me. Initially, it was the pressure and over-keenness to do well. Again, I was confused about things in batting. Probably, I was also desperate to make it to the senior India side. Again, the pitch and conditions at Roshanara Club where Ranji games were played, were seam and swing bowlers over friendly. But now, I have just decided to keep on scoring and be at my fittest best so that when the call comes I do justice to my talents.

Please tell readers how the quality of education you have had has helped you grow as a cricketer and a person?

I am grateful to my parents to have provided me with a quality education. Till the eighth class. I studied at Delhi Public School. Noida and after that I joined Modern School, Barakhamba Road from where I passed my class 12. My stay at Modern School really helped me to grow both as a cricketer and as a person. The self-confidence and independent thinking which I have developed have been largely due to my schooling and college education at St. Stephen's where I am in the final year.

Finally, please tell readers about your autobiography 'The Sky is the Limit.'

I have been maintaining a diary for almost a decade-80% of the book was completed before the 2012 under-19 World Cup India won under my captaincy. The remaining portion was completed after our win. The book also gives a lot of insight on the people who have made me what I am today and also what I have learned from the greats of the game.

RANDHIR SINGH – A FINE SHOOTER AND SPORTS ADMINISTRATOR

ALIVE – MARCH 2015

For many years the Maharajas of Patiala and later, their descendants, have been encouraging, participating in and administering sports. The senior most member of the family at present,in sports, is 68 year old Randhir Singh who was in December 2014 named for the prestigious honorary membership of the IOC after having served as a full member of the world body from India for the period 2001 to 2014. Randhir is the second Indian to get this honour. The first was the great Ashwini Kumar. I met Randhir Singh at his residence and the visit was truly an enriching experience as Randhir had so much to share.

Please tell readers about the people in your family who have contributed greatly to sports, sportsmen and the Olympic movement in India.

The first person from my family I ought to mention is my great-grandfather Maharaja Rajindra Singh. He was the first person in our family to get involved in international sports.This was in the 1890s. He took great interest in the development of Cricket, Wrestling, Polo and Hockey. The great cricketer Ranjitsinhji came to Patiala then and spent some time there.

My grandfather Maharaja Bhupindra Singh was keen on all sports. His Polo and Cricket teams were among the best in India. He was a fine shooter too. Bhupindra Singh was the person who presented the Ranji Trophy. The Ranji cricket tournament was initiated in 1935.

Maharaja Bhupindra Singh's son Maharaja Yadavindra Singh – my uncle – was a very good cricketer in addition to being an excellent sports administrator. He played a Test for India against England at Chennai in 1933-34 and scored 24 and 60. He served as the President of the British Indian Olympic Committee from 1938 to 1947 and President of the Indian Olympic Committee from 1947 to 1960. He was instrumental in organising the first Asian Games in Delhi in 1951.

His brother Raja Bhalindra Singh – my father - was also a useful cricketer who did well in first-class cricket. My father served two terms as the President of the Indian Olympic Association – 1960 to 1975 and 1980 to 1984. He was instrumental in organising the 1982 Asiad in New Delhi.

Please tell readers about your achievements as a shooter.

After making my debut at the national level in 1964 at the age of 18, I soon made it to the international level. In my little over three decades as a shooter, I represented India in the Clay Pigeon trap event in five Olympics – 1968 Mexico, 1972 Munich, 1976 Montreal, 1980 Moscow and 1984 Los Angeles. In 1964 in Tokyo, I was a reserve. I also represented the country in four Asian Games- 1978 Bangkok, 1982 New Delhi, 1986 Seoul and 1994 Hiroshima. I wish to add here that at Hiroshima I was both a senior official (President and Secretary General of the Olympic Council of Asia) and a participant too. My outstanding performances in the Asian Games were first of all a gold medal in the 1978 Games and an individual bronze and a team silver in the 1982 New Delhi Games. I have also won a bronze badge in the 1978 Edmonton Commonwealth Games.

You have also had a great record as a sports administrator. Please mention your achievements.

I have been a member of the International Olympic Committee from 2001 till 2014. In December last year, I was made an honorary member for life. From 2012 to 2014 I was Vice-President of the Association of National Olympic Committee (ANOC). I was also the Vice-President of the Commonwealth Games Federation from 1998 till 2007. The posts of Secretary General of the Indian Olympic Association from 1987 till 2014 and the Olympic

Council of Asia from 1991 were also held by me. Finally, I was the founder Secretary General of the Afro-Asian Games Council in 1998 and was instrumental in the organisation of the only Afro-Asian Games in Hyderabad in the year 2003.

How have you been honoured for your contributions as a shooter and organiser?

As a shooter, I was conferred the Arjuna Award by the Government of India in 1979 while as a sports administrator, I have received the Merit Awards from the Olympic Council of Asia in 2005 and the Association of National Olympic Committee in 2006. Last year, I received the Olympic Order (Silver) from the International Olympic Committee.

I am very happy to add that my second daughter Sunaina and my nephew Raninder are already in sports administration while my youngest daughter Rajeshwari is a very promising shooter. I am confident that they will continue to do the family proud.

How and why are our shooters performing much better these days?

For the last fifteen years, or so after the achievements of Col. Rathore and Abhinav Bindra in the Olympics, other shooters in India have begun to feel that they can also do very well in the international stage. Top class foreign coaches have helped too. The Government ensures exposure for our shooters. Private sponsorship is available too. More youngsters are taking to the sport. For all these reasons our shooters are doing much better now. I wish to add here that in our time, shooters only went to participate while nowadays, they go to win medals.

Finally, how can we bring about a proper sports culture in our country?

All schools must have playgrounds with proper facilities and coaches who love sports and being with children. They must have a discerning eye to spot talent. There must also be a lot of state-run academies to train budding players. The government – state in particular - must ensure that this happens.

Parents and children have started taking sports more seriously as apart from making children more fit, sports also plays a big role in securing college admissions. The other attractions are jobs and becoming world famous. The state governments have started giving huge incentives to sportsmen and women who win medals at the national and international events. The Central Government has also started a pension scheme for medal winners in international events. Again, Arjuna Awardees get free first class railway passes for travel. Private sponsorship is increasing for really talented players. A sports culture will surely develop.

BISHAN SINGH BEDI –A GREAT LEFT ARM SPINNER

ALIVE – JULY 2015

The Kolkata Test between West Indies and India in 1966-67 started on 31 December 1966. It is remembered by all for the riot that took place resulting in a day's play being lost. But for the genuine lovers of the game the Test was significant as it marked the Test debut of the then 20-year Bishan Singh Bedi, the classical left-arm spin bowler, who was a relatively unknown player till two weeks before that Test. Bedi went on to play 67 Tests and in the process captured 266 wickets at 28.71 a piece. He also captained India in 22 Tests one of which was India's record fourth innings chase vs the West Indies in the third Test at Port of Spain, Trinidad. I met the great left-arm spinner and spoke to him about his coach, his Test debut, cricketers and cricket in general.

To start with who was your coach and what did he instill in you?

Gyan Prakash Sir, my coach ensured first of all that my cricket sense was of the highest level and secondly, he taught me how to keep cool under pressure and when the batsmen were plundering runs off me. To be merely a quality player is of not much use if one does not have cricketing sense, temperament and courage.

Your cricketing life turned from a nobody to somebody in the space of the last 15 days in December 1966. Tell us about it.

In the first half of December in 1966, I learned that I had been selected to play for the Prime Minister's XI vs the West Indies at Delhi. Believe me, I only believed in mastering the art of bowling by practising a lot. When I was 12 to 13 years of age. I heard in the radio commentary that two of our bowlers had taken nine wickets in Test innings – Subhas Gupte 9-102 vs. West Indies in 1958-59 at Kanpur and Jasu Patel 9-69 vs. Australia in 1959-60 also at Kanpur. These two performances inspired me. **I wish to mention here that the first Test I saw was the first Test I played in.** Then came the match at Delhi from 20-23 December 1966. In that game. I took 6 for 139 off 51 overs in the first innings including the wickets of Sobers and Clive Lloyd. In the second innings, my figures read 1 for 57 off 32 overs and after the game, I learned that I was to join the Test squad for the Kolkata Test. Just before the start of the Test I was told that I would play. In the Kolkata Test, the West Indies batted first on a slowish turner. I bowled 36 overs and took 2 for 92- eleven of my overs were maidens. I had the wickets of Basil Butcher and Clive Lloyd - a youngster then. India lost the game by an innings and 45 runs on a wicket made worse by the riot that took place. My bowling was impressive enough for me to play in the third Test at Chennai. In the Chennai Test I had 1 for 55 and 4 for 81 off 28 overs. The rest by God's grace is history.

Please compare the Indian side's performances on the three tours of England in 1967, 1971 and 1974.

In 1967, we were a side which was quite inexperienced in English conditions. Despite our playing well in patches early on and with consistency later we lost all Tests. We went in the first half of the English summer and it was quite wet.

In 1971 we went in the second half of the summer and we had a balanced side which was used to English conditions. We batted well, fielded brilliantly and Chandrasekhar bowled really well in the Oval Test.

In 1974 we were poorly prepared and casual too. We had no business to be bundled out for 42 at Lord's.

What about the Indian side's two visits to Australia in 1967-68 and 1977-78?

In 1967-68 some of our batsmen were unable to cope with the bounce but overall we played quite well with three of the four Tests fairly well fought. Chandu Borde in the first Test and Mansur Ali Khan Pataudi in the last three Tests guided us well.

In 1977-78, I led the side and we lost a closely-fought series to a weakened Australian side 2-3. Our players put up a good performance but to be honest, the umpiring was poor. For example at Melbourne, when Chandrasekhar bowled a batsman, he appealed to the umpire. The umpire said he is bowled but Chandrasekhar asked him, "Bowled he is but is he out?"

What about our first Test series win abroad in 1968?

Oh, yes, we beat New Zealand 3-1 in the four-Test series. We batted well, our spinners except at Christchurch were too good for the New Zealand batsmen and most important of all our close-in fielding was superb. Mansur Ali Khan Pataudi led us very well.

Tell us about India's great win over the West Indies in 1976 at Port of Spain (third Test).

We were set 403 for a win and full marks to Gavaskar, Mohinder Amarnath and Vishwanath for seeing us through. We won the Test scoring 406 for 4. It was only the second time in cricketing history after Don Bradman's team that a side scored over 400 in the fourth innings and won.

What about the 1978 tour of Pakistan?

I do not think it is proper to use the cricketers for so-called diplomacy. Relations between India and Pakistan have to genuinely improve before we play each other. In 1978, Pakistan was a good side but you cannot imagine how hostile the atmosphere was. It was very difficult to play normally.

What do you feel about the IPL?

It is a disaster for Indian cricket. Very soon we will not have a Test side. Every year something stupid keeps happening in this tournament.

What are the reasons for all the mess in the DDCA and the BCCI?

The problem is that most officials despite holding honorary posts do not wish to give them up. Only if the Maker calls them then they give up their posts. All the scams and corruption are caused by these people.

What are your views on DRS?

I have mixed feelings on DRS. If it is followed, it must be compulsory for all countries. All things required must be available on all grounds where Tests and ODIs are played. Personally, I would leave decisions to be taken by the on-field umpires.

Could you tell readers about the role of a Cricket Manager in the Indian side as you have been one yourself.

When it was introduced it was a new concept. The players were not ready for it then and honestly they are still not ready for it. The reason for this is we are not truly professional.

You have been one of the greatest left-arm spin bowlers the world has seen. Please tell readers what is needed to be a quality spin bowler.

To become a quality spin bowler one has to put in hours and hours of practice. Endurance and perseverance are a must. One has to keep on bowling. One cannot become a quality spin bowler by bowling 4 or 10 overs.

What are your opinions on Mansur Ali Khan Pataudi and Ajit Wadekar as captains?

Mansur Ali Khan Pataudi was by far the best captain. He was the first captain who made us feel that we are first Indians. That is why, under him, we played as a team. Wadekar was a bit too defensive and honestly he reaped the fruits of the work done by Mansur Ali Khan Pataudi.

What about Tendulkar?

Tendulkar is a very special cricketer. Tendulkar and cricket are one. He is totally dedicated to the game. The commitment is amazing. No wonder he reached such great heights.

What are your opinions about Gavaskar, Vishwanath, Vengsarkar and Mohinder Amarnath as batsmen?

Gavaskar is the greatest opener the game has produced.

Vishwanath is a master batsman for whom batting was an art. If there is any batsman I will pay to watch, it is him.

Vengsarkar was a gutsy player of the highest calibre. He played pace and spin equally well.

Mohinder Amarnath was a technically sound player who was fearless against the fastest of bowlers.

Please tell us about the other three spinners who bowled with you.

Prasanna was a genius who was probably one of the best off-spinners the world has seen.

Chandrasekhar was a real match-winner. On his day he could demolish any opposition.

Venkataraghavan was a quality off-spin bowler who was very competitive.

How was E.D. Solkar as a close-in fielder?

Solkar was an extraordinary close-in fielder – the greatest ever. He was the one who made the four of us spinners so great. Venkat, Abid Ali, Wadekar, Gavaskar and Vishwanath were also very good close-in fielders.

Finally, Bishan who was the best batsman you have bowled to?

Without doubt Sir Garfield Sobers of the West Indies. There will never be another all-round cricketer like him – a genius of a batsman, a fine left-arm paceman, a more than capable left-arm spinner and an outstanding fielder especially close to the wicket.

SUDHA CHAUDHRY – FORMER INDIAN WOMEN'S HOCKEY OLYMPIAN

WOMAN'S ERA – OCTOBER (FIRST) 2015

The first Indian women's hockey team to participate in the Olympics was the 1980 Moscow Olympic side. Most of that Indian side went on to win the gold medal in the 1982 Asian Games at New Delhi. 54-year-old Sudha Chaudhry was the centre-half of the Indian team in both those tournaments. Sudha is considered the best centre-half Indian women's hockey has ever produced. I met Sudha, who works for the Northern Railway, at her Delhi residence and spoke to her about her hockey career and women's hockey in India today including the women's hockey team which has qualified for the 2016 Rio Olympics.

Please tell readers how you took to hockey.

My early life was spent in Meerut. I come from a Jat family and in those days the idea of Jat girls going out to play games in public was not taken too kindly. In 1975, when I was about 14 years of age, I went off to play a hockey match at the Meerut stadium after only telling my mother. I had picked up hockey watching and reading about Indian stars. My family members came to the stadium and found that not only was the atmosphere good there but my game had impressed the people who mattered.

How did your hockey career begin?

In 1976, women's hockey became a serious sport in U.P. when former Indian men's hockey captain K.D. Singh selected 15 girls to be trained and form a team in Lucknow. My name had been recommended for the camp and so I did not have to undergo any trial. The training was of the highest quality and taken very seriously. K.D. Singh was assisted by another Olympian Jaman Lal

Sharma. Both the Olympians taught me the basics of dribbling, passing and the art of anticipation. I also picked up the art of converting penalty corners from Jaman Lal Sharma in particular. These great players were both inspiring and encouraging. The training sessions were in the morning and the evening. In the day we studied. I graduated from Lucknow University.

When did U.P. form a good women's hockey side and what were the state's performances at the national level when you played for it?

By 1978, U.P. had a women's hockey side that could match the top teams. In 1978, we lost to Punjab in the final of the National Championship in Kolkata while in 1979 we won the title in Jaipur defeating Maharashtra in the final. From 1981 to 1985 I represented Railways in the National Championship.

When did you first play for India in a major tournament?

After attending the national camps in 1977 and 1978, I was selected to represent the Indian team in the World Championship at Vancouver, Canada in 1979. We performed quite well without much success. The period from 1980 to 1982 was great for Indian women's hockey in that we participated in the Olympics, won the first Asian Championship in Kyoto, Japan in 1981 and the gold medal in the 1982 Asian Games in New Delhi. In 1983, we participated in the fifth World Cup in Kuala Lumpur but did not do too well despite having a good side.

What were the main reasons for the Indian team doing quite well during the period 1979 to 1983?

There were two main reasons for our good performances during this period. The first one was that our team which was young and lacking in experience in 1979 became more skillful and united as the years went by. The understanding between the players was good. The next big reason for our performances was the presence of our coach Balkrishan Singh. The former Indian Olympian had a very positive influence on me in particular and the team in general. Balkrishan Singh was a great judge of talent. He would improve the basics and motivate the players. He gave me a lot of individual attention. Even in matters of strategy or systems, he would not hesitate to experiment. He would get the best from each and every player. In the 1980 Moscow Olympics, he coached the men's team that won the gold. He was unfortunately not with us as coach.

Please tell readers about the Indian women's hockey side at the 1980 Moscow Olympics.

In those days, as was the case in the very early part of this century, it was not easy to qualify for the Olympics. Only the six top sides in the world then qualified for the Olympics. In 1980, a number of countries withdrew due to political reasons and so the Indian women's team participated. We tried our best at Moscow. Unfortunately, we failed to win a medal. Here I wish to mention that we knew about our participation very late. Again, Balkrishan Singh was not with us as coach. We also arrived in Moscow a couple of days before the tournament which did not give us time to get used to the conditions and the artificial turf. Finally, most of our players found it difficult to adjust to playing on artificial turf. We should have prepared better. Despite everything, we drew 1-1 with Zimbabwe, the final winners, in the league stage. The Olympics is a very special event and unless one is at one's best all the time it is difficult to be successful.

During this successful period of Indian women's hockey, in which tournament were you at your best?

I feel it was in the 1983 World Cup in Kuala Lumpur. Personally, I felt I was at my best as a centre-half. In fact, people who mattered in hockey, present there were of the opinion that I was the best centre-half in the tournament.

What would you suggest to the present Indian women's team which has qualified for the 2016 Rio Olympics?

My congratulations and best wishes to the players. The team has some outstanding players in vice-captain Deepika Thakur, Rani Rampal and skipper Ritu Rani in particular. Our players must not allow balls to bounce off their sticks when stopping or trapping because they provide top players an opportunity to score. I feel they should play freely without inhibition. The team has nothing really to lose so if it plays freely giving everything it has who knows what can happen. I wish to add here that qualifying for the Olympics is much easier now. I feel that our 1982 Asian Games gold medal-winning side should have made it to the 1984 Los Angeles Games and the 2002 Indian women's side which won the Commonwealth Games at Manchester was also good enough to make it to the Olympics.

You have been an outstanding centre-half. What qualities must a player possess to be an excellent centre-half?

A centre-half must be good at all aspects of the game – be it attack, defence, distribution and coverage of the ground. He or she must have a proper reach and possess perfect anticipation. An ideal centre-half must be confident and very fit too.

Have you been involved in coaching the Indian women's hockey team?

Yes, from 2002 till 2005. In 2005, I was coach-cum-manager of the Indian women's side which was successful in an international tournament in Singapore. I have also been coaching the Northern Railway team for whom I played till 1995.

SUSHIL KUMAR- INDIA'S FIRST INDIVIDUAL OLYMPIC DOUBLE MEDAL WINNER

ALIVE – NOVEMBER 2015

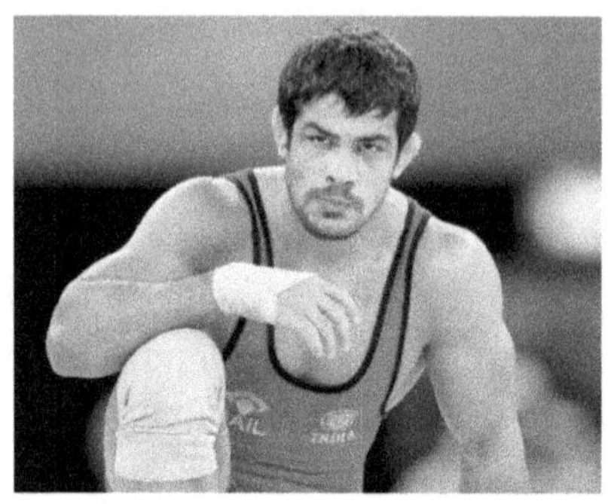

In the 2012 London Olympics, wrestler Sushil Kumar won the silver medal in the 66 Kg Freestyle event. **In the process, Sushil became the first Indian sportsman to win individual medals in two successive Olympics. In the 2008 Beijing Olympics, Sushil had won the bronze medal in the same event and category.** The Government of India conferred on Sushil the Arjuna Award in 2005, the Rajiv Gandhi Khel Ratna Award in 2009 and the Padma Shri in 2011. I met Sushil, who is presently Special Officer on Duty (Sports) with the Government of Delhi, at his office. To his credit, despite his very busy schedule, Sushil gave proper time and spoke about his early life, the people who helped him grow in the sport and how he has been able to do well.

Sushil, please tell readers about your early life and how you took to wrestling.

I hail from a middle-class family. I was inspired to take up wrestling by my father Mr. Diwan Singh and cousin Sandeep. Sandeep later stopped competing as the family could only afford to support one wrestler. This was how I took to wrestling.

Where did you first train to become a wrestler and who were your coaches?

I started training at the Chatrasal Stadium's *akhada* in Delhi at the age of 14. I was trained at the *akhada* by coaches Yashvirji and Ramphalji and later by Satpalji.

Is wrestling a violent sport?

Wrestling has very clearly defined rules. Sometimes, in the spirit of competition, people get hurt. But, it is not a violent sport.

What lessons did you learn after training in the *akhada*?

Apart from learning the art of wrestling, we learned discipline, respect for elders and loyalty. We were made to realise that to do well one had to be keen and determined to succeed. Hard work, perseverance and belief in oneself were a must if one wished to reach the top. To become a top-class wrestler one has to have all these traits.

What is your training schedule like?

We train in two sessions- morning and evening for three hours each. Wrestling requires a significant amount of cardiovascular endurance. Our work-out programme includes different exercises and rope climbing too to build strength and endurance. For developing stamina, we play other games too like Basketball, Volleyball, Badminton and Football. We also have to ensure that we have the right diet and take sufficient rest.

What role has your family played in your achievements as a wrestler?

Right from the time I started taking wrestling seriously, my family has done everything possible to ensure that I succeed as a wrestler. My cousin Sandeep gave up wrestling so that I could take to the sport. My parents would ensure even till the 2008 Olympics that I would have the necessary dietary supplements by sending me the best milk, ghee and vegetables. I am a strict vegetarian. Their sacrifices and blessings have helped me a lot in my progress. One of my coaches Satpalji, a fine wrestler himself, not only coached me but also served as a friend, philosopher and guide. I am fortunate he is my father-in-law. So I have the support of all my family members.

What were your main successes at the junior level in international wrestling?

My first success came at the 1998 World Cadet Games in Moscow when I won the gold medal in my weight category. Honestly, it gave me the feeling that I could win medals- even golds- at the international stage. This was followed by another gold medal in the 2000 Asian Junior Wrestling Championship in New Delhi. This win convinced me that I could do India proud at the international level- juniors and seniors.

At the senior level what were your medal-winning performances before the bronze you won at the Beijing Olympics in 2008?

In 2003, I won the bronze medal at the Asian Wrestling Championship in New Delhi. The same year, I won the gold at the Commonwealth Wrestling Championship in London. I again won gold medals in the Commonwealth Wrestling Championships in 2005 at Cape Town and in 2007 at London.

Tell us about your feelings when you went to the 2008 Beijing Olympics.

My first Olympics was in 2004 in Athens. I was a youngster then and participating in the Olympics that year overawed me. I was placed 14th in the 60 Kg weight class. I learned a lot at Athens and prepared myself well for the 2008 Olympics. The international competitive exposure before the 2008 Olympics helped me a lot. In the 2008 Olympics, I took part in the 66 Kg weight category event. I got the bronze medal defeating Leonid Spiridonov of Kazakhstan in the bronze medal deciding tie. It was a great moment for me and millions of Indian fans as it was only India's second Olympic medal in wrestling after K.D. Jadhav's bronze in the 1952 Helsinki Games.

Please tell readers about the silver medal you won in the 2012 London Olympics to become the first Indian to win two individual Olympic medals in successive Olympics.

The 66 Kg weight category was ideal for me. Before the London Olympics, I had two big wins. In the 2010 World Wrestling Championship in Moscow, I won the gold and became the first Indian to win a world title in wrestling. The same year, I won the gold medal in the 2010 Commonwealth Games in New Delhi. The competitions and the training camps we attended in the U.S.A. and Belarus helped me to win the silver in the London Olympics.

The final was held inside three hours after my semi-final win over Kazakhstan's Tanatarov. After the semi-final, I was vomiting and was suffering from dehydration. I had also picked up a neck injury. In the final, I fought as hard as I could but the Japanese Yonemitsu was better on the day. True, I lost the gold medal but at least I became India's first Olympic silver medalist in wrestling. After the London Olympics, I won the gold in the 2014 Commonwealth Games in Glasgow. In the 74 Kg final I defeated Qamar Abbas of Pakistan.

You had broken your collar bone and injured your right shoulder and have not been taking part in big competitions for quite some time. How is your collar bone and shoulder and what are your preparations like for the Rio Olympics?

My injury is improving and my practice schedule is becoming normal. I skipped the World Championships in Las Vegas this year as I was not fully fit. There are six more qualification tournaments for the Rio Olympics starting from March 2016. I will take part in them. Once I make it to the Rio Olympics, I will try to do India proud again.

Finally, what must India do to become a force in world sports?

The Government and corporates must invest in sports. The people running sports in our country must identify, train and support talented and mentally strong sportsmen and sportswomen from a very early age providing them with the best equipment, facilities, training and competitive exposure. It must be ensured that these sportsmen have the right education and most important of all become financially self-dependent.

RANI RAMPAL –STAR STRIKER OF INDIAN WOMEN'S HOCKEY

WOMAN'S ERA – NOVEMBER (SECOND) 2015

Rani Rampal, the star striker of Indian women's hockey, is a complete product of the hockey academy in the government school at Shahabad Markanda (Kurukshetra District) which was made internationally famous by Baldev Singh the Dronacharya award-winning hockey coach. Rani Rampal, who comes from an economically weak family has risen to great heights because of her talent, determination to do well and also the desire to ensure that her family leads a better life. Her parents have also totally supported her. I met Rani Rampal during the training camp that was held in Delhi recently and spoke to her about her early struggles, her successes and Indian and international hockey.

Rani, please tell readers about how you got into the hockey academy at Shahabad Markanda.

I hail from a very poor family. Somehow, when I was about six years old I showed a keenness to learn hockey. My father and mother felt that I should take up the game and so supported me. My father took me to Baldev Singhji, the coach and requested him to see if I could be trained. Baldev Sir initially refused to take me and told us to go. The next day my father again took me to the coach. On the second day after watching my movements and running, the coach agreed to train me. He told my father that he had initially refused to take me as he felt that I was from a very poor family wondering whether I could afford the time to play the game seriously and also the fact I was below 8 – the age at which he first trained the children. So my father's determination and my interest helped me join the famous academy two years earlier than others.

Please tell readers about your coach and the training you received at the academy.

What I am as a hockey player is because of Baldev Sir. I owe almost everything to him. Seeing that I was very poor he gave me a hockey stick and kit so that I could play and learn in the academy. He was very strict as a coach and there was no room for complacency in the academy under him.

What was the training schedule like in the academy?

The years I spent at the academy were the most difficult (physically) yet most beneficial (I became the player I am) periods of my life. In the academy, the coach followed the same schedule throughout the year. Irrespective of where we lived, the trainees had to report at the academy by 4.45 a.m. as practice would start at 5.00 a.m. and go on till 7.00 a.m. There were trainees of different age-groups so the type of training would differ. The emphasis in the morning was on the basics and fitness. I used to go to attend the training by cycle early in the morning. My mother would pack food for me – both snacks and some lunch. After practice, we would attend classes in school till 2.00 p.m. From 2.45 p.m. till 6 to 6.30 p.m. we would have match practice. A slight variation in timings was there depending on the season. There was no question of skipping school under the pretext of being tired. At the end of the evening practice we would return home. Believe it or not our coach was always the first to arrive.

How did your coach help you to become a quality player?

Apart from teaching me the basic skills of ball control, trapping, dribbling, passing and tackling, Baldevji instilled in us virtues such as punctuality, discipline and hard work. He developed in us the desire to play attacking hockey.

Before I come to your career to date, please tell readers about your contribution towards India qualifying for the 2016 Rio Olympics.

The match that decided whether India would clinch the crucial fifth place in the World Hockey League semi-final at Antwerp, Belgium and book a berth for the Olympics was against Japan. By God's grace, I scored the winning goal in the must-win game against Japan to help India win a place in the 2016 Rio Olympics. Though I scored, it was the team as a whole which put up a really spirited performance that day. We all realised that our hopes of playing in the Olympics rested on that match and so we gave it everything.

Rani, you have been a star and captain of India's junior women's hockey side. Please tell readers about Indian women's hockey's best performance to date at the junior level.

Without a doubt, our junior team's best performance during the time I have been associated with it was during the junior World Cup in August 2013. I was the vice-captain of the team which won the first-ever World Cup bronze medal in Monchengladbach, Germany. I was adjudged the 'Player of the Tournament'. In the final vs. England, I scored the only goal in regulation time and again twice in the penalty shoot-out. India won 3-2 via the penalty shoot-out after the regulation time of 70 minutes ended 1-1.

Apart from your outstanding performance against Japan at Antwerp which helped India qualify for the Rio Olympics, what has been your most outstanding performance or performances at the senior level?

I have had a number of fine performances in leading senior-level competitions but the one where I first hit the headlines was in the final of the Champion's Challenge II tournament held in Kazan, Russia in June 2009. In the final vs. Belgium, I scored four goals helping India win. I was adjudged the 'Best Young Player of the Tournament' and was also the top goal scorer. I wish to mention that I was 14 years and 6 months old when I made my debut for India in this tournament. The other memorable performance of mine was in the 2010 women's World Cup in Rosario, Argentina where I scored seven goals. I was conferred the award for the 'Best Young Player of the Tournament'.

What other distinctions have you earned as a player?

In 2010, I was included in the FIH women's All-Star team of the year. The same year, I was included in the Asian All-Star team based on my performances in the Asian Games. These are some of my other main awards. But more than awards, I wish to see India as a medalist in the Olympics during my playing days.

RITU RANI – INDIAN WOMEN'S HOCKEY CAPTAIN

WOMAN'S ERA – DECEMBER (FIRST) 2015

Ritu Rani, the talented Indian women's hockey mid-fielder, who is capable of scoring goals when required, is the present captain of the Indian women's hockey team. Ritu Rani made her debut for the Indian senior team before she was 15 years old in 2006. Since 2006, her consistently good performances and her mature approach have seen her being made the captain of the side in 2012. She has remained captain since then,and the team under her leadership recently qualified for the 2016 Rio Olympics. I spoke to Ritu Rani during the training the team was undergoing in New Delhi recently about her hockey career and her experiences,particularly at the International level.

When and how did you take to hockey?

I was in class six when I was taken to Mr. Baldev Singh, the Dronacharya award-winning hockey coach, who used to run a hockey academy in my hometown Shahabad Markanda. Baldev Sir felt I had the aptitude and talent and so agreed to coach me. He was the one who taught me discipline, punctuality, the basics of the game and what one needs to do to become a top- level player.

Tell readers about girls hockey in Shahabad Markanda (Kurukshetra District).

Baldev Singhji's untiring efforts have been responsible for the success of girls hockey in this place. His dedication, discipline, punctuality and the desire to impart sound skills to youngsters had to be seen to be believed. Once stars were produced, the craze among the girls in the area to take to the game increased. The government school where he also coached has a hockey academy which boasts of an artificial turf. Indian women's hockey captains and players have come from Shahabad Markanda and so more and more youngsters are taking to the game in this area.

Have you had other coaches?

Yes. I have had quite a few coaches at different levels. The two others I remember a lot are M.K. Kaushik and G.S. Bhangu.

What have the foreign coaches been able to instill in you and your team-mates?

Foreign coaches have also played their part in our development. Apart from the basics, their stress is on total hockey, structural formations and team-work.

When did you first make it to the senior India side?

The first time I was selected to represent India at the senior level was in 2006 at the World Cup in Madrid. At the age of 14 years nine months I played for India in the Doha Asian Games that year.

Which other major competitions did you represent India before being made captain of the Indian team?

In 2009, I was a member of the Indian side which won the Women's Hockey Champion's Challenge II in Kazan, Russia. In 2010 I also represented India in the Commonwealth Games, Asian Games and the World Cup.

What successes have the Indian women's team achieved after you took over as captain in 2012?

In 2013, India won a silver medal in the Asian hockey Champion's trophy and a bronze medal in the Asia Cup at Kuala Lumpur that year. Last year, our team won bronze in the Incheon Asian Games. This year, our team finished fifth in the World League semi-final at Antwerp, Belgium. This fifth position helped us to qualify for the 2016 Rio Olympics – the first time the Indian women's hockey team has achieved this distinction. In the 1980 Olympics, the Indian women's side participated as a number of teams had withdrawn.

How do you compare our team with the top Asian countries?

Skill-wise I feel we are as good as them, though their basics are very sound and they are less prone to making simple errors. Where they are better than us is in terms of speed-whether it is getting to a free ball or in recovery. This speed does unsettle us. However, we are improving all the time.

Why are the European sides much better than us?

The biggest advantage which European countries have is that their coaching is uniform and continues until they reach the highest level. The emphasis is in producing multi-role players from a very early age. Tactics and strategy are introduced quite early and this continues to the highest level. The basics are perfected early. Some of those countries have had the greatest penalty corner specialists or drag-flickers and so youngsters wish to emulate or even better them. The players get to play on artificial turf very early in their careers. Finally, they are given tough competitive exposure at every level in their careers. That is why European sides are much better than us.

How can Indian women's hockey reach the top bracket in World hockey?

First of all, hockey must be encouraged at the school level. Artificial turfs must be sufficiently available for interested youngsters to practise on them. Committed coaches with an eye for talent must be available where youngsters train. The national coach must meet coaches all over the country as often as possible so that techniques, rule changes and other inputs can be shared with the coaches so that the trainees benefit. Competitions must be regularly arranged so that the players get to play in tight situations and under match pressure from an early age. Top quality players must be specially taken care of.

What are the things that will basically attract young girls to the game?

The game and its players must be given proper publicity. Again, incentives in the form of jobs and attractive prize money are a must if young girls are to take to the game. Many of the players come from the lower middle class or poor families. Therefore job security is a must. The job too must be respectable- appropriate to the level the player has reached. In this context, I wish to mention that the Railways and the Police are providing jobs. However, it would ideal if Banks and other PSUs also helped in this regard.

Please tell readers how the Indian women's hockey players have tackled the problem of change in coaches at the national level.

Most of us, despite being young, are experienced players. We absorb the best things from all coaches who have been associated with us but follow the present coach wholeheartedly as we need to be united to do well. Most important of all we are representing India.

DEEPALI DESHPANDE – INDIA'S JUNIOR AND YOUTH SHOOTING COACH

WOMAN'S ERA – DECEMBER (SECOND) 2015

The Indian youth and junior shooters performed well in the Asian Air Gun championships which were held in the last week of September in New Delhi. One of the main people responsible for this success was former Olympic shooter Deepali Deshpande who is a Sports Authority of India coach and has been Chief Coach for youth and junior shooters since November 2012. I met Deepali Deshpande during the championship and spoke to her about her playing and coaching career.

When did you take to competitive shooting seriously?

In 1993, I completed my degree in Architecture from the L.S. Raheja School of Architecture. From 1994, I have been participating in shooting competitions till 2007 though I did participate in the women's rifle prone event during the national selection trials held in Pune in September 2012.

What were your main achievements at the international level?

I have won medals including gold in international events but the achievements that stand out are first of all winning a silver medal in the 10 m Air Rifle team event in the 2002 Busan Asian Games along with my teammates Anjali Bhagwat and Suma Shirur. Again, early in 2004, I won an individual silver in the Asian Shooting Championship in Kuala Lumpur which enabled me to win a quota for the 2004 Athens Olympics. Finally, I consider my participation in the 2004 Olympics quite an achievement.

Who have been the people who have made all this possible for you?

Everyone in my family, my husband – an architect, my in-laws and even my daughter have all co-operated with me. My coaches have helped me in different ways. But the person I wish to make special mention of is Mr. B.P. Bam, a retired I.G. of Police and a sports psychologist. He helped me in a number of ways by giving me total support and encouragement.

You mentioned that some coaches played an important role in your success. Who were they and how did they help you?

My first coach was Mr. Sanjay Chakravarthy. He developed in me an interest in the sport and taught me the basics. The first foreign coach who was associated with Indian shooting in the early nineties was a Hungarian Tibor Gonczol basically a pistol coach. He contributed a lot to Indian shooting and also greatly helped the leading Indian shooters then. It was Gonczol who established a proper system so that Indian shooting could grow. He standardized areas like selection trials, coaching and accountability. He ensured total transparency. He was bold and believed in getting things done. He even gave valuable inputs to players like me.

In 1999, another Hungarian coach Lazio Szucak initially came for a year and then returned to stay from 2005 till 2008. Szucak changed our outlook to shooting. When he first came, we had little or no international exposure to Shooting. He made us realise the importance of good equipment and quite honestly introduced all of us to the World of Shooting.

From 2009, Indian shooters including myself benefitted from Stanislav Lapidus- a coach from Kazakhistan. Technically he was very good. All the advanced skills and technical know – how we have, is due to him.

You have been the chief shooting coach for the youth level and junior shooters since November 2012. How do you go about your assignment?

I get great satisfaction in giving to youngsters what we never got when we were at that age. Basically, I deal with shooters under the age of 21. It is not difficult to teach youngsters the right technique from scratch. What is difficult to do is to remove the incorrect techniques which trainees have picked up and then teach them the correct techniques again. We try to develop in the trainees the correct mind-set. I do get about 70 trainees every year but since some of them have been with me for a couple of years I put players of a level in a group and I deal with different such groups. We have 15- day camps twice or thrice in a year in New Delhi. The top three from the junior and youth levels are given more extensive training. Those who become good enough to participate in international tournaments are given more training and practice before the competitions. This system has helped in making our shooters at the youth and junior level better and they should do well at the senior level later.

What do our women shooters need to do to win Olympic medals?

First of all our women shooters in particular must improve their physical fitness. Honestly, health consciousness among our youngsters is lacking though efforts are being made to improve the situation. Again, we need to be stronger and tougher. However, with the youth and junior programmes we are having and the competitive exposure our seniors and juniors are getting the day is not far when our women shooters too will win medals in the Olympics.

Why are women shooters of the countries who are top in shooting much better than our shooters?

Shooting is primarily an equipment game. European countries are very fortunate that the shooting equipment is manufactured there. So their players (including those of Russia) have easy access to the best equipment. Again, shooting as a sport has been going on at a high level for ages in those countries. Top class infrastructure is easily available for people living there. The systems of training, selection and competitive exposure are well laid-down. There are plenty of top-class coaches also available. Then, physically they are much stronger and fitter than us because they have an established sports culture. In many of those countries serving in the army for a certain period is a must and so they get shooting exposure there. For all these reasons their shooters do much better than ours.

What qualities does one need to possess to become a top-class shooter?

There are certain important qualities one must possess to become a top-class shooter. A person must possess both a good IQ vis-a-vis the sport and a high-level EQ too. Keeping cool in tight situations is a must. A top-class shooter only concentrates on the moment even if he or she has been doing well. For example, a top-class shooter when doing well will never think of big future things like the gold medal, and the honour he or she may get if he or she wins while playing. He or she will only continue to play well till the end of the match or matches. He or she must be very observant and a quick learner too.

How does Shooting help a youngster?

Shooting helps a youngster in many ways. First of all, it ensures that the person maintains proper fitness. The sport is one where one has to compete with no one but oneself. The better one becomes the better one performs. The sport thus brings about self-improvement in a shooter. It helps youngsters to be focussed and to think logically and rationally. Overall, it helps in personality improvement.

Finally Deepali, how have you been honoured for your services to the sport?

The Government of India conferred on me the Arjuna Award in 2004. This award was for my prowess as a shooter. I hope I can bring a lot of honour to the country by my coaching.

PARIMARJAN NEGI – A FINE CHESS PLAYER

ALIVE – FEBRUARY 2016

23-year-old Parimarjan Negi who has been one of India's best chess players decided to take a break from the game in 2014 wishing to seriously continue with his academic pursuits. Parimarjan is studying in the United States of America. He had come down to Delhi for the vacation. I met Parimarjan at his residence and spoke to him about Chess and his experiences in the game.

Why did you take this break from Chess at your age and when you were successful?

I was keen to study and become academically qualified. I felt that it was the right time to take a break from Chess and devote time to my studies. I am confident that I can get back to full-time Chess once I finish with my academics.

Please tell readers when and how you first took to Chess.

From a very early age, I started liking the game. I started learning it even before I was five years old. I was fortunate to study in Amity International School, Saket, New Delhi. The school encouraged me all through to maintain my education and also aspire for an ambitious future in Chess.

What were your big achievements at the junior or youth level?

My notable achievements include a gold medal in the 2002 Asian Youth Chess Championship at Tehran and the 2003 Commonwealth Youth Chess Championship at Mumbai both in the under-10 category. I also won titles at the national level.

Apart from having won the senior national title in 2010, please mention some of your big achievements as a chess player at the senior level.

On 1 July 2006, at the age of 13 years four months and 20 days, I became the second youngest GM ever, second only to Sergey Karjakin, the Ukranian-born Russian when I earned my third and final GM norm at the Chelyabinsk Region Super Final Championship at Satka in Russia. I also became India's youngest GM in that competition. In 2010, I was conferred the Arjuna Award by the Government of India. I won the 11th Asian Continental Chess Championship held in Ho Chi Minh City, Vietnamin May 2012. Finally, in 2014 I was part of the Indian men's side that won the bronze medal in the Chess Olympics held in Tromso, Norway.

Which year saw you become a 'man' in the Indian and possibly the World Chess scene?

The end of 2005 till the middle of 2006 suddenly saw me, a lad of 13, become a top player. I became a GM at that time.

You just mentioned the term 'GM,' i.e., Grand Master. Please explain how these levels are attained.

Ratings of chess players are based on the points they reach. These points ratings keep rising. However, generally if one attains 2400 points, he or she is an International Master. 2500 points mean a Grand Master while above 2750 points means the player is in the top-tier.

What would you say is the ideal age to take to Chess?

The best age to take to this game is between the years of five and eight. At that age children observe things sharply and also pick up things very quickly.

How does Chess help a young person to develop?

Chess is a mental game but to be successful in it one needs to be fit, disciplined and mentally strong. If one attains a high standard in the game, not only does one develop the qualities mentioned, he or she also becomes analytical which in turn helps a person in decision – making.

What is so special about Viswanathan Anand?

The greatness of Viswanathan Anand is that despite becoming older, he has been able to maintain his fitness, energy levels and the desire to do really well. You must remember it is difficult to play and defeat younger players who are top class. As a player, Anand was very good at every aspect of the game. He also helps and encourages youngsters from all sports who perform well.

How are we Indians at the world level?

In the men's category, we have Anand in the top-tier as he is invited for all the major competitions. Harikrishna is also in the top-tier but unfortunately, he does not get too many invitations. This will hopefully improve.

In the women's category, we are better off with Humpy and Harika very high in the world rankings.

Is Chess a worthwhile profession in our country?

Yes, for the top players it is. They are pretty well-off. Nearly all the leading players get respectable jobs due to their prowess in the game. The prize money too is improving. But, one has to be a player in the top drawer to be really successful money-wise.

Finally, what is the organisation of Chess like in the top chess-playing countries?

The top chess-playing countries like Russia have a great tradition in Chess. They have had a number of world champions. These world champions have served as role models in their country. There are also numerous quality chess academies which have top-level coaches. In the academies, the trainees get used to high-level competition. The best players also get the opportunity of participating in tough competitions at home and abroad from a very early age and so gain the experience of playing well in pressure situations from that age itself. Since most of the top chess players of the world are in that part of the world and Europe, their top players get far more exposure at the highest level competitions than our players.

In India, we have a number of good players in the second tier – the one below the top one where we have only Anand in the men's category at present.

SHANTHA RANGASWAMY: TORCH - BEARER OF WOMEN'S CRICKET IN INDIA

WOMAN'S ERA – MARCH (FIRST) - 2016

62-year-old Shantha Rangaswamy is one of the pioneers of women's cricket in India. She was a fearless batter, a useful bowler and a bold leader who never bothered about reputations. Of the 16 Tests she played for India, Shantha captained the country in 12 Tests. She also captained the Indian ODI side in 16 of the 19 matches she played. In 16 Tests Shantha scored 750 runs at an average of 32.60 and took 21 wickets. In the ODIs she was more successful with the ball taking 12 wickets. Shantha was the first Indian woman cricketer to be bestowed the Arjuna Award in 1976.This is what Shantha said to me about her career and women's cricket in India.

How did you take to playing cricket?

I grew up in a joint family where there were around 20 cousins. We had a big compound and the friends of my cousins would also come home to play cricket during the weekends. That is how I was initiated into the game of cricket right from my childhood. Seeing my interest in the game, my father presented me with a cricket bat when I was eight years of age. Unfortunately, I lost my father when I was twelve. I should mention here that my father was a state basketball player while his brother had been captain of the Indian basketball team.

Who was the person who ensured that you and your six sisters grew up well to be successes in life?

Without a doubt it was my mother. It was my mother who brought us all up ensuring that we pursued our varied interests without neglecting our studies. She realised the passion I had for sports and accordingly helped me. If I am a graduate who became a

General Manager in a bank with no promotions under the sports quota; later on, it was because of her. In a family of seven sisters, four became engineers, one a doctorate, one a double graduate and the least qualified was me.

Initially, when there was no platform for cricket which sports did you play?

During this period I represented the Karnataka State Ball Badminton side for two years. The Karnataka side dominated the game at the national level for decades. I also led the Karnataka Softball side being its first captain. Of course, I kept on practising cricket and bettering my skills all the time.

Who are the people who coached you in cricket?

I learnt the game on my own but it was refined by Saluz Nazareth (Bengaluru), P.S. Vishwanath (Bengaluru) and Arjun Naidu (NIS, Patiala). But the major role in my development as a cricketer was played by Pradyut Kumar Mitra of Bengal who taught me a lot about the finer points of the game.

When did you first represent Karnataka in the National Women's Cricket Championship?

It was in the second National Championship held in Varanasi in November 1973. I captained the Karnataka side. In its maiden appearance, Karnataka made it to the final where it lost to a vastly superior Bengal side. I was adjudged the best all-rounder of the tournament. I represented Karnataka for 21 years and we made it to the final ten times. My only regret is that we never won the national title even once in those ten occasions. The only consolation for me was that I led the South Zone side to victory on three occasions in the inter-zonal championships played for the Rani Jhansi Trophy.

What role did the pioneering women cricketers like you, play in ensuring that women's cricket in India has progressed to the extent it has today?

In 1975, Australia toured India while in 1976, New Zealand and West Indies toured India. According to me, perhaps the biggest contribution by all of us who represented India in the formative years was that as Founding Fathers (Mothers) we played well which was a major contributory factor for ensuring the longevity of the game in our country. Had we lost badly, perhaps it could have accounted for the early demise of the game like some women's games that started with cricket but perished early. I am proud of the fact that I was also one of India's early women cricketers. I wish to add here that the responsibility on the pioneers to do well helped those players to develop a steel-like resolve and also enjoy responsibility. This experience certainly made me a stronger person in life.

How did the entry of the Board of Control for Cricket in India in Women's Cricket help it?

To start with, the pension scheme was introduced for players who have represented India in a certain number of Tests. The present players are placed in central contracts getting a fixed sum for a year depending on their performances. They are also paid a good amount for every series they play. Again the facilities for playing and the grounds have greatly improved.

What is the best memory you have of your international career?

I have had the honour of being India's first official cricket captain. I also have the distinction of being the first Indian woman cricketer to get a Test century. However, the best memory I have is the 1976-77 Indian tour of New Zealand where under my captaincy our side did not lose a single game despite playing against a team whose country had had women's cricket for five decades. At that stage, women's cricket in India in comparison to New Zealand were two-year-old babes.

Finally, how are you still pursuing your passion for cricket?

I am currently the Chairman, Indian Women's Selection Committee under the aegis of the Board of Control for Cricket in India. I also write and broadcast on cricket.

Note:- In 2017, Shantha became the first Indian woman cricketer to be awarded the BCCI's C.K. Nayudu Lifetime Achievement Award for services to the game.

JITU RAI – PISTOL KING OF INDIA

ALIVE – APRIL 2016

One of the best pistol shooters in the world is 27-year old Jitu Rai. Jitu, who is modesty personified, is known as India's 'Pistol King.' In early March this year, Jitu, who has returned from a break due to abdominal surgery, beat a strong field which included former Olympic champion Pang Wei of China, to win the gold in the men's 50 m pistol event at the ISSF World Cup in Bangkok. Jitu has won five World Cup medals to date in the air pistol event. I met Jitu, an Arjuna Award winner, at the Dr. Karni Singh shooting range in New Delhi and spoke to him about his life and achievements in shooting.

How did you take to shooting?

I am basically from a middle-class family in Nepal. My village is in the middle of a forest. I was born and brought up in that forest. My father used to farm before he joined the army. My father died in 2006 and then I shifted to India from Nepal. In 2007, I joined the 11 Gorkha Regiment as a sepoy. I was not interested in shooting in the beginning. The army coach G.R. Garbaraj Rai forced me into it. Today, I am really grateful to him.

Why did you take up pistol shooting?

My coach said that my hands and other physical attributes were best suited for pistol shooting and so following his advice I took to it.

Please tell readers about your main achievements over the last few years.

Although I qualified for the finals of two World Cups in Munich, Germany and Changwon, Korea in 2013, my big successes began in 2014. In 2014, at the ISSF World Cup in Munich, I won a silver medal in the 10 m air pistol event. Soon after, in Maribor, Slovenia, I won two medals-silver in the 50 m pistol event and gold in the 10 m air pistol event. In the process, I won three medals in the World Cup in the space of nine days. I also became the first person to win two medals for India in a single World Cup.

At the 2014 Commonwealth Games in Glasgow, I won the gold medal in the 50 m free pistol event with a Games record in both the qualification and the final. At the 2014 World Shooting Championship in Granada, Spain, I won India's first quota place for the Rio Olympics by winning a silver medal in the 50 m free pistol event. My last big success in 2014 was the gold medal I won in the 50 m free pistol event at the 2014 Asian Games in Incheon by upstaging the world champion Jin Jong-oh of South Korea. I also won a team bronze in the 10 m air pistol event.

In 2015, I won medals in the World Cup and Asian Shooting Championship while in 2016 I won the gold medal in the men's 50m pistol event in the ISSF World Cup in Bangkok. After this success, I feel I am on the right track to do really well at the Rio Olympics.

You have achieved so much in so short a time. Who are the people who have helped you to achieve all this?

The first person I wish to thank is my first coach when I joined the army – G R Garbaraj Rai who not only forced me into pistol shooting but also taught me the basics. The Indian Army has had a major role in my development and improvement as a shooter. They have helped me in every possible way – be it job security, time to concentrate on my sport, equipment, training facilities, the best foreign coaches and a lot of motivation. Vijay Kumar, the London Olympic shooting silver medallist, has also guided me at every stage. Others have also helped. I, too, have not only worked hard but have also been fortunate to have had the blessings of my mother.

Which win of yours would you rate your best to date?

Without a doubt it will be the gold medal I won in the 50m free pistol event in the 2014 Asian Games in Incheon. The competition in Shooting in the Asian Games is really tough. I upstaged the world champion Jin Jong-oh to win India's first gold in the Games.

What is it that you are most proud of as a pistol shooter?

I am proud of the fact that I am the first Indian pistol shooter to be regarded as one of the best in the world. I am praying to God that I do achieve something big in the Rio Olympics.

What do you feel you would need to do to win a medal in the Rio Olympics?

I will have to work on a much higher level- participate in tough high-level competitions. God's grace and the good wishes of the nation are a must. Most important of all, on that day I must be perfect in execution and totally relaxed. Then I reckon a medal will be a reality – hopefully Gold.

ANIRBAN LAHIRI – A TOP CLASS INDIAN GOLFER

ALIVE – MAY 2016

The Rio Olympics will be held in August this year. After the 1904 St. Louis Olympics in the USA, Golf is staging a comeback as an Olympic sport and will be one of the medal events at Rio. Anirban Lahiri is almost certain to make it to Rio.

Anirban Lahiri, India's No. 1 golfer, strikes one as a thoughtful professional but a polite person who values his time. 2016 is a big year for Anirban, as it is the first time he has a full card for the PGA Tour. I met Anirban at the Delhi Golf Club during the Hero Indian Open and spoke to him about his early days, his career and making it to the top level in the game.

How did you get initiated to Golf?

I learned how to play golf from my father Dr. Tushar Lahiri, a doctor in the Armed Forces, and a recreational golfer too. We would chip and putt together and that is how it all started.

Who coached you early on and gave you the correct basics?

I was fortunate to have a good professional teacher in Mr. Vijay Divecha. I was also lucky to have easy access to equipment and of course practice facilities.

When did you join the Asian Tour and what were your major wins?

I joined the Asian Tour in 2008. I picked up my first victory in 2011 at the Panasonic Open. I also won the 2012 and 2013 SAIL-SBI Open.

When did you break into the top 100 in the Official World Rankings?

I broke into the top 100 in the Official World Golf Rankings for the first time in March 2014 following a consistent season which included two wins on the Asian Tour — the CMIB Niaga Indonesian Masters and the Venetian Macau Open.

How did you make it into the top 50 of the Official World Golf Rankings and qualify for the 2015 Masters Tournament?

Two big wins on the European Tour in early 2015 enabled me to make it to the top 50 of the Official World Rankings and qualify for the 2015 Masters Tournament. The first one was in February 2015 when I won my first European Tour title at the Maybank Malaysian Open and a few weeks later, I won the Hero Indian Open.

How was the year 2015 really outstanding for you?

After qualifying for the Masters, the year 2015 went really well for me. First of all, on 10 August, I won a competition for the longest drive achieving 327 yards in an event before the Major. On 16 August, I finished joint fifth in the 97th PGA Championship in Wisconsin — the best ever by an Indian in a Major. In that month too, I became the first Indian to shoot sub-par scores in all four rounds of a Major in the PGA Championships at Whistling Straits. In September, I became the first Indian to qualify for the prestigious biennial Presidents Cup between the International team and the USA.

Looking back,what did you do to reach the top level?

Lots of people play the game with different goals in mind. However, for me, I have played it with the intention of seeing how better I can be and what is the best I can be. In my golf career, I started with the PGTI and then moved up — the Asian Tour, the European Tour, the Masters and finally to the PGA. There is no shortcut. One just has to keep pushing oneself if one wishes to reach the top. One has to push the barriers and not get intimidated at any stage.

How would you assess your game over the last three to four years?

My game has evolved over the last three to four years. I have had good rounds but I have not been consistent. But I am learning. I am adapting to conditions better and feeling more comfortable playing across Asia, Europe and the USA.

What are your plans for this season?

The target will be to win on the PGA Tour, be in contention for the Majors and the World Golf Championship (WGC). I also feel that I can be a contender at the Rio Olympic Games and hopefully get a medal for India.

Finally, what does India need to do to have half a dozen Anirban Lahiris?

This is possible but it will take time and needs a lot of planning. First of all, the Government must ensure that people with the talent and skills for the game, whether they have the money or not, are given all the facilities and encouragement to take to this game. It must be made clear to the youth that there is money in the game and so it can be a career. There must be as many public courses as possible in all towns and cities. Practice and coaching facilities and equipment must be available at moderate costs. Regular age-group competitions should be held so that the best talent can be picked up and groomed. Once the numbers increase, the talent will also come to light. Everything needs to be planned from the grass-root stage and in a few years given the right training and competitive exposure India will surely have even more than half a dozen Anirbans. Of course, all this has to be properly monitored so that deserving players get a proper deal.

SSP CHAWRASIA –GOLFER WHO OVERCAME DIFFICULTIES TO REACH THE TOP

ALIVE – MAY 2016

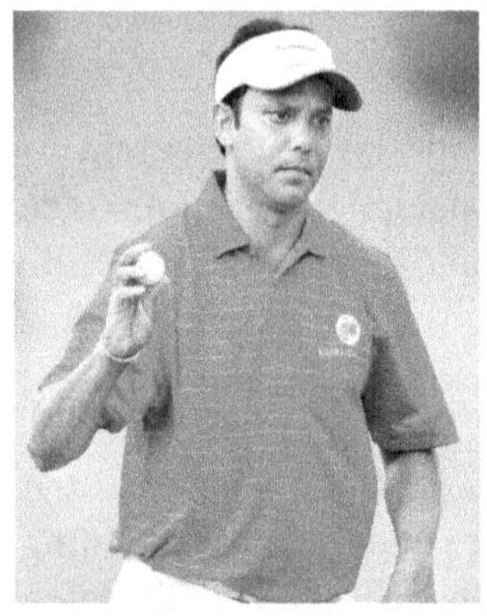

Shiv Shankar Prasad Chawrasia is an extremely level-headed, modest person who despite his huge achievements has not forgotten his roots. This has been one of the main reasons why this 38-year-old golfer has been a huge success despite his humble and difficult early life. I met Chawrasia at the Delhi Golf Club after he had won the 2016 Hero India Open defeating the previous year's winner and much higher ranked Anirban Lahiri in the process and spoke to him about his early years which were difficult and his subsequent rise as a golfer.

Tell us about your early life.

My father worked as the greenskeeper at the Royal Calcutta Golf Club. So I virtually grew up on the golf course so to say.

What difficulties did you face while establishing yourself as a top professional at least in India?

It was very very difficult in the beginning. One could only watch and dream. There was no equipment and no opportunities. Then one day a member of the club was kind enough to help me. He was Mr. Neil Law. He helped me with equipment. The learning part I used to do through observation and practice whenever it was possible. I worked a few years as a caddie before turning a professional in 1997 at the age of 19.

When did you first hit the head-lines?

It was in the 1999 Indian Open in Calcutta when I finished runners-up to Arjun Atwal in the final.

Please tell readers about your great win in the 2008 Indian Masters.

The 2008 Indian Masters had golfers such as Ernie Els, Thomas Bjorn, Maarten Lafeber and Ross McGowan along with Indian golfers Arjun Atwal, Gaurav Ghei and Digvijay Singh vying for the title. The event, which I won with a score of nine under par, earned me not only my first European title but also a purse of $ 2,39,705. I was the only player in the tournament to achieve sub-par rounds on all four days.

When did you make it to the Asian Tour?

I joined the Asian Tour in 2006 after winning eight Indian Tour titles. That year in the Hero Honda India Open, I narrowly missed out on winning the title. The title, which was won by Jyoti Randhawa, was decided by a play-off.

How about your second European Tour title in 2011?

In February 2011, I outclassed England's Robert Coles to win the $ 1.8 million Avantha Masters title at the DLF Golf and Country Club and collected $ 300,000 as well as a diamond – studded trophy.

Your win in the 2016 Hero Indian Open must have done you a world of good. What were your feelings?

For me, winning the 2016 Hero India Open was a dream come true particularly because I have been runners-up four times before including 2015. The win was very important for me as this is the year of the Rio Olympics and the points would help me qualify. I wish to add here that in 2015, I was a member of the Asian team that played Europe.

Why have you been given the name 'Chip-putt-sia'?

Because of my short game which is mainly based on chipping and putting.

How did you work on your game to go up the ladder?

I have been coached in my earlier days by Pritam Saikia and Sandeep Verma but honestly I feel my success so far has been due to honesty of effort, hard work, keen observation and correct application of whatever I have learned. My wife has also been a source of great encouragement.

How has Golf helped you improve your life?

Whatever I am today is because of Golf. It has helped me to grow as a person, earn a lot of money and see the world.

How can Golf be made a sport which all Indians from all classes can take to easily?

The Government must go all out to help this sport to grow in the country. There is a lot of money in the game so it can be a source of livelihood for many. The government must set up public courses — at least three or four in all towns and cities. Equipment must be made available at moderate rates. Even coaching and playing facilities must be available at moderate rates. All these must be strictly supervised so that the facilities are put to proper use.

What are your future ambitions?

My immediate wish is to make it to the PGA tour. Again, on a long-term basis, I wish to set up a foundation that will help needy, keen children with a talent for Golf, with equipment. I am ready to share my technical know-how with those youngsters.

KAPIL DEV – A CRICKETER WHO CHANGED INDIA'S FORTUNES IN THE GAME

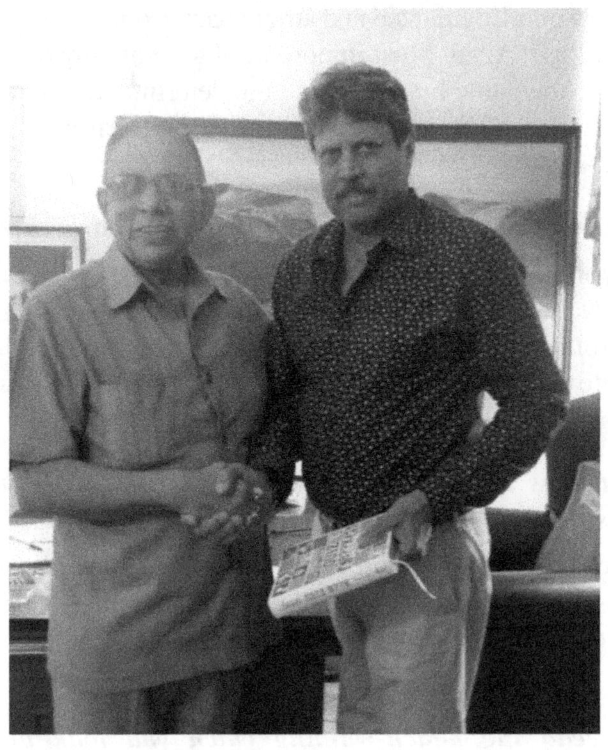

Kapil Dev is one of the greatest sportsmen India has ever produced. He was the one who made it possible for India to become world champions in limited overs cricket- leading India to a win in the 1983 World Cup final defeating the reigning champions West Indies at Lord's. No one can ever forget Kapil's great 175 not out vs. Zimbabwe at Tunridge Wells - a knock that helped India reach 266 for 8 in 50 overs after at one stage being 17 for 5.Again, who can forget his out of the world catch of the great Vivian Richards when the master batsman seemed unstoppable in the 1983 World Cup final. **I, Vijayan Bala, met the great Kapil Dev at his office in Delhi on 16 June 2016 to present him a copy of my sports quiz book 'The Complete Indian Sports Quiz Book.' Before**

the presentation of the book, Kapil and I had a conversation on Kapil's approach to life and cricket and also certain memorable instances in cricket and well-known cricketers.

How did you make it to the Indian side at such a young age?

I had a very good, dedicated and strict coach from an early age. He was Desh Prem Azad. Most important of all, not only did I have a passion for the game but I also had the determination to succeed. Therefore, I worked very hard and tried to learn as quickly as possible.

How does one keep one's balance after tasting early success?

It is very important to be born in a family where the elders instill the right values. Outside, it is essential to have the right type of people around you. It helps a lot if one has one good friend. Again, we need to be focussed on what we wish to accomplish and keep away from distractions.

Briefly tell us about that memorable 175 not out which you scored vs Zimbabwe at Tunridge Wells in the 1983 World Cup.

That knock of mine did turn the match in India's favour after we were in a bad position. However, I must make it clear that it was my day and I believe that if a day is yours, you can achieve anything that day.

Please recall the match-winning catch you took of Vivian Richards in the final of the 1983 World Cup.

Such catches can be taken by experienced fielders with safe pairs of hands.It was a good, crucial and match-turning catch but certainly not the best catch a fielder can take.

What do youngsters need to keep in mind to be successful in life?

First of all, youngsters must be happy to go to school. School must be fun for them. Teachers or elders must be able to identify their strengths early. Then the youngsters must focus on their strengths and work hard with passion and single-minded devotion to achieve their goals.

Your views on Sachin Tendulkar.

Sachin was an extremely gifted player. He worked very hard to ensure that his God-given gift produced the maximum possible results. He is probably the most focussed cricketer India has produced. However, I still maintain that he could have achieved much more than he did.

Among the fast bowlers, you played against which three will you rate the best?

Wasim Akram, Malcolm Marshall and Sir Richard Hadlee. Not only, did these three great pacemen have genuine pace but they could also play around with the ball much to the discomfort of the batsmen.

SAKSHI MALIK – INDIA'S FIRST MEDAL WINNER IN RIO OLYMPICS

WOMAN'S ERA – SEPTEMBER (SECOND) 2016

Days were passing by with India not having won a medal in the Rio Olympics. It was then that the 23-year-old Sakshi Malik who was representing India in the 58 kg. category women's freestyle wrestling event picked up a bronze medal – India's first at Rio - by her sheer courage, determination and fighting spirit. Sakshi also became the first Indian woman wrestler to win a medal in the Olympics. She is the fourth Indian lady to win a medal in the Olympics with badminton star P.V. Sindhu winning silver soon after Sakshi's bronze. I met Sakshi, also a holder of a Master's Degree in Physical Education, at her residence at Rohtak soon after her return from Rio.

Who inspired you to take to wrestling?

I was inspired by my paternal grandfather Chaudhary Badlu Ram who was a wrestler himself.

How did your parents support you in your desire to become a top-class wrestler?

Girls were not thought well of if they took to wrestling as it was generally regarded as a male sport. In fact, only in 2002, we girls were allowed into the sport in Haryana. Society objected to my participating in the sport but not only was I determined, my parents too, totally backed me. I never gave up the sport despite my mother fearing that my face would spoil and some of my relatives taunting me.

When did you take to wrestling in a proper manner?

When I was twelve years old. I joined the akhara in Chotu Ram Stadium, Rohtak, where Ishwar Singh Dahiya– a twelve-time

Bharat Kesari used to coach aspiring wrestlers. After a few months of training my coach made me practise and fight with the boys because I seemed too strong for the other girls. Fortunately, I was able to make the boys struggle too. Ishwar sir taught me a lot and was my coach till 2009,i.e., for five to six years. Mandeep then became my coach and he still helps me.

What is your normal training schedule like?

We train for about six hours in a day– both morning and evening. The training includes both physical training and practice bouts. We have to do about 500 sit-ups every day. Since our schedule is so rigorous, it has to be backed by a diet that will keep us physically strong, energetic and mentally alert.

What is your training like when the Olympics are about a year or so away?

For instance, about one and a half years before the Rio Olympics, our training and practice schedules became very rigorous. Apart from training and practising in India, we were given international exposure too. We had roughly two months training and bouts in Madrid (Spain) and Sophia (Bulgaria). We were also made to understand the tactical aspects of the game especially what should be done against which opponent.

Please tell readers about how you qualified for the Rio Olympics.

You will be surprised to know that I was not even the original choice to represent India in the Rio Olympics in the newly introduced 58 kg. freestyle wrestling category. Geeta Phogat was the first choice. However, during the first Olympic qualification tournament in Ulan Bator (Mongolia) in April 2016. Geeta, slated to fight in the repechage event pulled out at the last minute citing injury. The Wrestling Federation of India was not pleased. In December 2015, I had upset Geeta in a Pro-Wrestling bout. So for the second and final Olympic Games qualification at Istanbul, Turkey in May 2016, I participated. By God's grace, I secured the quota for the Rio Olympics by winning the silver medal. In the semi-final, I defeated China's Lan Zhang.

What have been your major achievements at the international level before the Rio Olympics?

In 2010, I won a bronze medal in the Junior World Championships. In 2013, I won a bronze medal in the 63kg. category in the Commonwealth Championships in Johannesburg. 2014 saw me win a silver medal in the Commonwealth Games at Glasgow in the 58kg. category. I also won a bronze medal in the 60kg. category in the 2015 Asian Championships in Doha. Finally, I qualified for the Rio Olympics by winning a silver medal in Istanbul, Turkey in May 2016.

You won India's first medal in the Rio Olympics. Describe for the benefit of readers how you won the medal.

I was defeated by Russian Valeria Koblova who made it to the final. This meant that everyone whom the Russian had beaten along the way made it to the repechage. I was determined not to let this chance of winning a medal go. I outclassed my first opponent Orkhon Purevdorj of Mongolia 12-3. An hour later I faced my next opponent Aisuluu Tynybekova of Kyrgyzstan. Initially, I was a little tense and nervous and with barely a minute and a half to go, I was trailing 0-5. My coach, Kuldeep Malik sir, then yelled out to me to get free from my opponent's grip and topple her. Following my coach's advice, I broke free and forced my rival on the mat (2-5), then once again (4-5) and again to take a 7-5 lead. The opponent's protest at that stage was overruled and I was declared winner 8-5. I had earned India a bronze – my country's first medal at the Rio Olympics after a twelve-day wait.

What was your immediate reaction after winning the medal?

I was so thrilled and excited that I leapt into the arms of my coach. He lifted me on his shoulders and did a victory lap with myself draped in the Indian tri-colour.

What do you feel you need to do to win a better medal in the 2020 Tokyo Olympics?

I am more experienced and confident now having participated and done reasonably well in the Rio Olympics. I will be rectifying the errors I made at Rio and will be definitely more aggressive in future.

What qualities does one need to possess to become a top-level wrestler?

Apart from strength which has to combine with tactical intelligence, a wrestler in order to become top class needs to be dedicated and have a proper diet and take sufficient rest.

What must India do to produce a lot of top-class wrestlers?

Wrestling must be encouraged at the grass-root level. There must be residential academies where the trainees are carefully selected and looked after properly. Dedicated coaches are a must so that proper care is taken regarding the stay, training, diet and mental health of the trainees.

Finally, what is your message for the girls in our country?

The country must realise that we girls are no less than the boys in any field. We girls can achieve anything if we get the opportunities and encouragement. I hope the girls get inspired and reach greater heights in the future.

DEEPA MALIK – INDIA'S FIRST WOMAN MEDALIST IN PARALYMPICS

WOMAN'S ERA – OCTOBER (SECOND) 2016

Deepa Malik, the 46-year-old sportsman, coach and motivational speaker achieved the distinction ofbecoming the first Indian lady to win a medal in the Paralympics. Deepa achieved this feat when she won a silver medal in the F-53 shot put event during the 2016 Rio Paralympics on 12 September. I met Deepa, a 2012 Arjuna Awardee, at her Gurgaon residence and spoke to her about her life, sporting career and how she achieved the unique distinction in the Paralympics. Speaking to Deepa and listening to her was a truly wonderful experience.

What were the sports you enjoyed playing till 1999?

I enjoyed playing all the games. However, I did reasonably well in Basketball and Cricket making the state side. Biking was also a sport I really liked and it was through this sport I found my husband.

You were not born with a disability. Please tell readers what exactly happened.

My physical problems were first noticed in 1975 when I was five years of age. I felt a weakness in my lower limbs, So in 1976, my father took a special posting to Pune so that I could be seen by the best doctors in the Armed Forces Medical Hospital there. The healing process and treatment lasted for about seven months then. In December 1977, I was operated on for a tumor in the upper spinal column. The cyst was removed and the whole process lasted eight to nine months. After the rehabilitation process, I started to walk again. In fact, I became an active and normal person. However, in the first half of 1999, complications arose and the doctors felt the tumor was bad and a cyst had become too big. So I was operated on. This was on 3 June 1999. Things did not improve and so I was finally operated on a week later. Since then I am in the wheelchair.

What has been your approach to life after you realised you have to spend the rest of your life in a wheelchair?

I have never taken my handicap as an excuse. In fact, it has become my strength. Disability has given my life focus and sports a direction. This whole journey of ability out of disability has made me evolve as a better person- more inspired and more worthwhile.

While reading about sports events related to disabled people, one comes across terms like F and T followed by numbers. Briefly explain what these denote.

F stands for field events like high jump and throws while T denotes track events like athletics for example. The number mentioned denotes the category or level of disability.

What are the special requirements for the disabled participants?

For disabled participants, special arrangements have to be made. First of all the place must be totally barrier-free. Special throw frames with platforms are required. Team escorts are a must to help out. The gymnasiums must also provide wheelchairs in a barrier-free environment. Toilets must be suited to the needs of the disabled participants.

You have made it four times to the Limca Book of Records. What were the achievements that led to it?

The first occasion was in 2008 when I swam against the current one km. in the Yamuna River. I took to swimming as part of my recovery process. The following year I became the first Indian woman to ride a bike – a special one. The third occasion was in 2011 when I drove across nine high altitude passes in nine days (Leh–Ladakh)– the highest motorable road. I was the first woman in the world to attempt it. Incidentally, I am the first person ever to receive a license for an invalid (modified) rally vehicle. Finally, in 2013, I drove 3278 km from Chennai to Delhi – the longest distance driven by a paraplegic woman. For these achievements, my name was included in the Limca Book of Records.

Before you participated in the 2016 Rio Paralympics what were your major successes?

I had participated successfully in two Asian Games – 2010 and 2014. In the 2010 Asian Games in Guangzhou, I won a bronze medal in the Javelin throw event and became the first Indian woman to win a medal in the Asian Para Games. In the 2014 Asian Games, I won a silver medal in the Javelin throw event. I wish to add here that in the shot put event I had thrown far enough (A Level) to qualify for the 2016 Rio Paralympics. Before the Rio Paralympics, I won two medals in the Oceania Asian Championship in Dubai. The medals I won were gold in the Javelin throw event and silver in the shot put event.

How did you prepare for the 2016 Rio Paralympics and win the silver medal?

After the 2014 Asian Para Games, I learnt that I had qualified in the shot put event for the 2016 Rio Paralympics. So I gave up the Javelin throw event and started working on shot put. I appointed a new coach soon after the Incheon Games in 2014. This coach remained with me till the 2015 World Championship in Doha. At Doha, I found to my utter dismay that I had shown no improvement at all as compared to what I had achieved in Incheon. I realized that I was back to square one. An analysis showed me that due to muscular problems my performance was being affected. So we appointed a bio-mechanic specialist in Mr. Vaibhav Sirohi. He started working on the physical aspect, i.e. strengthening of the muscles and ensuring maximum effectiveness. Vaibhav felt the need of a nutritional expert so that the diet could be taken proper care of. As a result Mr. Chirag Sethi, a nutritional expert, was hired. While the physical and dietary aspects were being looked after, I felt that the skill training aspect was being neglected. At that stage my husband Col (retd.) Bikram Singh Malik – a sportsman himself– gave up his job so that he could help me and monitor my skill and overall training. The skill training would take place in the evening. In the day time he would drive me wherever required so that I did not feel tense or over-exhausted. He read up all possible material and studied videos so that he could help me in the skill part which I felt I had neglected. So I had a 24x7 skill coach. Our society was also kind enough to provide me space for my practice. My elder daughter Devika, who is a qualified psychologist, along with Dr. Priti Agarwal – a professional psychologist ensured that I was emotionally fine and totally relaxed. Because of Priti and Devika, I was able to prepare in a cool, confident manner for the 2016 Rio Paralympics. My younger daughter Ambika also helped a lot. Another person who I wish to make mention of is Taj Mohammed – a domestic help. Taj helped and motivated me as if he was going to win a medal. Apart from helping me on the field of play and at home, he always prayed for my success in his Friday prayers. Mr. Rao Inderjit Singh M.P., the Sports Authority of India, the Haryana Government, the Target Olympic Scheme, friends and my own open attitude also contributed to the Rio achievement. So this is how I achieved what I did in Rio.

Any regret after the 2016 Rio Paralympics?

I do feel that had I started training for the 2016 Rio Paralympics following my and my team's methods immediately after the 2014 Incheon Asian Para Games, I probably would have won the gold at Rio. This is probably the only regret.

How long do you wish to continue participating in international competitions?

My wish is to continue to represent India in and till the 2020 Paralympics and of course all the competitions in between. My immediate focus is on the two World Championships next year – the IPC World Championship in July in London and the IWCA World Championship. In 2018, we have the Asian Games and Commonwealth Games too. I hope I can continue to bring glory for India in all these competitions.

What message would you like to give disabled people in particular and women in general?

For disabled people especially women I wish to say that we should have faith and self-belief. It is not our fault that we are or have become disabled. We just need to discover our potential in our respective fields for which we were born, work hard and simply go ahead positively.

For women, in general, I wish to say a truly liberated lady is one who has time for her job– the work she does, her family and most important of all time for herself too in which she regenerates herself by pursuing her interests so that she stays happy and motivated.

RISHABH PANT: A STAR KEEPER – BATSMAN IN THE MAKING

ALIVE – DECEMBER 2016

Coach Tarak Sinha has produced many Indian players over the years. The latest youngster under his care who seems likely to make it to the top soon is the 19-year-old Delhi wicket-keeper-batsman Rishabh Pant. I met Rishabh recently during the short break for the Delhi Ranji Trophy team in mid-November and spoke to him on his experiences and how he has been able to make it to the national and international (Jr. level) limelight so soon.

You are basically from Meerut. What made you come to Delhi?

Right from the time I was very young my father was very keen that I play cricket seriously. In 2009-10 Sonnet Club which is coached by the well-known coach Mr. Tarak Sinha advertised for cricket trials in order to get fresh young talent. I went for the trials and was selected. I played under-14 and under-16 for Rajasthan but was constantly in touch with Tarak Sinha Sir. After the under-16 level, I have been with my coach.

How has Mr. Tarak Sinha helped you to develop as a cricketer?

Sir has ensured that I become better and better both as a cricketer and as a person. He taught me the basics of the game bringing out the best in me as a player. He taught me how to survive in Delhi cricket. He taught me the value of qualities such as patience and perseverance. Finally, I have also learnt from him what I need to do to be a successful cricketer in this professional and competitive world.

You were vice-captain of the Indian under-19 side that played in the 2016 under-19 World Cup at Dhaka. Please tell readers about how it felt like representing India.

It is a very special feeling when one wears the blue Indian jersey (night cricket). It gives one a lot of confidence and self-belief. One feels that one must perform well and one's desire to achieve maximum success increases.

Please tell readers about your most memorable performances in the 2016 under-19 World Cup.

I had two memorable batting performances in that tournament. The first one was against Nepal in the Group D match on 1 February. I scored 78 off 24 balls. In the process, I broke the record for the fastest recorded under-19 fifty achieving it in 18 balls – one ball faster than the previous mark. In that innings, I hit nine fours and five sixes. On 6 February, I got a hundred in the match vs. Namibia which put India in the semi-final. In that game, I scored 111 off 96 balls inclusive of 14 fours and two sixes. On that day I was also recruited by Delhi Daredevils for the 2016 IPL at a sum of Rs. 1.9 crores.

Why did the Indian side perform disappointingly in the final against the West Indies?

We should have won the final. We did not play upto expectations that day. Again, I too got out in a most negligent and embarrassing manner. The bowler was Alzarri Joseph who was bowling at over 140 Km.p.h. I was batting from outside the crease. The delivery I got out to I had left outside my off stump. I did not drag my feet back in the crease after leaving the ball. The wicket-keeper Imlach, much to my dismay, broke the stumps and I was out stumped. It was a huge disappointment for me and my team.

You had the great Rahul Dravid as coach in that competition. What was your experience like?

Initially, we were quite frightened at the prospect of having Mr. Rahul Dravid as our coach as he is a cricketing legend. On meeting him and talking to him, we found that he is a very good person who talked freely with us. We could go to him at any time with our problems. He gave us a lot of confidence and we learnt discipline by just watching him. During a match he would allow us to play freely but expected total commitment.

You had mentioned about being recruited by the Delhi Daredevils for the 2016 IPL. What was your experience like?

For one who is quite young it was great for me to be selected by one of the franchises at quite a good price. The experience was great as one played with and against top international players. One not only got the opportunity to learn but one was also paid well.

You made your Ranji Trophy for Delhi last season. What was your first season for Delhi like?

It was my dream to make the Delhi Ranji side before playing the under-19 World Cup. I am glad that I realized it. I played a couple of matches and got a fifty on my debut vs. Bengal.

You started this year's Ranji season with a hundred. Please tell readers about that knock.

In the first Ranji match I played this season I got 146 vs. Assam at Vadodara. I played 124 balls and hit 13 fours and eight sixes. I shared a 220 run partnership for the fourth wicket with Nitish Rana (146) and Delhi won the match by an innings and 83 runs.

Your next innings was a huge 308 vs. Maharashtra at Mumbai. How did you steel yourself to get such a big score?

At the start of the season, I had set my mind to get atleast a double century this season. The Maharashtra match turned out to be a huge opportunity for me as Maharashtra batting first scored a massive 635 for two declared. I settled down to the task of helping Delhi take the first innings lead. I got 308 off 326 balls and hit 42 fours and nine sixes. Unfortunately, despite useful knocks by others we fell 45 runs short of Maharashtra's total. Our not taking the first innings lead hurt me deeply.

In your fifth match for Delhi vs. Jharkhand in the first week of November you scored a century in each innings. Please tell readers about that game.

This was a match in which Delhi was forced to follow on. In our first innings, I scored 117 off 106 balls inclusive of 9 fours and 8 sixes. I shared a 187 run fourth wicket stand with Unmukt Chand (109) but we had to follow on. Following on, I got 135 off 67 balls inclusive of 8 fours and 13 sixes. I reached 100 off just 48 balls– the fastest hundred in Ranji Trophy. The match ended in a respectable draw.

This year for the first time Ranji matches are being played on neutral venues. What do you feel about it?

I am very happy as I am performing well. The biggest advantage of this practice is that there is no home team advantage. Both sides have to play in new conditions.

What has been responsible for your tremendous form especially with the bat this season?

During the off-season, I worked very hard with my coach and physical trainer. All my work and practice was planned well in advance and I followed it to the tee. Again, my team coach and captain have encouraged me and told me to be myself. My mother in particular has ensured that I play without any tension in my mind.

What are your other interests?

Cricket takes most of my time. However, when I am free I like playing games like Table Tennis and Badminton. I also like watching movies.

Finally, any message for school children?

Yes. All school children infact, all young people must remember that if we have the talent and perform, the people who matter can delay but never deny your entry.

DIPA KARMAKAR- INDIA'S MOST SUCCESSFUL GYMNAST

WOMAN'S ERA – FEBRUARY (FIRST) 2017

23-year-old Dipa Karmakar is, without doubt, India's finest gymnast to date. In the 2014 Glasgow Commonwealth Games, she became the first Indian woman gymnast to win a bronze medal. She also won a bronze medal at the 2015 Hiroshima Asian Gymnastics Championships. These performances resulted in the Government of India conferring on her the Arjuna Award for 2015. The year 2016 proved a great year for Dipa. In April, she became the first Indian woman gymnast to qualify for the Olympics. At the Rio Olympics, Dipa narrowly missed winning a medal- finishing fourth in the women's vault. The Government of India honoured Dipa by conferring on her the Rajiv Gandhi Khel Ratna Award for 2016. The Tripura Government promoted her to the post of Assistant Director. I met Dipa recently in Delhi and spoke to her about her career in Gymnastics.

When and how did you take to Gymnastics?

To be frank, gymnastics is in my blood as my father who is a weightlifting coach with the Sports Authority of India was initially getting training in gymnastics before he switched to weightlifting. I started practising gymnastics at the age of six first with madam Soma Nandi as coach. After being coached by her for about three years, madam Soma Nandi's husband Bisheshwar Nandi sir took me under his wings. I have been with him since then. Whatever I have achieved has been due to both of them.

What role has your coach Bisheshwar Nandi played in your achievements to date?

I owe all my success to him. He is, of course a tough taskmaster. But all the same, he is a concerned person too. He ensures that I stay fully focused both during training and competitions. With him around, I am just left to concentrate on my routines and sharpening of my skills. It was again, under his guidance that I did get to do the Produnova Vault which I think has had a major say in my getting to where I am now.

Please explain to readers the Produnova Vault.

The Produnova Vault or the headspring double front is an artistic gymnastics vault consisting of a front handspring onto the vaulting horse and two front somersaults off. The vault currently has a 7.0 difficulty score and is the hardest vault performed in women's artistic gymnastics. This vault has been so named because the first person who performed it was Russia's Elena Produnova in 1999. In fact, it is so difficult that even its inventor Elena Produnova handled it standing up first once in her career. Dipa is one of the five people in the world to have performed this successfully.

What about foreign coaches? Are they a must for big successes?

Look at P.V. Sindhu and Sakshi Malik. They got India medals with Indian coaches. Whatever I achieved at Rio in my first Olympics was all due to my Indian coach. I am confident that if I work hard and follow my coach's advice more religiously I will win a medal in the 2020 Olympics. Our performances have shown that Indian coaches are not inferior to their foreign counterparts. In fact, I feel that an Indian coach will work much harder to ensure that our tri-colour flies high.

What about facilities for training and practice in India?

The facilities and infrastructure that we have at the Indira Gandhi Indoor Stadium in Delhi are as good as the ones abroad. The government and the Sports Authority of India have assured us of all the required help. Even the Gymnastics Federation of India is doing its best.

Your biggest achievement was qualifying for the Rio Olympics. Please tell the readers about it.

Honestly, I wanted to qualify for the Olympics in November 2015 during the World Championships at Glasgow. Unfortunately, I finished fifth when a podium finish was required. In the Rio qualifiers at Rio in April 2016, my first vault, the Produnova, gave me 15.066 points, the highest among 14 competitors. But a poor show in the uneven bars (11.700) took me down before 13.366 and 12.566 points in beam and floor exercises respectively pushed up my all-round total to 52.698 points. That was enough to push me into the top 30 and ensure a place for me in the Rio Olympics.

Hours after qualifying for the Rio Olympics, I clinched the gold in the vaults final at the test event of the Rio Games by scoring 14.833 as my best effort. Many top stars were not there as they had already qualified for the Rio Olympics.

Please recall for the benefit of readers your performance in the Rio Olympics.

In the qualification event of the vaults in the Rio Olympics, I finished eighth with a score of 14.866 and qualified for the final. My performance in the other events – uneven bars, balancing beam and floor exercise was not so good. I was in the sixth position before the final round but a strong performance from Canada pushed me to the eighth spot- the last qualifying place for the final. In the final, I finished fourth with 15.066 points. I lost the third place and bronze medal to Switzerland's Giulia Steingruber who had 15.216 points by just 150 points more.

What were your feelings on your return?

I remember telling my parents before leaving for Rio that they need not worry about my return as I would take an autorickshaw from the airport and return home. I was truly touched by the warm welcome I got from thousands of people from all over the country. I was glad to know that millions of Indians stayed awake at night to watch me perform. I am grateful to God for everything.

How do you plan to win a medal in the 2020 Olympics?

I am confident that my coach will help me to win a medal in the 2020 Olympics. I will listen to him more religiously, and follow all his plans-attending camps-both national and abroad and take part in the strongest possible competitions specially abroad.

What sacrifices did you have to make to reach this level?

From an early age, I have had to ensure that my body was very fit and supple. As I progressed as a gymnast, I had to totally cut out on sweets and chocolates. Again, due to competitions and training camps, I had to stay away for long periods from my family and friends. In fact,only after the Olympics, I ate some sweets.

Finally, please give a message to our youth especially girls.

First of all, do not let the state you come from prevent you from progressing. Remember, if you have the talent and get a good guide you will surely progress. Respect and carefully listen to and follow what your parents, coaches, teachers and seniors tell you. Be enthusiastic, hardworking and devoted.

GURBACHAN SINGH RANDHAWA – ONE OF INDIA'S GREATEST ATHLETES

ALIVE – MARCH 2017

Gurbachan Singh Randhawa is without doubt one of India's finest men's athletes ever. The 77-year-old athlete is perhaps the most versatile athlete the country has produced as he excelled in the high jump, javelin, 110m hurdles and the decathlon events. He was an Asian Games gold medalist in the decathlon in 1962 and had the distinction of representing the country in two Olympics – 1960 Rome and 1964 Tokyo where he finished fifth in the 110 m hurdles event. I met Gurbachan Singh Randhawa – an Arjuna Awardee in 1961 and Padma Shri in 2005 - at his residence in New Delhi and spoke to him about his early days, his first Olympics in 1960 and also his own achievements.

How is it that you took to Athletics?

I come from a family that has excelled in athletics. My father was an excellent sports person being a top class athlete. He was brilliant in the long jump, hurdles, discus, high jump and triple jump.

My elder brother H.S. Randhawa, an all India university champion in 110m hurdles and the best athlete in Punjab University, was a former Chief Athletics coach at the National Institute of Sports (Patiala). So, it was but natural for me to take to athletics.

How successful as an athlete were you in your school and college days?

I won a number of events at the school and college levels. I was the star athlete (best athlete) of Punjab University excelling in the hurdles, the high jump and many other events.

Who was your first coach from outside the family and how did he guide you?

It was J.S. Saini. He was associated with me from 1960 till 1966. He suggested to me that I should concentrate on the decathlon.

Please could you explain what decathlon is?

Decathlon is derived from the word decade which means ten. There are ten events, comprising three jumps, three throws and four races. Races include 100m, 400m, 1500m and 110m hurdles. Jumps include high jump, long jump and pole vault. In throws, it is shot put, discus and javelin

When did you first achieve great success at the national level?

It was in the 1960 Delhi National Championships. In that championship, I broke Dr. C.M. Muthiah's decathlon national record with a tally of 5793 points. I was able to prove my versatility by also winning the high jump, javelin throw and 110m hurdles at that Nationals breaking four national records over a span of two days. After this National, the national selectors took notice of me.

Please tell readers about your outstanding feats in an Indo-German Athletics meet in Delhi in the early 1960s

A German athletics side visited India in the early 1960s. In that Indo-German meet at the National Stadium, I stood first in the 110m hurdles, high jump, long jump and javelin throw events.

Was the 1960 Rome Olympics your first Olympics?

Yes, it was. At the age of 21, I was the baby of the team.

Why was the 1962 Asian Games at Jakarta memorable for you?

At the 1962 Asian Games in Jakarta, I won the gold in the decathlon event. My tally of 6739 points was 550 points more than silver medalist Shosuke Suzuki of Japan. I also finished fifth in the 110m hurdles and javelin throw events at Jakarta. The crowning glory came when I was adjudged the best Asian athlete by a panel of International Track and Field statisticians on the basis of the Asian Games performances

How did you prepare for the 1964 Tokyo Olympics?

A shoulder injury after the 1962 Asian Games at Jakarta forced me to leave the decathlon and concentrate on the hurdles. I was fortunate that Hungarian coach, Jozel Kovacs, who was a visiting coach at the National Institute of Sports (Patiala), not only taught me the art of warming up but also gave me some useful advice.

Again, I was fortunate to be given the opportunity of competing extensively in Europe before the 1964 Tokyo Olympics

Please tell readers about your performances in the 1964 Tokyo Olympics

Before I talk about my performances, I wish to state that in Tokyo I was the skipper of the Indian contingent. I was lucky to get into the semi-finals as the fastest loser with a timing of 14.3 seconds. In the semi-finals, I finished second with a personal best timing of 14 seconds which was also a national record. The final was to be staged only 45 minutes later, just enough time for a massage and a quick nap. The final had a line-up consisting of two Americans, one Soviet, a Frenchman, three Italians (the Italians were competing with the American for supremacy) and myself- the lone Indian. In a tough race, I finished fifth 0.2 seconds behind the fourth runner and 0.3 seconds behind the bronze medalist.

What were the weather conditions like on the day of the semi-final and final?

That day in Tokyo it was raining and the track was wet. The temperature during the semi-final was 14.2^{0} C and the humidity was about 96%. During the final, the temperature was 13.4^{0}C and the conditions were wet. Believe it or not, the *kachchha-baniyaan* that I wore for the semi-finals was completely soaked but I stuck with it for the final.

Which organization did you serve?

I joined the CRPF in 1958. I also served with the Intelligence Bureau and the Indo-Tibetan Border Police. I retired in 1994.

How were your services recognized by the Police?

I was awarded the Home Minister's Gold Medal for the best All India Police Athlete on six occasions. I have also been awarded the Police Medal for Meritorious Service in 1978 and the President's Police Medal for Distinguished Service in 1990.

In what capacities have you served Indian Athletics?

I have been fortunate to serve Indian Athletics as a coach, talent scout and Chairman of the National Selection Committee. I have also been the Advisor on Sports to the Vice-Chancellor, Punjabi University.

What qualities do you look for in youngsters who wish to become top athletes?

First of all, I see their physical structure – athleticism, secondly,their dedication and thirdly,their attitude to a good coach. Once the trainee has the talent and the right attitude, he or she will be given exposure in competitions.

The performance will be monitored. Consistency is also an important virtue.

How can sports be properly made a valuable part of our school education?

The government must ensure that all recognized and affiliated schools have proper playfields, sports facilities and equipment, committed and properly qualified sports teachers with an eye to spot talent. The school timetable and exam system must encourage sports. Schools must aim to produce champions.

HARENDRA SINGH – A FINE HOCKEY COACH

ALIVE – APRIL 2017

18 December 2016 was a great day for India's Junior hockey coach Harendra Singh when the Indian hockey side which he carefully selected, trained and moulded became the first host country to win the junior World Cup hockey title in Lucknow defeating Belgium 2-1 in the final. The win was India's second in the tournament having won it for the first time in 2001 in Hobart, Tasmania, Australia. Harendra was also associated with the 2001 side till he was asked to join the coaching staff of the Indian hockey side for the 2000 Olympics. I met 50-year-old Harendra Singh, the Dronacharya Awardee, at his residence to speak with him about the junior World Cup success and his playing and coaching career.

How did you take to hockey?

I was born in Chhapra, Bihar. I studied in the village school till class V. In class VI, I joined Union Academy in Delhi. It was at Union Academy that I started playing hockey. In school, I was coached by Hawa Singh. We had a very good team.

How successful were you as a player at the university level?

I studied in Delhi University- the first year in Kirori Mal College and the other two years in Khalsa College. For the years 1985, 86 and 87, I was adjudged the best sportsman of the year for Delhi University. I also captained the combined universities side in 1986 and 1987.

Please tell readers about your playing career till you made it to the Indian side for the 1990 Beijing Asian Games.

My performances for the combined universities were impressive and soon I rose to be a dependable full back for Mahindras and

Customs in Mumbai and Maharashtra from 1987 till 1990. The Maharashtra Government honoured me with the Shiv Chhatrapati Award in 1990. That year I moved to Indian Airlines and did well for them in national tournaments and the national championships. The Indian Airlines side was a very powerful team at that time and my consistent performances helped me to be selected for the Indian side that went to Beijing for the 1990 Asian Games. India won the silver medal. I played for Indian Airlines till 1998,i.e. till the time I became coach of the side. As a player, I also received tips from 1956 Olympian and coach Hardayal Singh and other seniors.

Who motivated you to take to hockey coaching?

In 1995 I went to play for F.C. Lyon in the hockey league in France. I continued to play there until 1998. During this period I played six months in France and six months for the Indian Airlines in the main tournaments. In Lyon, I met Tony Fernandes, a brilliant inside left from India, who had migrated to France in 1965. Tony was coaching in France. He was the first person to motivate me to take to coaching.

What coaching courses have you undergone?

After I took to coaching in 1998, I have been attending coaching courses of different types conducted by the FIH (International Hockey Federation) since 2000. These courses include special and high-performance ones. In 2014, I qualified as an FIH coach- the only one from India.

When did you start coaching hockey?

In 1998, I returned to India after my playing stint in France. On my return, I was asked by Mr. M.S. Balakrishnan, then Secretary (sports) in Indian Airlines and Senior Vice President of the then Indian Hockey Federation to start coaching the Indian Airlines side from 13 September that year. The Indian team had not performed well in the 1998 World Cup so new coaches were to be appointed at the National level. The meeting to appoint the coaches was to take place in Chennai. At about that time Indian Airlines with me as their coach won the All India MCC hockey tournament in

Chennai and I was asked to coach the National Junior side with CR Kumar. That is how it all began.

What qualities must a good coach possess?

To be a really good coach, one must have an eye that can spot talent. One must possess sound knowledge of the sport and have the courage of conviction when it comes to backing players whom one thinks is good. One must be innovative and prepared to experiment. One must look upon coaching as a vocation and not a job as we are guiding players- sometimes youngsters. We also need the support and understanding from the people who run the game.

Who is the hockey coach you admire the most?

Without a doubt, I rate Ric Charlesworth of Australia as the best coach. He is a real all-rounder – a qualified medical doctor, a successful cricketer and a world-class hockey player. He is also a great administrator and coach. He has the unique distinction of being a high-performance director in hockey and cricket in Australia. It was unfortunate that we in India could not get the best out of him. He is a true mentor. I wish I could have worked with him.

As a coach, when you get a bunch of players to prune down, what yardsticks do you keep in mind?

I am grateful to God that he has given me the power of intuition to choose the right player. As a coach, what I initially observe is how a player passes and receives the ball and also the way the player positions himself or herself when tackling or passing. Match temperament, fitness, durability and attitude are other qualities I took for in youngsters.

Your biggest success as a coach was the winning of the junior World Cup at Lucknow in 2016. Please tell readers how the victory was achieved.

I first met the probables at New Delhi's Dhyan Chand Stadium on 25 April 2014. That day itself I worked on a blueprint for success in the 2016 junior World Cup, touching on the skill, fitness and mental aspects required. I feel our win in the December 2014 Sultan of Johar tournament really set the ball rolling. This victory, a little more than six months after I took over the team, gave the players the belief that they were on the right path and my methods as coach were correct. They really began to listen to me. Even during the run-up to the junior World Cup our winning the Asia Cup, the Eurasia Cup and the Four-Nations tournament also gave us a lot of self-confidence. In the four Nations tournament in Valencia, our opponents were Belgium, Germany and Spain. The team became a cohesive unit and the players realised that only collective brilliance would help realise the collective dream. The team blended as a family, with there being no room for ego, dispute and indiscipline and thus no superstar. This is why we won the title despite being down at times.

The great Ric Charlesworth said that the structure of the junior winning side was good. Please elaborate.

Other Indian sides had the class of individuals while this team had the class of a team. The players of this team will do well in even a new group as they have understood the concepts of a team. Please remember that while brilliant players can win matches, brilliantly united teams win tournaments. This is what Ric Charlesworth meant by good structure.

What has led to the overall improvement in Indian hockey over the last few years?

Ever since Dr. Narinder Batra took over as Hockey India Chief in 2014, Indian Hockey has really started moving in the right direction. Dr. Batra's becoming FIH President in November 2016 was a great boost for Indian hockey. Dr. Batra has ensured that there is a proper hockey calender which is religiously followed. He has ensured that Indian hockey has the best infrastructure, facilities and equipment. The planning is done by him and experts. The selectors and the coaches get all the freedom to do their jobs well. There is no interference. We now have atleast 100 newly laid astro-turfgrounds in our country. Most of these grounds have floodlights. The world's best hockey players now participate in a competitive professional hockey league in our country.

Our players- men, women, senior or junior now get maximum international match exposure be it in India or abroad.

How has the Hockey India League helped?

The Hockey India League has brought professionalism into our hockey at all levels- players, coaches and umpires. Our players have become more skillful, technically better and more confident and assured particularly when facing reputed foreign players. Their physical fitness, thinking and execution abilities have greatly improved. Of course, those involved in the league are financially better off and find their lives more secure. Spectators also get to see many top class players in action. Since every one treats it as a profession, the quality has risen. For me as a coach, it was a great experience coaching players from different countries with their own styles of play and moulding them into one unit.

How have the changes in hockey rules in the last few years helped Indian hockey?

Changes like four quarters in a match, self-pass and top of the circle free hit have helped our players who are very speedy. We have also started using the rolling substitutions much better now. Four quarters in particular are very helpful for our players who are fast but need more time for recovery. Again, the four quarters helps us to use our players more effectively and at the right times.

Finally, do you have plans to improve coaching standards in India so that one day we can have many top-level Indian coaches like you?

I feel that we need more top-level Indian coaches in our country. I am not averse to coaching coaches now- not the ones already into it though. India has given great players but not great coaches. Without a number of quality coaches, we cannot have a constant and regular supply of top-class players. My wish is to become a coaches' mentor. Only if one has his or her own coaches can one execute any long-term plan or vision. I hope I can achieve this dream of mine for the long-term benefit of Indian hockey.

G.R. VISHWANATH – A BATTING GENIUS

HINDUSTAN TIMES (DELHI) – 12 FEBRUARY 2018

G.R. Vishwanath was the original wristy artist in Indian cricket. The batting great who turns 69 on Monday was the first from India to score another century after making one on Test debut – 137 against Australia in Kanpur in 1969. But he won a legion of admirers for his batting feats during a 91-Test career. After retirement, he had served as chairman of the national selection committee, and it was his panel that selected Sourav Ganguly and Rahul Dravid for the 1996 tour of England where both made a big mark. An avid golfer these days,

Vishwanath took a trip down memory lane with me at his residence in Bangalore.

What qualities should one possess to be a successful Test batsman?

The two most important requirements for a successful Test batsman are a sound technique and a cool temperament – the ability to remain unruffled in tight situations. One must know how to relax. The important thing is to take each Test match as it comes as each Test match greatly differs from the other.

What made Sunil Gavaskar such a batting phenomenon?

The great qualities possessed by Sunny were a perfect technique, an unruffled temperament and great powers of concentration. The greatest thing about him was that whatever the level of the match he played, he never threw his wicket away.

Which Test innings would you rate as your best?

It is a difficult question to answer as I have played quite a few really fine knocks. A crucial knock from the point of view of my Test career was my 75 not out against England in the second innings of the fourth Test at Kanpur in 1972-73. I had fared poorly in the first three Tests and in the first innings of the fourth Test. There was also talk about dropping me. In the second innings, we were 39 for 4 with a first innings deficit of 40, when I played that knock which saved both my country and myself from embarrassment. My confidence was restored and I got 113 in the next Test at Mumbai becoming the first Indian to score a second century after making a century on Test debut.

The innings you described was crucial for your Test career. Which innings would you rate as your best?

Without doubt, my 139 in the second innings of the third Test at Kolkata versus West Indies in 1974-75. We had lost the first two Tests of the series and there were three more Tests to go. A loss at Kolkata would have meant the loss of the series. At Kolkata, we conceded a first innings lead of seven runs. I top-scored with 52 in our first innings score of 233. In our second innings, despite my 74 - run stand with Farokh Engineer (61) we slumped to 152 for 5. Madan Lal (15) and I then put on 40 for the sixth wicket. After that Ghavri (27) and myself put on 91 for the seventh wicket to help India reach a fine total of 316. West Indies, set a winning target of 310, were bundled out for 224 to lose the match by 85 runs. India thus reduced the 2-0 lead West Indies had.

Please tell us about your century on Test debut against Australia in the second Test at Kanpur in 1969.

I was selected in place of the great Chandu Borde. Captain Tiger Pataudi made it clear to the chairman of the selectors Vijay Merchant that I had to be in the first eleven and not be a reserve. In the first innings, I got out for zero. Merchant mentioned my failure to Tiger Pataudi. I was doubly nervous as first of all, I, a 20-year-old, was making my Test debut and secondly I had got out for zero in the first innings. While I was waiting for my turn to bat in the second innings, Tiger Pataudi told me to relax saying not to worry and that I would do well when my chance to bat came. My captain's words eased my tension and I went on to score 137 in the second innings against a quality attack which had good pacemen and spinners. My innings ensured India did not lose.

Can you talk about B.S. Chandrasekhar's great spell against England in the Oval Test in 1971?

That spell of Chandra's (6 / 38) went a long way in helping India win the Test and series – India's first against England in England. That day, Chandrasekhar was at his magical best and the English batsmen were so mesmerized that they just did not know how to play him.

What was the Indian team's batting high during your Test career?

It was the third Test against the West Indies at Port of Spain in 1976. In our second innings, we were set 403 to win and we achieved the target scoring 406 for 4. We won by six wickets. It was the highest successful run chase bettering Don Bradman's Australian side's 404 for 3 versus England in 1948. Initially, we played with the intention of saving the game. Only at tea did we feel we could win and batted accordingly with Brijesh Patel putting the finishing touches with an aggressive 49 not out. Before Patel's fireworks, Sunny scored 102, I got 112 while Mohinder Amarnath made 85. There were very good partnerships too.

What was the 'low' in Indian batting during your Test career?

It was definitely our 42 all out in the second innings of the Lord's Test vs. England in 1974. That day the wicket was all right. Only the conditions were typically English – gloomy and with a heavy atmosphere. Pacemen Chris Old and Geoff Arnold exploited that and bowled exceptionally well. They were very accurate too. We did not have an answer that day.

You played a bit of one-day cricket too. Which knock of yours do you rate the best?

My best innings in this kind of cricket was without a doubt my score of 75 out of 190 against West Indies at Birmingham in the 1979 World Cup. It gave me a lot of satisfaction as I scored against fast bowlers of the calibre of Andy Roberts, Michael Holding, Joel Garner and Colin Croft.

You have played against some of the best fast bowlers. Who would you rate the best?

Of those I played against, Andy Roberts of the West Indies was the best. He was a really quick bowler with great control and extraordinary variety. He used to bowl two bouncers – the second one was such that one never saw it till it hit you. I was quite thrilled to score a lot of runs against Roberts at his fastest in the 1974-75 series. Graham McKenzie of Australia whom I played against in my debut series in 1969 was also a great fast bowler - deceptively quick and possessing great control over swing. Imran Khan and Richard Hadlee of New Zealand were also top class fast bowlers. Dennis Lillee was not at his fastest when I played him. So I have not really considered him.

Finally, any disappointments?

Yes, the way I had to leave Test cricket. I did have a poor tour of Pakistan in 1982-83 but so did many others. Again, I was finding too much Test cricket a bit strenuous. I did want a short break from international cricket. Unfortunately, the break proved to be permanent.

ABHINAV BINDRA – INDIA'S FIRST OLYMPIC INDIVIDUAL GOLD MEDALIST

ALIVE – JULY 2018

Abhinav Bindra is still India's only individual gold medal winner in an Olympics. He achieved this feat in the 10m air rifle event in the 2008 Beijing Olympics. I met Abhinav recently and spoke to him about the sport, his greatest moment in it and sports in India in general.

You are the first Indian and so far the only one to win an individual Olympic gold medal. What were your feelings after you won the gold medal?

I was relieved, contented and satisfied after my achievement. I was also proud as I had become the first Indian to achieve that feat. I was grateful to God that my continuous hard work and preparation had paid off. Honestly, I had prepared hard to perform well – winning the gold medal was an unbelievably great moment for me.

What does one need to do to become an Olympic champion?

The most important things a person must have or do to become an Olympic champion are first of all to possess the will to succeed, to work very hard, persevere, persist and develop the ability to absorb failure. Of course, one has to have the mental fortitude but it will always be a combination of one's technical skills which must be strong, and one's physical fitness and durability for one to succeed. The mental part also cannot be neglected. In the end, one has to get everything right together to be successful. I followed the holistic approach to my training concentrating on all three aspects – technical, physical and mental.

Your comments on the achievements of our shooters particularly the younger ones in the recent 2018 Commonwealth Games.

Since the silver medal India won in the 2004 Olympics, Indian shooting has been making rapid progress. With our successes in shooting in successive Olympics – 2008 and 2012 – young shooters in India have taken to the sport in fairly large numbers. Again, regular and proper training for young shooters has been organized for quite some time now. The success of our younger shooters in the Commonwealth Games means that we can expect success in the tougher challenges to follow.

How do you rate our prospects in Shooting in the coming Asian Games?

The competition in the Asian Games will be much tougher than what we encountered in the Commonwealth Games. But I am confident that we can perform as well as we have talent which has done well in tough competitions. Since Shooting is a day to day sport our shooters can do well as they are working hard to get better and better.

What do you feel must be done by India so that it becomes a sporting nation?

First of all, our Government needs to decide whether we want to become a sporting nation and whether Olympics sports are a priority. If they are, then we need to invest in it. We need to have patience and we need to invest long term. Top class coaches who are dedicated and have an eye for talent have to be recruited. Then games have to be started and developed from the grassroots level. The process of talent spotting and grooming should follow. But, the problem in India has been that we wake up to Olympic sports once in four years. When the Olympics comes, the media and the public show interest. If we do not get results, there is disappointment which is first followed by negativity and then total quiet. So, we first of all need to decide whether we wish to become a sporting nation and whether Olympic sports do mean a lot to us. Then the other things will automatically follow.

How according to you should Sports be a part of school education?

Schools must ensure that the physical education teachers selected are ones who are not only passionate about the sports they have specialized in but also possess the ability and keenness to spot and groom genuine talent. Primary and even middle-level teachers must be interested in sports. Ofcourse, sports must be an essential part of the curriculum with children playing atleast three to four games at the primary level mainly for fun. Proper incentives must be given to excellent sports persons and the school authorities must ensure that the lost academics of these sports persons are made up. Again, once children start loving sports, the values which sports teaches must be inculcated in them.

Finally, what are the benefits one gets from Shooting as a sport?

The great thing about the sport is that we concentrate on and aim at getting better and better. The sport helps us to focus better and goes a long way in improving our mind and body coordination.

SUDHA SHAH – A PIONEER IN INDIAN WOMEN'S CRICKET

WOMAN'S ERA - AUGUST (FIRST) 2018

60-year old Sudha Shah, one of the pioneers of women's cricket in India, became in June this year, only the second Indian women's cricketer after Shantha Rangaswamy (she won it in 2017) to receive the Board of Control for Cricket in India's C.K. Nayudu Lifetime Achievement Award for her services to the game. Sudha, a right-hand batsman and off-spinner, has served the cause of Indian women's cricket for over four decades-first as a player, then coach and finally as a selector. I chatted with Sudha on her well-deserved award and her experiences in Indian women's cricket.

Congrats on your receiving the C.K. Nayudu Lifetime Achievement Award from the BCCI in June this year.

Thanks. I cannot say how happy and honoured I am at receiving this honour. All the sacrifices made and the hard work put in have been recognised by this Award. It feels really good.

I understand your family was involved in cricket. Could you tell readers about your family?

My father was a Gujarati and my mother was from Kerala. My father was the Founder-Secretary of the Tamil Nadu Women's Cricket Association (TNWCA). I have an elder sister- Meena Dalal nee Shah who played for Tamil Nadu and South Zone. My sister, later on, became Secretary of TNWCA after she stopped playing. My brother Arun played cricket for his school.

How did you start playing cricket?

I was keen on sports right from when I can remember. I used to play tennis ball cricket with the boys in my colony. When I was in my final year of school, we heard that the Women's Cricket Association of India was being formed. So my school friends and I started taking cricket seriously and began playing with a cricket ball. There was no looking back after that.

Who were the coaches who made you the cricketer you became?

L.J. Edmunds and Sushil Haridas (both Tamil Nadu Ranji players) were my first coaches. Then the late N.J. Venkatesan and Audi Chetty helped me hone my skills.

How and when did you represent Tamil Nadu for the first time?

In those early days the really keen players with basic ability were able to make it to the state side. I was fortunate to have been coached well which helped me in getting selected. I first played for Tamil Nadu in October 1973 in friendly matches against Bombay in Chennai. I then captained the Tamil Nadu side in the second National Championships in Banaras.

What were your achievements at the state and zonal levels?

I captained and represented Tamil Nadu from 1973 to 1997 and captained (several times) and represented the South Zone side from 1975 to 1997. I scored the first first-class century in the country (in women's cricket). My highest score was 139 n.o and my best bowling performance was seven wickets for three runs. Both these performances were against Kerala. I was also the first captain of the Madras University women's cricket team.

Please tell readers about your international career as a player.

I represented India officially from 1976 – 1991. I have played against Australia, New Zealand, England and West Indies at home and abroad. I made my debut for India in 1976 at the age of 18 against the West Indies. I played 21 Tests and 13 ODIs. In Tests, I scored 601 runs while in the ODIs I totalled 293 runs.

When did you become a coach and what were your achievements as coach of the Indian team?

I finished playing for Tamil Nadu in 1997. After taking a year's break, I became a coach in 1998- the first woman level 2 coach in

India. I was India's coach from 1999 to 2010 and again in 2014. When I was coach, we won the Asia Cup thrice; entered the final of the 2005 World Cup in South Africa. Again, we also defeated England in an ODI series in England in 1999 and won the first - ever T-20 match vs. England in England in 2006. In the 2009 World Cup in Australia, our team defeated Australia twice.

How else have you served the cause of cricket in Tamil Nadu and India?

I was a national selector in 2013 and 2015 while at present I am Chairman of the Tamil Nadu Women's Cricket Association Selection Committee.

Please tell readers about how things were when you were playing.

In those days, finances and sponsorship were hard to come by and we had to go round asking for help. We were more often than not left to fend for ourselves. During our playing days, we used to travel second class - unreserved too and play on corporation grounds or school grounds. We even stayed in classrooms and dormitories. The difficulties were there. But looking back, it was all part of our growing up.

How did the entry of the BCCI into women's cricket help it?

In 2006, the BCCI took over things and women's cricket in India benefitted greatly. The women's cricketers got better facilities and infrastructure. The players have started getting more money, exposure and publicity too.

What are your observations on women's cricket in India today?

Indian women's cricketers now give a lot of attention to physical fitness. Again, players like Harmanpreet have shown that our players can resort to destructive power-hitting. Unlike players of our time, today's players regularly hit big sixes. They do not restrict themselves to technique and playing along the ground. The only thing that needs to be worked on is our bench strength.

www.ingramcontent.com/pod-product-compliance
Lightning Source LLC
Chambersburg PA
CBHW061518020726
47502CB00006B/2123

* 9 7 8 9 3 8 7 4 5 6 7 4 7 *